Milo Devine and the Demagogue's Daughter

Brendan Landers

POOLBEG

Published 2001
Poolbeg Press Ltd.
123 Grange Hill, Baldoyle
Dublin 13, Ireland
Email: poolbeg@poolbeg.com
www.poolbeg.com

© Brendan Landers 2001

The moral right of the author has been asserted.

Copyright for typesetting, layout, design
© Poolbeg Group Services Ltd.

1 3 5 7 9 10 8 6 4 2

A catalogue record for this book is available from the British Library.

ISBN 1 84223 035 2

All rights reserved. No part of this publication may be reproduced or transmitted in any form or by any means, electronic or mechanical, including photography, recording, or any information storage or retrieval system, without permission in writing from the publisher. The book is sold subject to the condition that it shall not, by way of trade or otherwise, be lent, resold or otherwise circulated without the publisher's prior consent in any form of binding or cover other than that in which it is published and without a similar condition, including this condition, being imposed on the subsequent purchaser.

Cover Design by Splash
Typeset by Patricia Hope in Bembo 12/14.5
Printed by
Omnia Books Ltd., Glasgow

About the Author

Brendan Landers worked as a bus conductor in Dublin for seven years before emigrating to Canada. He is now a freelance writer/journalist. His award-winning short fiction has been widely published in Ireland and Canada. He is former Publisher/Managing Editor of *Ireland's Eye*, a magazine for Irish Canadians, and former editor of *Irish Canada News*.

He is married with one son. *Milo Devine* is his first novel.

For Mam and Dad

1

I should be shot as a fool for letting the bugger in the door. I should be shot dead as a dodo, as the mightily imbecilic uncrowned king of all *schmucks* and idiots throughout the world to infinity and beyond.

I should kick my own arse.

But it's a miserable, maudlin, woebegone Monday morning and I'm having a bad, bad day of it. I've been having a few of them lately. I'm in a funk. It's maybe a middle-age crisis, I tell myself – old Father Time seditiously having his inevitable way with me. My subconscious is, I reckon, having trouble adjusting to the possibility that I'm past my prime. Whenever that was.

Not to mention the fact that I had a skinful of booze last night and my nerves, like my judgement, are in anything but the best of form.

I'm in bits.

And I'm thinking maybe I'm becoming slightly

unhinged. Just a tad. Enough to keep me off balance. Maybe I'm going slightly bonkers in the maelstrom of my presumed crisis. I'm getting old.

I'm slowing down.

Stiffening up.

Getting older.

I certainly feel it.

Jaded.

Some days.

That's the kind of day it is.

Wakey, wakey, Milo.

There was a time (and it's not so long ago) when I fancied myself as being always (almost) on the ball. Totally, like. I prided myself on my capacity to spot trouble on the wing and dodge it with casual ease and even a splash of panache. I used to be smart – cute as a hoor, if you'll pardon the expression – when faced with adversity.

I was quick on the uptake.

Past tense.

This morning it's like someone has taken a chainsaw to my once well-honed sense of self-preservation. Misfortune comes knocking on my door and, in a moment of weakness and extremely bad judgement, a moment that will change my life forever, I say Open Sesame.

Joe McGonagle is Trouble Incarnate. He's adversity on legs. What's worse is I know it. He's a player in the drama of my history. A minor architect of what has probably been the major misfortune in my heretofore existence. And like a dope I just sit here and I let him walk into my office and into my life.

On a sunny Monday mid-morning in September.

A doozy of a hangover makes a rusty, inhospitable cranial home for the few brain cells I have left and an apparently no longer requited *grá* for my current sweetheart, Maria, is squeezing a clamp on my aching, breaking heart. But, even taken together, these debilitating conditions are no excuse for a screw-up like the one I'm in the process of making. They're just two more reasons for extraordinary caution. Between them, however, they've sucked the vigour and clarity out of my bones and left me rudderless, like an empty, dispirited desert ship drifting on the shifting, uncertain sands of another pointless, dehydrated Monday.

The simple truth is I'm in no fit state today, physically or psychologically, to be dealing with a shrewd operator like McGonagle.

And I know it.

I let him in anyway.

I don't know why on earth. Curiosity maybe. Masochism. Or a fuck-it-all sense of abandon bred out of my listless humour.

Anyway, I let him in. When Angie rings up from downstairs.

"Send him up," I say.

A proper gobshite I am.

He breezes in the door like a Moonie on speed or one of those quick-tongued silverstreak snake-oil salesmen you see in old Hollywood movies on late-night television. All smiles and glittery teeth and *bon vivant* and movement.

He's across the room in a flash and heartily pumping my arm.

I'm discombobulated. I dip my head to look at my arm going up and down, up and down. In my toxic mind's eye I have an absurd, Dali-like vision of a gusher of oil shooting out through the gaping hole of my mouth. That's how spaced out I am.

"Milo, my old flower, long time no see. How's it going?"

He says.

He's looking good. He has a tan. A full head of black hair — no evidence of Grecian 2000. His body is firm. He's working out, by the looks of him. And dressing sharp. Classy khaki trousers with creases in the legs that would cut butter and a navy woollen jacket hanging loosely off his shoulders. White shirt with a Calvin Klein logo on the pocket. A light-blue silk tie with silver fishes on it swimming up to a perfect Windsor knot.

A yuppie Irish cop for fuck's sake.

Back in the old days, when we worked together, he was just another rumpled, grey-suited, shiny-elbowed, whiskey-pickled Special Branch man. The millennium is obviously treating him well.

The cunt.

Cops have never looked so good. It's the times that are in it, I suppose. Prosperity. Consumerism. The Celtic Tiger and all that.

I'm looking pretty sharp myself, if I may say so. I'm wearing a blueblack calf's leather jacket, the texture of which is as soft as a baby's arse, a white linen shirt, black cotton pants and Hush Puppy loafers over black cotton socks. I look after myself. I might feel like the inside of a rat's colour-coordinated arse, but I like to keep up appearances.

I sit, get cosy in my chair, put my feet up on my desk, nod at the empty client chair.

"Hello, Joe," I say.

Cool as cucumber.

I reckon.

He sits.

"How's business, Milo?"

"Great," I say.

Business is poxy.

"We don't see enough of you nowadays, Milo. You're missed down at the Garda Club. You shouldn't be a stranger, y'know."

I grunt.

I'd be Captain Boycott in the fucking Garda Club.

"What can I do for you, Joe?"

"Straight down to business, is it? No messing with Milo. You haven't changed a bit, but I've always liked your style."

"I'm a busy man."

"Good for you. We're always glad to see one of our own do well."

One of our own, my bollix.

"It so happens I'm here to put a bit of business your way," he says.

"You want me to keep an eye on your better half, is it?"

He chuckles dutifully.

"No, Milo. I have no need to be worrying on that score, touch wood." He gives the desk a knock with his knuckles. "I'm here unofficially, off the record, on behalf of my boss."

"Which boss?"

"The Gaffer."

I groan.

The man McGonagle calls the Gaffer is Archie Cooley, the leader of the not-so-loyal Opposition. And our future Taoiseach, if the pundits read the cards right. He's been in opposition for four and a half years, but his demeanour has never suggested that he perceived himself as anything other than Taoiseach-in-waiting.

Cooley is the walking, talking personification of patriarchy — *how's your father, givvus a job, I'm your man, trust me Jack and here's a shivvy up your arse, me old segocia.* He's a legend in his own lifetime. He's Ben Cartwright, Teddy Kennedy, Eamon de Valera, Cuchulainn and Benito Mussolini, all rolled up into one larger-than-life, super-political demagogue.

As you may have deduced, I'm prejudiced against the man.

He was nicknamed the Gaffer for his merciless heavy hand when — many moons ago, but well on his way up the greasy pole — he was the party's chief whip. With the lift of a lethal eyebrow and a surgical finesse, Cooley has in his day dispatched more than his fair share of Hungry Harrys and ignoble wannabes to the political abyss. If politicians by nature are sharks, he's the mother of all great whites.

Jaws.

McGonagle is Cooley's official driver. His gofer, his minder and, some say, his private soldier of fortune.

"McGonagle," I say, "you must know I don't take political jobs."

Irish politics at the best of times is a dangerous game. Here and now, with speculation rampant about the durability of the various IRA and loyalist paramilitary ceasefires, with the possibility of a renewed war waged by republican fundamentalists, with guns and Semtex buried in bogholes all over the country and God knows how many factions and potential splinter groups scrambling for access to the weapons for after, to meddle in the dark side of politics, to inadvertently, even, lift the wrong lid, is tantamount to Russian roulette. It's a mugs' and thugs' game and you'd want to be stark raving mad to play at it.

Time was, and not so long ago either, I was neither a mug nor a thug, but, it would appear, the voices whisper in my ear, times and people change and you're no exception. Muggins, Milo, they say.

McGonagle puts his hands up, palms facing me, as if putting me at ease. He's grinning from ear to ear, like a man would with nothing to hide.

"Hold your horses, Milo. This one is not political. Straight up. On my honour. This is personal."

"Right," I snort.

When it comes to politicians, especially wide boys like Archie Cooley, the personal has a way of subtly and then not-quite-so-subtly transmogrifying into the political, and tenderfeet more often than not are vanquished in the murky depths of the smoke and mirrors.

Cooley has been around the block and back again. In one way or another his figure has dominated public life in Ireland for the best part of the past thirty years. He's been written off into political oblivion and come back again so many times his enemies call him the Dracula of Irish politics.

In his heyday, legend has it, he was a holy terror and they say each and every Dublin wall has a different story to tell about his carousing, his philandering and his wheeling and dealing. He was the most handsome man in the country, they say – Ireland's Most Eligible Bachelor. His fondness for the ladies was notorious. As was his buccaneering approach to business and pleasure. And the people lapped him up. They took a vicarious delight from his wanton independence. His spirit of adventure. His devilment.

In his heyday he was involved in subterfuge up to his eyeballs. It's common knowledge in police and political circles, throughout the bloody country for that matter (his netherworldly intrigue is part of his allure) that when the troubles broke out in the North at the end of the sixties he had a hand in funnelling the money that bought the weapons that armed the re-emerging IRA.

In the late 1970's, although he'd publicly split with the Provisionals and had supposedly turned his back on the gun, rumours were rife that his shadowy peers in the party ran the rackets in the six counties with a Kalashnikov-toting private army. In the early 1980's, there was talk of pre-perestroika Russian money refilling the party's depleted coffers.

Not that Cooley himself ever had any need of Soviet money. He inherited a pile of dough. His father was a navvy who went to work on the buildings in London after the war. He saved his money, went into business for himself and made a fortune. Came back home to Dublin in the late sixties, built a large portion of the emerging suburbs and doubled his fortune. He retired in the mid-eighties and Archie took the helm of the family business. Coasted for a few years, until the Celtic Tiger began to roar and then plunged into real estate development. Sent the family fortune into the economic stratosphere. The Cooleys won't have to worry about the price of potatoes for generations to come.

Nowadays, with the party's private army up North disowned and presumably disbanded, it's reconcile this and build a bridge across that, but, like a lot of the windy-bagged predators of his generation in Irish politics, he's got more than his fair share of blood on his hands.

And the smart money has him running the country after the next election, which is due any day now.

Go figure the fickle finger of fate.

And do anything but despair, I dareya.

Nowadays, with his eye on the big political prize, he's Mother Teresa when it comes to talk of virtue and Mahatma Ghandi when it comes to talk of peace, but, if you ask me, Cooley has never been anything but his own man and normally I wouldn't touch him or his world with a forty-thousand-foot pole.

Normally.

"Straight up, Milo," says McGonagle. "Absolutely no politics. Cross my heart and hope to die." He crosses his heart with a finger like we used to do when we were kids. "This is strictly personal."

Inside myself I roll over. Really, I should just say thanks but no thanks and send the man on his merry, diabolic way. Deep down in the roots of my heart and soul I know this. My hunch knows it. My intuition knows it. My very bones know it. My guardian angel is at panic stations roaring in my ear chuck him out, *chuck him out, chuck him out, chuck the motherfucker out*.

But I'm a bloody eejit.

"I'm not promising anything," I hear myself saying, "but I'm listening."

Fuck.

Says my guardian angel.

"Attaboy, Milo," says McGonagle.

"So what's the story?" I ask, my sails more or less windless now.

"It's to do with Nuala. The daughter," he says.

Nuala Cooley.

A blast from the past for Milo. Just the mention of her name sweeps the years away and lights a lusty fond glow in my belly. Many, many moons ago, Nuala and I danced around the maypole together for a couple of memorable seasons. She was a wild one then. And since, or so I'd heard on the grapevine. A chip off the old block, according to the street and the gossip columns. Just like her da was in his prime, say the wags. But I know better. There's goodness in Nuala that never afflicted her father. And decency. Passion, by God. And not a little sadness. My memories of her are nothing but happy and warm, with a touch of bittersweet, almost tenable mystery to whet the perpetual glow of remembrance.

"You remember Nuala?" says McGonagle, throwing me a lewd wink. Showing his sensitive side.

"I remember. What's she up to now?"

"That's what the Gaffer wants to know. She's gone missing."

"That's playing true to character for Nuala. More power to her. So, what's the problem?"

"Her father is worried about her."

I give a short snort, as if to say I'll be looking out my window tonight, having invested my savings in a parcel of swampland in Florida, hoping to catch sight of a flock of pigs flying across a blue moon.

"Ah, you're a hard man, Milo. You've lost your faith in human nature."

I look him in the eye and the seconds tick by.

Eventually he shrugs.

"And her timing is bad," he says. "There's an election on the cards."

Ah, there's the rub.

"And your Mister Cooley is anxious lest the bold Nuala pop up *à la carte* on page three of *The Star* or the front page of *The Daily Mirror* sucking Prince Andrew's big toe or smoking one of Bill Clinton's cigars — is that it?"

"You're a cynical man, Milo. The truth is, it's a bit of both — paternal caring and political anxiety. But what's the harm in you finding her?"

"Maybe she doesn't want to be found."

"We're not asking you to drag her home screaming. Just make sure she's safe and secure."

"Why me? Why don't you use your own people?"

He taps the tip of his nose with a forefinger.

"Confidentiality," he says. "You know the way things are. Everything is politics, Milo, despite what freewheeling romantics like you would like to think. The Gaffer has his friends on the force. But where there's friends in politics and policing there's enemies also. There are those with no fondness for the man. People with other allegiances, who wouldn't be averse to seeing him done down. And we don't want any untoward leaks to the press at this particular moment in time."

"With an election due?"

He rests his arms on the desk and leans over, glamming me full on the eyeball. It's real masculine stuff, *mano-a-mano*, this eyeball-to-eyeball shit, and on my good days I couldn't be fucking bothered, but McGonagle is bringing out the worst in me. I glam him back. I'm acting like a bloody dinosaur.

He's reeking of down-home cornball sincerity. If you don't know him you'll give him all your trust. If you do, you'll give him an Oscar. Or, if you have any sense (which I apparently don't, says my guardian angel), a wide berth.

We're glamming away.

He moves his eyes.

Yafuckinhoo.

"All I want you to do, Milo, is come out and talk to the old man, listen to what he has to say. We'll make it worth your while."

He reaches into his breast pocket and his fist comes out wrapped around a stack of bills. He spreads them out on the desk before me. I count them with my eyes. Three hundred smackers. Fifteen twenty-punt notes. All brand new. Fresh out of the bank machine. From where I sit I can smell the ink off them.

"Three hundred bills, Milo, for a couple of hours of not even work. A social call, if you like."

I look at McGonagle. His face doesn't move.

I look at the bills.

My mouth waters.

What can I say?

Times are hard.

"I just talk to the man? No commitment?"

"No commitment."

I pick up the money.

I'm suckered.

Hook, line and sinker.

2

I pocket the money and tell McGonagle to get lost for an hour while I tend to some business. Not that there's a hell of a lot to tend to. Four of my men are on contract work, shadowing shoplifters and pickpockets and kicking derelicts and junkies out of a suburban shopping mall on the southside. I've got a man and a German Shepherd on the night shift watching a few warehouses down on the docks and a deal almost cut to check out security for a supermarket chain.

Otherwise things are quiet.

I call my contact at the supermarket and make an appointment for tomorrow. Then I take some time to mull over McGonagle, the Gaffer and Nuala and what I could be letting myself in for.

I'm a bit ticked off at myself for breaking one of my golden rules — no politics or politicians allowed in my life. But at the same time the three hundred bills and promise of more easy money are a compensation not to be sneezed at. Life is tough for the small businessman. Besides, I tell myself, maybe Cooley is on the up and up this time. I have a hard time swallowing that one, though, so I divert my thoughts to more plausible pastures.

It would be nice to see Nuala again.

A glad diversion with Maria giving me the runaround.

I don't think I'd call what Nuala Cooley and I had together love.

It was more an infatuated friendship and probably all the healthier for that and the fact that we both felt there wasn't any danger of either of us getting screwed up by Cupid's poison arrow. At least that's what we told each other.

It was back in my early days at Special Branch and I was still eager for the job and life in general. More years ago than I care to remember. There's been a lot of water under the bridge since then.

Nuala was just coming out of her teens. She had a hearty, in-heat glow off her and she was exuberantly curious about the mysteries and temptations of life and young womanhood.

So was I.

The timing was perfect.

We were both ripe for the plucking. And we plucked with happy abandon. For a couple of glorious years, on and off, we danced the light fandango and turned cartwheels across the floor, by golly, and there wasn't one sour note to the whole affair.

We had the world by the tail and we swung it.

We never fought. Not one little tiff, even.

In retrospect, I suppose it was one of the happiest times of my life, though I never suspected so then.

You never do, do you?

When our relationship ran its natural course we casually drifted away from each other. No recriminations. No tears. No heartbreak or soul-searching or post-mortems. No blues.

We stayed friends.

We still sent each other Christmas cards. And, if we bumped into each other in town of an evening, we'd go for a drink, have a laugh and maybe hit the hay together, though it had been a couple of years now since I'd seen her.

More or less since Maria came into my life.

But it was a good one, the way Nuala and I had with each other.

It's a bit perverse to be taking money off her old man to find her, but I figure if he's going to send someone after her, it may as well be someone like me, someone who's on her side and not his.

She never got along with the Gaffer.

It's not surprising, really. When I was going out with her, Nuala was a free spirit, wild at heart and champing at the bit, and he was a control freak. Sometimes he even used the cops to keep an eye on her. She told me she suspected that she initially took to promiscuity to spite the old man. Then she discovered she liked it so much she didn't want to stop.

That was back in the days before the plague of AIDS and we could afford to be free and easy with our affections. Nowadays, I wonder what passionate, virile young men and women do to burn off the excess heat, to contain exploding passion, and I shiver.

After me, there was a string of men in Nuala's life. I kept my ear to the wire, maintained an interest. Dublin is a small town. To my knowledge she'd never met the Love Of Her Life.

The rest of her life had been just as eclectic. Two years of philosophy at Trinity College, a year in the United States, a fling with dope and another with the women's movement. Most recent word had her dabbling in the production end of movie-making. That's a world that would suit her.

So I figure the beef between her and the old man is still the same, time hasn't tempered anything.

Maybe she's in provocative mode and he's got

the shits up him with an election due that she's going to pull some stunt that will leave him with egg all over his face and cost him precious votes. She's done a vanishing act and he wants to find her so he can keep an eye on her. Maybe he knows I was cosy with her once and he reckons maybe I can be a bridge across their troubled waters.

What's the harm?

Any danger of Nuala getting pissed off with me for taking the forty pieces of silver?

Nah.

She'd get a kick out of the Gaffer greasing me.

The old man is probably making a mountain out of a molehill anyway. She's probably getting an all-over tan on some nude beach on the Mediterranean or in happy *ménage à deux* in Spiddal or the Lake District, enjoying a romantic fortnight with her latest *paramour.*

So what if I pocket the Gaffer's money and I find her? She makes a phone call, puts the old man at ease and we have a bit of a giggle. Maybe we get to spend some time together. Some long days and nights. Lordy, lordy. That's a notion that settles easily in my mind. I've been down in the dumps, man. I could do with some celebration, some happiness, some Nuala in my life.

I could use some quality time with a good female friend.

I daydream a bit about the possibilities and the remuneration and the more I think about the proposition that's just come into my purview, the more amenable to it I become.

I figure I'll hear the Gaffer out and, if everything looks kosher – fuck – what the hell, I'll go for it.

3

McGonagle picks me up just before noon. The car is a black Beemer, with wine-coloured leather upholstery on the seats. The interior smells of male prosperity. Cigars, cologne and power. The air above the expansive back seat is heavy with the weight of the decisions made there.

McGonagle is on his own.

I go sit in the back.

He looks at me in the mirror, makes pyramids out of his eyebrows. He nods at the seat beside him, back at me in the mirror again, as if to say who do you think you are, royalty, putting on your airs and graces?

"What are you doing back there?" he says.

I sniff, make a show of inhaling the ambience of prosperity.

"I'm getting a taste of how the other half lives. Do you mind?"

He shakes his head.

"You're a nutcase," he says. "What are you?"

"A nutcase," I say.

I play along, but I'm not paying much attention. I'm making the best of the moment. I'm enjoying myself, getting cosy in the comfort, looking out the window. And, I guess I'm just a kid at heart, but I'm getting a bit of a kick out of the notion of McGonagle chauffeuring me around.

"You don't expect me to sit with the help, do you?" I say.

He looks at me in the mirror again, making sure I'm serious.

"Cheeky bugger," he says.

He puts the Beemer in gear and moves into the traffic.

In my day, in my jobs, I've travelled many the time as help in up-market cars. I never came close to owning a really expensive vehicle, but with the business and the life I've had, I've kind of got used to the feel of occasionally travelling first-class. Today in the Beemer I'm remembering the first time I rode in a rich man's car.

I was in fifth year in secondary school and I'd made fast friends with Davy Mullen. Davy and I couldn't have come from more different social milieus. His family was upper-middle-class. His father was a prominent barrister. But Davy and I got close. We still are.

One Saturday afternoon, unbeknownst to his parents who were away for the day, Davy borrowed the family car. It was a Jaguar XJ6. He drove up my road, parked the car outside our house and knocked on the door. I lived in a corporation estate where the residents thought second-hand Cortinas were posh, never mind Jags. We only saw the likes of them on the telly.

I came out and saw the car and I was thrilled skinny. A Jag come to pick up Milo. This was status, man. A touch of class.

We got into the car and before we were halfway around the block all the little kids were out on the street, running after us with awe on their faces and calling Davy a rich swine.

We never left the street that afternoon. I think every kid in the neighbourhood got a go around the block in the back seat of Davy's old man's Jag. It was a sweet afternoon. We kept Davy so late that when he got home his folks were there already and he was in hot water.

But he made a friend of me for life.

Now I'm sitting in the back of the Gaffer's Beemer, smelling the affluence, letting myself be driven off towards God knows what shenanigans, and I'm remembering the pleasure, the novelty, the sheer delight my friend brought to me and the kids on my street by coming to call on me in his old man's Jag.

My office is on the southern side of St Stephen's Green. Today it's the tail end of summer on the cusp of autumn and there's a touch of moisture in the air, but it's still sunny and the office crowd converges on the Green with sandwich bags, burgers or fish and chips and Styrofoam cups of coffee.

For the next hour the suits will share the park with the hippies and the homeless, the punks and the pensioners. I often spend the lunch hour in the Green, feeding the ducks and earwigging the chatter, the banter and the eloquent derision Dubliners are so expert at.

That's Dublin town for me — the ebb and flow and turbulence of derivative chitchat at lunch hour in St Stephen's Green on a weekday. You can keep your Molly Malone, your Jimmy Joyce walkabouts, your Floozie in the Jacuzzi.

Just give me the wags on the Green.

We leave the Green behind us and head for the suburbs on the northern side of the city.

I grew up on the northside and I still make my home there. I wouldn't live anywhere else. Unless, of course, I won the lottery and the Costa del

Erotica or somewhere sunny on the southern arse of Spain or France or Monaco maybe became an option.

But, barring such unlikely sudden riches, as long as I live in Dublin, or Ireland for that matter, the northside will always be home to me. Living there keeps me humble. Northsiders know what's what and they give short shrift to pomp and circumstance or delusions of grandeur. They're down to earth and that suits me. I like my people as I like my whiskey. Straight up.

The Beemer sails along like a yacht on placid waters and McGonagle keeps his peace. He sticks a CD into the stereo and his fingers tap the steering wheel, keeping slow time with Van Morrison singing *Have I Told You Lately That I Love You?*

I'm impressed. Van The Man is quite a stretch for a one-time hillbilly like McGonagle. Time was his musical repertoire consisted of Big Tom and the Mainliners, the Wolfe Tones and a few choruses of *The Black Velvet Band* at closing time. It's a sure sign that rock'n'roll has come of age and lost its edge when redneck Irish cops like McGonagle are listening to the same tunes as the trendies. Once upon a time it was like east and west — never the twain shall meet.

Maybe there's hope for the human race after all.

We cruise past Talbot Street. I'm reminded of a famous Dublin character from days of yore – the venerable Matt Talbot, a reformed drunk and obsessively religious man who slept on boards to deny himself comfort and devoted his life to whipping and hurting himself in the name of Jesus. Despite the rise of the Celtic Tiger and the prevalence of consumerism and agnosticism, many sturdy souls remain in this town who would pay sentimental homage to a strange, tormented man's relentless masochism and the not-so-distant days when self-flagellation was a virtue.

That's Dublin for you. It's a breeding ground for eccentrics, oddballs, warped saints, crazy scholars and just plain old lunatics.

And the city embraces them.

Nowadays the whips are racked up on shelves in knocking shops off the Burlington Road. They're taken down and wielded for money by sassy, shameless whores in sequined tights and leather knickers.

And the city embraces them.

But nowadays when the lash cracks, Jesus isn't in the game and there's precious little virtue involved in lapping up the punishment. There's no beatifications in store, alas, for the good citizens who nowadays don the cloak and stoically bear the burden of flagellation.

I picture poor old Matt Talbot standing in his chains and halo just inside the Pearly Gates, squinting down on European Dublin in the early morning of the new millennium. Laughing at us. All is changed and all is stayed the same, the venerated masochist might whisper to himself, with a private little chortle. I fooled them all. Had a great time.

And got myself beatified into the bargain.

Through the North Strand we drive, where, in World War Two, German bombers, oblivious or uncaring of Ireland's hard-fought, convoluted neutrality, let rip their deadly cargo.

We pass by Fairview Park, where the fantastic flower-beds lay perennially, miraculously untouched and unvandalised by the homophobic gurriers who lurk in the bushes in hope of cracking a passing gay skull or two.

Past Clontarf and St Anne's Park, celebrated in the history books as the spot where the great warrior King Brian Boru laid waste to the Vikings and threw them back into the ocean. Forever enshrined in my consciousness, not for the heroic exploits and derring-do of the noble Brian, but for the memory of a balmy summer evening back in 1979 when I lost my cherry to hot-breathed, swift-handed Cecilia Duffy under a bush at the foot of Mount Everest, the tallest tree in the park.

Cecilia Duffy. Now there's a memory.

Ah, sweet, slinky, sure-footed Cecilia Duffy. You opened my pores to the brave new world of the pleasures of the flesh and I've built a monument to you at the crossroads on the main street of my fond nostalgia.

Where are you now, Cecilia, I wonder. What are you up to? What did you end up doing with your life? And are you still performing your miracles of revelation? Would you change a thing if you could do it all over again? What I'm trying to say in my awkward way is, I suppose, I'll always love you just a little bit and thanks for the memory.

When I travel along these streets I'm coasting on the highways and byways of my recollection.

Past Kilbarrack and Sutton we go and into Howth, the picturesque fishing village where Erskine Childers' yacht, the *Asgard*, landed with guns and ammunition for the War of Independence. You can't dodge history in this city.

I spent much of my childhood on the Hill of Howth. My maternal grandparents lived in the city, as did most Dubliners in their time, which was long before the advent of airbuses and package holidays. Howth was a village in the country, not the suburb it is now. Granda was a carpenter. He leased a plot of land in an idle field and built a two-room hut on it. That was the family's holiday home. Their place in the country. After he died my granny got into the habit of taking me with her for a fortnight every summer.

For that two weeks I'd spend my days roaming the heather, climbing trees, searching for birds' nests along the sides of the cliffs, playing cowboys. Often, I virtually had the hill to myself. I was Jesse James, Wild Bill Hickock, Bat Masterson and Geronimo all rolled into one white-hatted, two-gunned rider of the purple sage on the Hill of Howth. Many's the dastardly villain I sent to meet his Maker in the great panhandle in the eastern sky. I was the holy terror of the Pecos. The big shot of the Brazos. I was the king of the hill. Over the years I got to know the place like the back of my hand.

The hut is long gone now and the field it stood in is home to a riding stable that backs on to the Gaffer's estate.

We motor through Nobsville, sanctuary of the upper-upper-middle class, where public transport rarely shows its common face, there's nary a sight nor a sound of children playing in the streets and the driveways are filled with Mercs and Jags and Jeeps and Beemers.

Past the infamous eyesore that TV personality Jimmy Fay calls home. It's a cross between Gothic mansion and Spanish-style *hacienda*. Marble meets *adobe*. Sylvester Stallone in a Spaghetti Western.

Tacky, tacky, tacky.

Fay is one of Irish television's top earners. He launched his career as a country and western singer in the heyday of the showbands and when they wound down he tried his hand at politics. He sat on the backbenches of the Dáil for four years, but he got bored with that. He missed the limelight and moved into broadcasting. His star rose quickly. Now he has his own daily programme on the radio and a weekly chat show on the telly. He's the darling of the happy homemakers.

He could retire a wealthy man today and the up-and-coming happy faces of TV land are keen to see him on his way, but showmanship is in his blood and he's leery of leaving the arena.

His neighbours were over the moon when he moved to Howth a few years back and he was invited to all the parties, until his hosts opened their mail and perused the invoices billing them for his appearances.

He's known around here now as Mister High and Mighty.

The Gaffer's gaff is an unobtrusive ranch-house. Low-slung and elegant, it fits snugly into the contours of the landscape, showing a bit of class, a stark contrast to Jimmy Fay's *nouveau riche* ostentation. Cooley's house sits snugly atop the hill and regally overlooks the Irish Sea. On a clear day you can think maybe you see Wales over yonder. On the gatepost there's a sign made out of a thick oblong slice cut out of the trunk of an oak tree. The name of the house is carved into the oak and inked in emerald green embossed in gold.

Saoirse, it says.

Freedom.

McGonagle gives the nod to two Branch men sitting outside the gate in a blue Cortina. One of them puts a walkie-talkie up to his mouth and says something into it. Another copper comes out of the trees lining the driveway and opens the gate for us. There's an Uzi swinging inside his camouflage jacket.

Welcome to Freedom.

The driveway is a quarter of a mile up a slight incline bordering a forest of ash and beech and chestnut trees and rhododendrons. The foliage is giving us the hint that it's just getting ready to start changing colour. In another few weeks this drive will be resplendent with the glorious hues of autumn.

We're up at the top of the hill and my ears are popping from the altitude.

McGonagle drives around the back of the house and parks on gravel beside a huge bush sculpted into the form of a horse. On the lawn dropping away from the house similar bushes are cut into the shapes of more horses, hounds, hares and foxes.

"The man is mad keen on the hunt," says McGonagle.

"Bully for him," I say.

4

McGonagle leads me into a kitchen that's as big as my flat. And there he is. Lord Muck himself. He's standing beside the stove with his back to us, pouring water into a coffee percolator. He looks every inch the lord of the manor. He's dressed in riding clothes – black jacket and tight-to-the-skin cream-coloured pants – the gear the upper crust wear when they ride to the hounds.

He turns as he hears us come in and I'm face to face with the living legend – the man who will in all likelihood be in charge of the country's destiny for the next four or five years.

He's almost bald on top, but the white hair that remains he wears long, flowing down over his shirt collar. It's well tended, thick and rich and wavy, and it adds a dashing, cavalier touch to his appearance. He nods amicably at McGonagle.

"Joseph," he says.

McGonagle nods back, casually, but nonetheless deferentially.

"Boss," he says.

They're easy with each other. Comfortable. Like Batman and Robin or Holmes and Watson. Or Fred Flintstone and Barney Rubble. You can sense that they've been together a long time and have settled into an easy, mutually acceptable officer/enlisted man relationship. Boss and glorified privileged gofer. The scuttlebutt says that McGonagle's loyalty to Cooley is as close to absolute as you can get. My money says that enlightened self-interest and sordid shared secrets are the glues that bind this dynamic duo. Call me cynical.

Cooley turns all his attention on me and looks me full in the eye. The famous, ocean-blue, lady-killer eyes. They're so blue they're almost translucent and, looking into them, I get a hint of how gorgeous he must have been in his prime. But the longer I look into those baby-blues, the more I realise it's like looking at a two-way mirror. You can see yourself reflected in them, but you can't see into him at all. He's managed to pull a screen over the windows to his own soul.

It gives him an edge.

I'm into edges.

I reckon.

I'm Milo. I'm smart. I'm an ex-cop. I know about interrogation. The trick is to get the upper psychological hand (the edge, in other words) on the perp and you're halfway there already. What's the scoop on getting results out of interrogation? Get the edge. That's the scoop. I know.

So does the Gaffer.

I'm barely in the door, but he has the edge on me already by virtue of the fact that we're doing our business on his turf. The trick is now to take the initiative back. But he's a wily fucker. He knows that. He beats me to the move. He steps up and in, his face six inches from mine, invading my space. But he's all grace and manners. He has the art of one-upmanship down well. His breath smells delicately of peppermint. He flashes his pearly whites. He sticks out his hand.

"Mr Devine, I presume?"

I nod.

We shake.

"Thank you for coming at such short notice. I know your time is valuable. I appreciate you sacrificing it to come and see the likes of me."

He's a slick one all right. Smooth as silk. He's the perfect host and the words slide out of him like cod-liver-oil snakes down your gullet and slithers through your digestive system to have its irrefutable, relentless way with you.

"Sit down, gentlemen, please," he says. "Sit. I presumed you wouldn't have eaten and took the liberty of preparing some lunch for us."

He ushers us over to a table that would comfortably seat the Last Supper. He has us sit. There's soda bread on the table and home-made brown bread. Cold meats, pickled onions, potato salad, crackers, a selection of cheeses and pâtés. I realise I'm starving. All I had for breakfast was two cups of tea and a KitKat.

Cooley brings the coffee and three mugs. He pours the coffee and ladles salmon pâté onto a cracker.

"Dig in, lads. Dig in. I'm a bit peckish myself. I've been out riding and the fresh air has given me an appetite."

He shovels pâté and cracker into his mouth. McGonagle and I dig in.

Lunch is peppered with small talk. His horse, Pirate Queen, is good for a flutter in Newmarket on Saturday, the country's budget surplus is going through the roof, and Cooley's wife Margaret made the brown bread.

After the meal we get down to business. McGonagle makes himself scarce and Cooley leads me into the lounge. The walls are papered a tastefully understated light-green with gold borders. He's partial to the green and gold, this guy. Persian rugs are scattered on the hardwood floor. A mahogany bar is to one side of a big bay window. On the other side is a Celtic harp that stands six feet tall, at least. It wouldn't surprise me to be told that it's the harp that strummed once upon a time through Tara's halls for the high kings of ancient Ireland.

The window looks out on the garden where we came in. Outside, a grey-haired plumpish woman wearing a tweed suit is tending a rose bed that's adjacent to a bush that resembles Bugs Bunny. I recognize her profile from the rare pictures I've seen in the papers. She's the Gaffer's wife.

Margaret Cooley, *née* Lynch, comes from a venerable old Irish acting family. During the forties and fifties, her father and mother were two of the leading lights of the Abbey Theatre. Margaret followed in their footsteps and surpassed them. She took to the acting like a duck to water – and why wouldn't she, said the wags, it being in her blood. The people loved her. They flocked to the Abbey to see her perform. She could have been a movie star, said the wags. They called her Ireland's Sweetheart.

Then along came the dashing, gorgeous Archie Cooley. A man on the make, with great things written large in his destiny – or so he'd have the world, and Margaret, believe. Ireland's Sweetheart met Ireland's Most Eligible Bachelor and that was that. For her. She fell head over heels for him. Gave it all up for him. Stayed home, looked after his needs and raised the children.

"Is Mrs Cooley the one with the green fingers?" I say, being polite.

"Yes," he says. "I don't have much time for that kind of thing."

He waves a hand at the furniture.

"Take a seat," he says.

I have my pick of a couch, a love-seat and an armchair, all covered in mustard-coloured leather. I flop into the love-seat. It's deep and cosy. Sitting in it is like floating on the Dead Sea.

Cooley pours drinks at the bar. Decent measures too. About five fingers of Crested Ten in heavy-bottomed glasses. There's a water cooler tucked behind the bar and he pours us each a half pint of water to chase down the liquor. I could grow into this life. He puts my glasses down in front of me and sits across from me in the armchair.

"*Sláinte*," he says.

"Down the hatch," I say.

We drink.

"Joseph tells me you're a friend of Nuala's?"

"It's been a while since I've seen her, but, yes, I like to think we're friends."

"Friends," he says.

He's gazing deep into the whiskey in his glass. The expression on his face is an invitation to share his pondering of the imponderable, as if he wants to invite my mind in there, to swim about with his in the whiskey vapours, to uncover the true meaning of friendship and pickle it.

"A true friendship endures over distance and time," he says.

Cooley the philosopher.

"I'll be perfectly frank with you, Mr Devine," he says. "It's no secret that my relationship with Nuala hasn't, at times, been as perfect as I would like. In many ways, in my private life, I'm an old-fashioned man, and children grow up so quickly these days. Do you have any kids yourself?"

I shake my head.

I wish.

"I haven't yet been blessed with a family," I say.

I'm starting to talk like him.

He nods, sympathetic already for the future he suggests is in store for me.

"Your time will come. And when you have a daughter of your own, you'll get a glimmer of the complete meaning of what I'm saying. Rest assured. No doubt the infamous generation gap is partly responsible for Nuala's disaffection. And public life takes its toll on personal relationships. The ordinary ups and downs of familial exchange are amplified a hundredfold in the glare of the omnipresent media. God knows, it's difficult enough for young people to come to terms with the demands and responsibilities of adulthood without the gutter press lurking ready to pounce and splash their little mistakes and, em, peccadilloes all over the front page."

Politicians sure like to hear themselves talk.

There's no need for me to say anything. He's not even looking at me. His gaze is diverted upwards, as though his audience is somewhere up there in the gods, close to the ceiling. He's playing to the gallery. He's working his way through his relationship with his daughter and, as is his wont being a politician, he's doing it by making an off-the-cuff speech and disseminating it in his head as he talks. That's what it looks like to me, anyway.

He catches my eye again.

"Don't get me wrong, Mr Devine. I know I could have been a better father. The demands of my life's work have been such that I haven't always been there for Nuala when she perhaps needed me. I make no excuses for myself. But it is important to me — at the outset of our relationship, as I hope to avail of your services and your good will — it is important to me that you understand that I love my daughter and I only want what's best for her and to protect her from the scavengers. And, believe you me, the scavengers are out there hovering."

I have to give it to the guy. He has a way about him. Charisma it is, and a tongue constituted of lyrical wax. Come the election, I wouldn't want to be running against him, debating with him.

"There are times," he says, "when I wonder if I made the right decision about going into politics. If I should have stayed in business. God knows, my life would have been easier. Things might have been different between me and Nuala. I would have had more time for her. I'm going to tell you a secret about myself, Milo."

I'm Milo now.

"I'm going to tell you something about myself that few people know — and I trust I can rely on your discretion?"

"Of course," I say.

What else can I say? The man is expounding pontifically, my body is drowsy digesting lunch, I'm sunk in the soft, seductive comfort of my mustard-coloured leather love-seat and the Crested Ten is mellowing me out. All in all, I'm being rendered uncommonly and uncharacteristically amenable to his lofty monologue. I'm being disarmed and I'm too languorously comfortable to bother fighting it.

"When I was a young man," he says, "I thought I had a vocation for the priesthood. I agonised over the notion and in the long run I decided to opt for family life and a layman's role in the church. I've never regretted my decision, understand. The business made me prosperous and my family, despite the occasional difficulty like the present one, has brought me much joy and fulfilment. But I often wonder if my decision — and it wasn't taken easily, let me assure you, Milo — I wonder if my decision to go into public service wasn't based on an unconscious inclination to live up to my spiritual vocation to serve my people."

He stands up and takes the empty glass out of my hand. My water glass is still full, all but forgotten on the coffee table beside my chair. We're knocking back the whiskey and keeping good time with each other. I feel the booze merge with the residue of last night's alcohol and freshen it up. *We're baaack.* I try to pull myself out of my languor, but I'm fighting a losing battle. It's *siesta* time, *amigo*. I could use a cup of coffee.

He goes to the bar and tops up our glasses. He hands me another five fingers of holy water and perches himself on the arm of my love-seat. Now he's looking down at me and, for the sake of good manners, I have to twist my body and tilt my head to look up. It's making me dizzy.

"Do you get my drift?" he asks.

I shrug.

He changes tack.

"Joseph tells me you used to be in the police force?"

"That was a long time ago."

"You're a man with a high regard for justice, I believe, Mr Devine."

I'm Mr Devine again. And Cooley is talking, albeit in code, about my falling out with my police colleagues.

"I believe in fair play," I say.

What I don't say is that being a cop, or (to be absolutely precise) not being a cop any more, loving my Maria unrequitedly and the vagaries of life in general have done their damage to my once pristine value system and my erstwhile creed of honour.

I don't say that my notion of what constitutes fair play these days is somewhat sketchy and tempered by the darker tendencies of my current moods. That the wind has been knocked out of my sails and I'm treading water on a glacially gradual tide of reconstruction. I don't say, nor do I concretely recognize, that in all likelihood I'm in a dismally vulnerable state.

I don't say it to him because I don't really say it to myself. But he's probably guessed it, the success of his life's work having likely been predicated on a capacity for astuteness in the reading of men.

"I admire a man with principles," he says. "And I admire a man infused with the spirit of free enterprise. It takes guts, especially in this country, even nowadays, with all that rampant prosperity and wealth out there, to turn your back on a secure job and a pension, to go out into the world and carve out your own corner of it. Joseph tells me you're doing just that, Milo."

I'm Milo again.

But Cooley is moving too fast. I know what he's up to. He's flexing his muscles, tilting at my old job, my old crisis, making hints about my ever-wobbly business. He's crowding into my space and manipulating it for dubious, probably nefarious, reasons of his own. And he hasn't been invited. And I'm pissed off. But I'm drifting, my head all woolly from the mixture of the booze, my melancholy and my dilapidated, hungover state.

I'm not on the ball.

"How is the business doing?" he asks.

"I'm getting by," I say, knocking back half of what's left in my glass. The love-seat is starting to close in on me and the pervasive smell of his expensive aftershave is getting up my nose.

"Excuse me," I say. "Is there a bathroom handy?"

He smiles amenably.

"Through the kitchen, down the stairs and first door on the left."

Through the kitchen, down the stairs I go and I take the first door on the left and thank Christ it's a bathroom. I drop my pants, sit on the bowl and piss. I've still got my drink in my hand. I suck it down and lay my forehead against the cool tiles of the wall. I gather myself.

Lunchtime drinking is a mug's game unless you're on your holidays or hanging loose. In control. If you want to play with the big boys, you don't play by their rules. You make up your own. Or else. I've been playing by the big boys' rules. Big mistake.

I lift my head and check out my temporary sanctuary. The bathroom is fucking huge. I'm squatting below and in front of what could very well be a Norman Rockwell print of the ideal American family (the Stars and Stripes is hanging on the wall in the background) sitting down to what must be Thanksgiving dinner. Turkey, squash, roast potatoes, good will and good cheer.

Shades of the Waltons.

But none of the comely Walton maidens ever turned to promiscuity to spite her old man.

Good night, John Boy.

I stand and zip up my fly. I splash water on my face and pat it dry with a towel that's as soft as a baby's arse. I drag my battered psyche back to the land of the living. I notice a jar of disposable toothbrushes and a bottle of mouthwash. I brush my teeth and have a gargle.

Back up the stairs I go and into the kitchen. There's coffee still in the pot and I fill my mug, knock half of it back and fill the mug again. I carry it into the lounge. The atmosphere in the room has changed. It seems colder. Feels like I've been gone for ages. The Gaffer is standing at the big bay window, looking out. I walk up and stand beside him. I look out. Margaret is gone. He feels me there and looks over.

"You have a fine home," I say.

"Yes," he says.

But he's been thinking despondent thoughts. The residue lingers in the air.

Apparently.

He looks sad. You can't read it in his eyes or on his face, but somehow his demeanour is full of an infinite, deep ruefulness.

I almost feel sorry for him.

We take our business back to the kitchen.

"I want you to find Nuala for me," he says.

"I know."

"Will you?"

"Why should I?" I ask.

"Because I don't know where she is."

"She's over twenty-one."

"Why shouldn't you find her?"

"Why did she go?"

"Honest to God, I don't know. You know Nuala. She's impulsive and unpredictable. This is not unlike her."

"So why are you so anxious to locate her, if this is so typical of her behaviour? It's nothing new. Why worry?"

He eyeballs me and his eyes are mirrors. They tell me absolutely nothing. His soul is buried deep behind those unfathomable orbs. He must be magic at poker.

"I'll be very candid with you, Mr Devine. Tomorrow, the Taoiseach is going to the Phoenix Park to ask our President to dissolve the Dáil and we'll be going to the people. It's time to face the puckout. By any count, this will be my last chance to become Taoiseach. I want the job and – let me be frank with you – the nation needs me. This is a time of great moment. Our country is at a crossroads. History is being made and its direction must be shaped. We have an opportunity at our fingertips to end the violence and suffering in this land once and for all. We have the chance to lay the groundwork for a new, perennially prosperous, united Ireland to emerge at some time in the near future. The country needs strong hands at the helm and I sincerely believe that I am the man to captain the ship, given the day that's in it. The competition simply doesn't have the brains or the bottle for the challenges of the times we live in. But the election promises to be a dogfight – very close – and I want to be sure no unexpected impediments drop in my path."

"Like Nuala?"

"Like Nuala taking it into her head to do something silly."

"Did you have a row with her?"

"Nuala and I are always having rows."

"About anything in particular?"

He shakes his head.

"About her attitude. My attitude. The meaning of life. The price of tea in China. That's the way it is with us. That's the way it's always been."

"Why would she want to upset your apple-cart, so, at this juncture?"

"You know Nuala. Why does she do anything? For attention. Revenge. For pure devilment. She *likes* to upset my apple-cart. And, cute as she is, her timing is usually impeccable. You may recall reading on page one of the tabloids, three elections ago, about her and her cannabis and skinny-dipping parties around my own pool, in my own home, while I was off on the campaign trail?"

Tsk, tsk, Nuala, you're a scamp.

"To be blunt, Mr Devine, my daughter can be a pain in the proverbial arse."

Coarseness – the proletarian touch. The punters must love it.

I look him right in the eye. My whiskey-induced funk has faded. I have my bottle back now.

"Fair enough, Mr Cooley. Now let me in turn be straight with you. I have two reasons for hesitating to take this job. One, maybe she doesn't want you to find her and if that's the case I might be betraying a friend. And two, nothing personal, mind, but I don't know you very well and a rule of thumb of mine is never trust a car dealer, an insurance salesman or a politician. You're a politician, Mr Cooley."

He squints over and lays a sympathetic fawn on me.

"I appreciate your honesty and I admire your loyalty to Nuala. Let me try to put your doubts to rest. Your succinct appraisal of the political profession is not without an element of truth. Machiavelli described politics as the art of deceit and I'm far too modest a man to argue with a philosopher of his stature. But I'm sure we can come to an accommodation that will overcome the barrier of mistrust and in doing so assuage your first reservation."

Only a politician could talk like this. He pours himself a cup of lukewarm coffee and tips the last of his Crested Ten into it.

"All I want to know," he says, "is that Nuala is all right and that she's going to behave herself. What if I was to propose that you find her, you tell her of my concerns, you listen to what she has to say and you report back to me with her full knowledge? We establish a line of communication and take it from there. Now what can be fairer than that?"

Aside from the fact that he sounds more like he's negotiating a hostage release than trying to reach out to his beloved daughter, I can't think of a single thing wrong with it. It goes the way my mind has been wandering.

"Seems reasonable to me," I say.

He sticks his hand across the table and we shake.

"Now," he says, "I want this to be strictly between you, me and the wall. And Joseph, of course. You'll be liaising with him."

Yabbadabbadoo.

"Understood," I say.

A wallet appears in his hand. He dips his other hand into it and fishes out some bills. I've never seen so much ready cash floating around in a day. Nobody seems to bother with chequebooks around here. He peels off ten one-hundred-punt notes. I'm counting them with my eyes. A grand. A fucking grand. In cash.

I hope I'm not drooling.

"This should do you," he says. "The taxman will be none the wiser. The job shouldn't take more than a few days. If it goes into next week there will be another thousand in it for you. All right?"

"Fair enough."

I reach over and take the cash. He clasps my hand with the cash in it in both of his paws and he stares intensely at me.

"And fuck the begrudgers," he says.

5

McGonagle materializes out of nowhere. He's a cross between Dirty Harry and Jeeves — a majordomo with a shooter stuffed down his servile cummerbund. Cooley deftly removes himself from the scene with a handshake and McGonagle steers me out through the back door.

He winks at me.

"You could do well out of this, Milo," he says. "If you do the job right the Gaffer might fix you up. You know the score. A word in the right ear and you could be set up for life. No more hustling and struggling and breaking your bollix chasing penny-pinching, piddly-arsed little jobs. He can put government contracts your way, as well you know. Money for jam. The Gaffer looks after his own."

Somehow the notion of being lumped in as one of the Gaffer's own makes me feel like a good scrub.

But the thousand *punts* is nonetheless snug in my pocket and there's the other three hundred stashed under a loose floorboard back in my office. I'm hitching a ride on the gravy train. And praying the juggernaut doesn't run away with me. Derail me. Once and for all.

"It's time you came in from the cold, Milo," says McGonagle. "When you've been on the inside, it's a lonely place out there where you are."

I grunt.

He snorts.

Male bonding.

"I hope you don't mind," he says, "but I've arranged for you to be driven back. I have to take himself to a meeting."

There's an unmarked Branch car parked beside the Beemer. I haven't ridden in a police car since I quit the force. The prospect is less than appetising. But McGonagle is already holding the back door open for me.

In I get.

"I'll be in touch, Milo," he says.

"Righto, lads," he says to his cohorts and he thumps the roof of the car.

Off we go.

The ambience in the cruiser is arctic.

The driver mumbles a begrudging, indecipherable

greeting as I sit in. He's a hunched and rumpled, medium-sized man with the dirty red hair of the travelling people. I remember him. He came into the Branch during my last few miserable weeks there. When I was an untouchable. He was quick on the uptake and gave me a wide berth. We never spoke more than two consecutive words to each other.

The passenger is a young guy I've never seen before, but the traveller has obviously had a word in his ear, because the youngster's head is standing at attention, his eyes locked dead ahead on the road. He's doing the right thing. Giving the cold shoulder to the pariah.

Me.

There's a *Daily Mirror* on the seat beside me. I pick it up, crack it open and make a fuss of pretending to read it. We drive all the way to town this way — me making a show of reading the paper and the two of them in the front in a silent huff over something that happened nine years ago and had nothing at all to do with them in the first place.

But that's a downside to the ancient Irish national character we haven't all outgrown yet — a peasant mentality with the attendant feudal inclinations, not to mention the all-encompassing, vituperative memory.

I make them stop outside a coffee shop and I run in and get an extra large cup of Colombian to take away. When they dump me outside my office it's almost three o'clock and starting to rain. The suits are long back at work and the punks, the hippies, the homeless and the pensioners have the park back to themselves again.

They're moving under trees for shelter.

I keep a bottle of Black Bush and a shot glass in the bottom drawer of my desk. For medicinal purposes. I pour myself a shot and knock it back. I pour another for sipping and I give the coffee an edge with a dram.

I'm a little rattled, despite myself.

The silent treatment in the cruiser took me back through the years to a time I don't care to remember. A time of grief, of disappointment, of grim solitude and ruthless isolation. A time that over the years I've come to look back on as my desultory agony in my own little Garden of Gethsemane.

My last few days in the Garda Síochána, the police force sworn to serve and protect peace and the Irish way of life.

I committed the Cardinal Sin.

I snitched.

Informed.

The IRA kills, exiles or kneecaps its informers, depending on the degree of transgression. The brotherhood of cops does worse. It persecutes them psychologically. Drives them up the wall. It's classic cruel and inhuman punishment. Cops blur the line between good and evil, between sanity and madness. They harass their traitors and turn them inside out with doubt and guilt and blame and indictment. It's nothing organised or orchestrated. It's just the way it is — the unwritten code of the boys in blue. It's tradition. The culture.

I don't know why I became a cop in the first place. I'm not exactly what you'd describe as enforcer material. My political and philosophical sensibilities are wet, as the Tories say, if anything. I'm more or less an idealist. I used to be, at any rate. Now I'm never quite sure what I am any more.

If I was to be psychoanalysed a shrink might come to the conclusion that I joined the cops to spite my old man. He was a rebel. He was an IRA man and an organiser for Sinn Féin when I was a kid. I still remember the monthly meetings at our house. Men would straggle in in ones and twos and sit huddled in our parlour to drink tea and smoke and plot conspiracies.

These were the only times our parlour door was ever closed.

I remember the burn of smoke in my eye when I put it to the keyhole to have a gander. I remember the muted hum of conversation that reminded me of the interminable recitation of the rosary at funerals.

I remember two cops sitting in a car a couple of doors down from our house and taking notes as the men came and went. I remember cops calling to the door to persecute the old man and him with the glint of steely defiance in his eye telling them to go take a hike and persecute some real criminals.

And when I grew up I joined the ranks of those whose job it is to harass and imprison conspirators like him. He never seemed to mind, though. I suppose he was glad I had a decent, secure, permanent job. His generation and class put great stock in a dependable weekly wage and a pension.

And he always took pains to differentiate between the bluebottle, the regular cop on the beat, and what he called the political police, the Branch. He was in a tricky situation there, as father to a growing boy. If he was too liberal in his animosity for the agents of the law I might easily have jumped to the conclusion that anything the law was opposed to was all right and he'd have a budding Billy the Kid on his hands. So he made the logical (to him) distinction between the regular cop and the politico.

Just as well so, in a way, that he was dead and gone when I joined the Branch in the early eighties. He wouldn't have liked it. I know that now – I've grown reflective as middle age encroaches on me. Back then I didn't know, didn't think and didn't care. I was hot to trot. I didn't think much about politics or my da and I was gung ho for promotion and the okay to carry a shooter.

That didn't last long.

The people I worked with were good soldiers – on the up and up – and my first couple of years in the Branch were relatively happy and carefree. But I soon learned, through bitter experience, that the old adage is true – when it seems like life couldn't get any rosier, adversity forever lurks around the corner, warming up to give you a kick in the bollix.

What brought about my undoing was the Christy Craven story.

Christy Craven was the golden boy of the Garda Síochána. He joined a few years before me, but he was famous before he enlisted. He played Gaelic football and he was the best in the world at it. For four years in a row, he captained his county team to victory in the All Ireland Football Final. He was the best mid-fielder in the country – in the history of the Gaelic Athletic Association, maybe.

Christy got an arts degree at Dublin University, but he didn't have much of a *grá* for the books. He had two loves in his life – Gaelic football and Betty Hanratty, a former Miss Ireland who returned his love. He got gold medals for the football and he married Betty. They had three kids in rapid succession. Christy doted on his family.

The Gardaí love their Gaelic footballers. Christy was a shoo-in for a job on the force.

Only three months into the job, he caught the Ranelagh Rapist. Some sicko had been terrorising the Dublin suburb of Ranelagh for a year. He'd raped five women. Women were afraid to go out on the streets alone. The police were under fierce pressure to catch the bastard.

Christy was walking his beat one night and he heard a woman screaming from up a lane. He went up the lane to investigate and caught the Ranelagh Rapist red-handed.

It was a fluke. The arrest virtually dropped into Christy's lap, so to speak. Nonetheless, the public and the politicians lavished their gratitude and relief on him. Christy was news again. He was a hero.

This wouldn't do his career any harm. He had it made. Or so it seemed.

But there was that fickle finger of fate lurking around the corner.

The drink destroyed Christy Craven. Whiskey got a grip on him and sucked him down into the pits.

Everybody conspicuously drank a lot back in those days. It went with the job and nobody was inclined to notice the early stages of chronic addiction. At the start of it, Christy was just like the rest of us — knocking back the pints every night and guzzling aspirins in the morning. He quickly moved up to the whiskey. Gradually, his first drink of the day came earlier and earlier until he was taking a large Jameson with his cornflakes in the morning.

His work suffered. He couldn't be trusted on the street. He was given warnings. He was sent away to dry out a number of times. Nothing worked. He couldn't get the monkey off his shoulder. Eventually, the brass gave up on him. They gave him a desk job. Christy became a filing clerk with whiskey breath and shaky hands.

Finally, Betty couldn't take it any more. She left him and took the kids with her.

That was the end of it for Christy. He didn't have the wherewithal to beat the booze. Life was hopeless. And empty with the family gone. Things couldn't get much worse.

Christy decided to kill himself.

His best friend was another copper named Joe Farrell. Joe was a decent man and he stood by his friend. He tried to help however he could, but there wasn't much he could do except be there to pick up the pieces.

One night, Christy and Joe were drinking with a bunch of us in the Garda Club. Christy got into his cups and told Joe that he was going to put an end to it all that very night. He was going to do himself in. Joe muttered all the right noises and took his time drinking his pint, thinking he should stay sober as it looked like he'd be putting Christy to bed. Again.

Christy went out to the jacks and didn't come back. We heard a screech of brakes from outside and a copper at the door told Joe that he'd seen Christy drive off like a maniac. Joe said fuck, knocked back his pint and went out after Christy.

It was about one in the morning and the streets were deserted. Joe found Christy's car wrapped around a lamppost. Christy had a small cut on his forehead where he'd hit the windscreen. Other than that, he was unscathed.

But there was a dead woman lying on the road, with pulp from her brain oozing onto the concrete like gooey caviar.

The woman was one of the travelling people. A woman of no property. A woman of no influence. No assets. No political clout. No power. She left a husband and five children.

Joe Farrell made a wrong call that night. He opted for a cover-up. He decided to save Christy's name and what was left of his career.

And hang the dead woman out to dry.

Joe stashed his own car around the corner. He called a pal of his in uniform to come to the scene.

He had Christy taken home and out of harm's way. He said he was driving Christy's car. He said the woman had run right out in front of him. A tragic death, but unavoidable.

I'm not a wimp or a prude. I believe in justice. And I believe in loyalty. I allow that anyone can make a mistake, even a cop. In my day I've left things unsaid and turned a blind eye on occasion to transgressions of one degree or another. I recognise the frailties of the human condition in myself and I make allowances for them in others. When the odd cop falls victim to an isolated aberration I'm prepared to look the other way.

But I believe in justice. That woman and her family had the right to justice. Not to mention compensation. Some things are just wrong and there's no two ways about it.

Word gets around. Everybody in the unit knew about the cover-up. The brass knew. I was sure of it. They had their spies and lackeys. Nothing went on that they didn't know about. The conspiracy seemed to have the tacit approval of the communal psychology. Some of us didn't like it. But we kept our peace and nobody talked about it. We held our noses and got on with the job.

Evil prospers while good men stay silent.

And the coroner's inquest loomed.

I waited and waited in vain for the brass to put

their oar in. Two weeks before the inquest I went to my boss and told him I was bothered. He said he'd look into it. A week passed by. Nothing happened. I went back to him.

Don't butt in was the message.

The days ticked by. The inquest got closer. I waited. Nothing happened.

I couldn't do the dirt. I broke ranks.

I did the right thing.

Finally.

I made a phone call to a reporter I was cosy with in *The Irish Times*.

And the shit hit the fan.

The case hogged the headlines for weeks. The brass assembled a committee of inquiry. Christy Craven went on disability leave. He was facing a manslaughter charge. Joe Farrell went back to walking the beat on some mountainside on the coast of Donegal. The dead woman got her justice.

Three months later, Christy put the barrel of a shotgun in his mouth and pulled the trigger.

A year later the inquiry put the whole thing down to a couple of bad apples and reassured the public of the flawless integrity of the police force.

I was long gone by then.

My reporter friend was loyal. He kept his source protected. My name was never mentioned in the papers. But nobody was fooled. It was a common knowledge that I was the stoolie. The supergrass. As far as the brotherhood was concerned I had the mark of Judas on me.

After all the hullabaloo died down they froze me out. My subsequent partners consisted of an endless rotation of new boys. When I walked into the cafeteria, the babble of conversation lost its exuberance. I found turds in my locker and piss in my shoes at the gym. The campaign of vilification was orchestrated by a small but powerful coterie of ring-leaders, hot-shots on the make and already well on their way up through the ranks. McGonagle was one of them.

My superiors made it clear that, if they had their way, in time I'd be spending my time keeping the peace among the mountain goats in Ballygobackwards.

Some of my colleagues came to me on the quiet and shook my hand and this was good. But they were powerless in face of the plodding, intransigent merciless machine of the brotherhood.

For me, all the joy was gone out of the job. Getting up in the morning and going to work was a bleak, demeaning, dispiriting sufferance.

I put up with it for five months.

Then I quit.

6

At a quarter to five half the whiskey is gone and, with all the booze and the remembering, I've got the blues. I hit the road. I'm homeward bound. I make my nest in a flat on Castle Avenue in the suburb of Clontarf, just three miles outside the city. Supper and a restorative shower might shake the cobwebs off my weary soul.

I sing along to a Willie Nelson tape as the traffic snakes through Fairview. I'm almost home when I find myself yanking the wheel, looping an impulsive loop back towards the Crescent in Marino, where my enigmatic sweetheart Maria rents the bottom flat in a renovated Georgian mansion two doors down from the house where Bram Stoker wrote Dracula.

I could use a woman's touch right now. Nuala Cooley's gaiety, come to think of it, would be the perfect antidote to my dissolute moroseness, but she's AWOL, so I put my pessimistic hope in the woman I reckon I currently love. Cruising by Maria's place I spot my competition parking his car. He's a gynaecologist in the Rotunda Maternity Hospital. He's toting a bunch of flowers and a bottle and he's ringing my Maria's bell.

Fuck it all, I say to myself.

Get the message, Milo.

Maria is quietly, doggedly, ruthlessly giving me the elbow.

Home, Milo.

7

A long hot shower puts some of the glitter back in my bones. I get into a T-shirt and sweat pants. I heat up a bowl of chili in the microwave and eat it watching The News on the telly. The government has leaked the scoop that it's going to the people. The race is on. It's time for the powers-that-be to shake each other's slithery hands, return to their respective corners and come out fighting.

The talking heads are full of beans, all excited at the prospect of an election and the overtime in store for them. One of them interviews the Gaffer going on about how he'll keep the country moving forward and infuse it with the confidence and energy to face the daunting challenges of the twenty-first century and the global economy.

I switch the channels and find a rerun of *The Simpsons*. That Homer is a howl.

An hour later a bell rings and jump-starts me out of a serious doze. The telephone. It's a quarter to eight and *Coronation Street* is on the box. I pick up the phone.

"Are you going for a pint?" says my good friend Davy Mullen.

The sound of his voice warms my blood. He's just what I need. James Taylor sang it right when he crooned about how good it is to know you have a friend in this cold and treacherous world.

Behind Davy's voice I hear glasses and bottles clinking against each other. I recognise the comfortable, muted noises of a quiet Monday evening in a pub.

He's in the Palace, he says, waiting for me.

I'm on my way, I tell him.

I splash some cold water on my face, take some Colgate to my teeth, put on a pair of old Levis and a sweatshirt. I turn off the telly and I'm off to see what's fast become a vanishing breed for Milo.

A man without an agenda.

Davy and I sat beside each other for our last three years of secondary school at O'Connell's Christian Brothers. The school was called after Daniel O'Connell, the Great Liberator, one of an abundant stream of great liberators eaten up by Irish history. The brothers took his noble name to heart. They wilfully ignored his non-violent ethos and struggled mightily, by any means necessary, and with varying degrees of success, to liberate us from the straitjackets of ignorance, temptation, materialism and worldly distraction.

While Davy and I sat at our desks, straining at the bit and wishing to High Heaven someone would liberate us from the oppression of a moribund, hidebound life under the rigid auspices of the Christian Brothers.

After we left school, although our lives took radically different directions, Davy and I stayed in touch. I joined the police force and he went to university. He always had his head screwed on. He planned ahead, organised his life. He studied history, got his doctorate and he now has more degrees than a thermometer. He ended up lecturing at Trinity College, his alma mater.

It's a cushy life, he says.

He got what he wanted.

While I fell in and out of a slew of relationships with all stripes of women, he married Lynda, his childhood sweetheart. They have three nippers and a comfortable home in the affluent environs of Dublin 4.

Davy has written a couple of history books. He's also into pop culture. He's a fountain of folkloric knowledge and he's made quite a name for himself as a captivating storyteller. He's a frequent guest on

TV talk shows and his name regularly pops up in the society columns. He's a celebrity and he gets invited to all the bigwig parties and functions. The big shots trust him as an unthreatening, if playful and sometimes sacrilegious, peer, and he moves easily along the corridors of power. He's privy to many secrets, knows where a multitude of bodies are buried, what skeletons live in whose cupboards.

He's a great man for a bit of gossip.

To all intents and purposes, he's a pillar of society, but he takes it with a pinch of salt. He has zero tolerance for the bent politicos, the craven apparatchiks, the mandarins, the corrupt captains of industry, the bagmen, the cartels and secret societies, the backscratchers, with their egos, their naked lust for power, their ruthlessness and what he describes as their lack of moral fibre.

They're pigs at the trough of the public purse. The corridors of power all converge on a cesspool. He says.

Davy puts a lot of store in moral fibre and he says it's a quality sadly lacking in certain good-old-boy sectors of Irish public life. So he thanks the stars for his independence and he guards it fastidiously.

"Have you lost your bloody mind?" he says.

I've just told him about my new case. He's aghast.

"Keep your hair on, Davy," I say.

But I know what I'm in for. A nuclear blast of the unvarnished truth. Some unwanted good sense, straight from the horse's mouth.

"I'm surprised at you, Milo. You, of all people, should know better. You must be off your rocker working for the likes of Cooley. You're a stupid gobshite."

He has a mouth on him, when he's of a mind to use it.

He is, of course, the voice of my own inner self, uttering the words I've avoided saying to myself all afternoon and evening.

"Cooley's kind are carnivorous by nature," he says. "They have no conscience. They use and abuse ordinary, vulnerable people just for the hell of it. For the entertainment. They're like kids in a Sam Peckinpah film, torturing insects for play. It's pathological. I spend time in the belly of the beast. I walk among them. I hear them talk. I see the way they operate. I know. And so do you. They don't give a shite about ordinary people. There's no such thing as justice, you know. You, of all people, should know. They threw you to the wolves before and left you with diddly-squat. You're out of your league, Milo. They'll eat you up and spit you out. Again. Get out of it. Get out of it now, while you can."

He's genuinely upset and worried about me and I'm touched by his concern.

"You're over-reacting, Davy," I say. "Anyway, it's handy money. A grand for a meagre week's work."

No sooner have I said it than he whips out with his pen and his chequebook.

"If you're that hard up for cash, I'll give it to you. No sweat. No strings. A thousand pounds, is it?"

I put my hand between the pen and the chequebook.

"Don't be a smartarse, Davy. Put your money away. And trust me. I can take care of myself."

He eyeballs me.

"Normally I wouldn't argue with you. But you haven't been yourself lately. I know you. You're in a funk. That woman has you all bent out of shape."

"Her name is Maria."

He snorts. He never liked her.

"Well, your Maria has you crooked. What's the story with her?"

I shrug.

"I'm in love."

"Hell's bells. At your age? You'll never learn. Trust you to fall in love with a farmer's daughter with the soul of a carpetbagger."

I leap to her defence.

"She's not that bad."

"Think about it, Milo. She's a daughter of the soil. And it's plain as the nose on her face that she's after a husband and kids and all the creature comforts of life. She's lethal for the likes of you. She wants roots, stability and relative prosperity. It's ingrained in her essence. She's after a man with the firmness of the earth and the predictability of the seasons. Not a gadabout like you. Nope. You're barking up the wrong tree there, pal."

He has me on the defensive.

"I have roots," I say. "I own my own home. And I'm stable."

He snorts again and snickers.

"In your own peculiar way. Not hers. Dream on, Milo. Look at the work you do. You're a thrill-seeker. People like her get involved with people like you for an adventure. You're a bit of a fling. In her old age you'll be a wistful memory of her youthful adventurism. She'll get a buzz out of telling her grandchildren how devil-may-care she was in her prime, going out with a private detective, a shamus just like Sam Spade. But as a long-term investment you're dodgy material to say the least. I'll wager a fiver you haven't even got life insurance."

I always meant to get it.

"It's on my list," I say.

He chuckles.

"Has she given you your walking papers?"

"Not in so many words. But she's staying out of

my way. And there's another bloke in the picture. A doctor."

"A doctor?"

"Yeah."

"Ouch. You're fucked, Milo. Fucked. With a doctor in the race, you're well and truly out of the running."

"Thanks for the vote of confidence."

"Such is life, Milo. Such is life. Besides the fact that she's a nurse and they have medicine in common, Doctor Kildare will give her everything she wants that you haven't got – prosperity, prestige, stability, holidays on the coast of lah-di-dah, free tranquillisers."

"Huh."

"Huh about sums it up, Milo. If you'll take my advice, you'll let her go. Play the field. Find yourself a flighty woman. An actress, if you'll excuse the cultural stereotyping. Or an artist. A brasser. A whore even. And take comfort from the knowledge that you're following in hallowed footsteps. The great Yeats suffered from the same affliction – unrequited love. He literally worshipped Maude Gonne. He was so mad about her he nearly drove himself demented. But she was enamoured with revolution and revolutionaries – she married the rebel, MacBride – so Yeats was in the ha'penny place. Didn't stand a chance. Now that I come to think of it, you have a lot in common with Yeats. You're a hopeless romantic, Milo."

"Bollix."

"You're no poet, though."

I try to bring the subject back around to the Gaffer, but Davy is off and away, his fancy taking flight. He's in his element now, rapturous with talking and theorising about Yeats, Maude Gonne and revolution. He's flying around the ivory towers of his own erudition. Nothing will bring him back down to earth.

"We men wrote the history books, Milo," he says, "and we wrote them to suit our own delusions. In our naïveté, we swallow the notion that Eve was fashioned out of Adam's rib. Of course it's all a load of shite. My thesis is that Eve was the original resident in the Garden of Eden and she was bored, so she plucked out one of her own ribs and created Adam out of it so that she'd have a toy boy to torture, to confuse and to persecute."

I go to the bar for two more pints.

At closing time we go our separate ways.

"I'll put out a few feelers," he says, "and see if there's any gossip floating around about Nuala or Cooley or the both of them."

I knew he would.

"Thanks," I say and I walk away.

"Milo," he calls after me.
I stop and turn to face him.
"Watch your back, my friend."
Softly, he says it.
He's serious.

8

I go to bed with a glow on. Davy's company has given me back myself for a while. But the glow diminishes as I think of the day that's almost done.

Davy is right, of course. Maria has me rattled. She's bad for me. Loving her has led me into a deep, dark forest of the heart and I can't see the woods for the trees. I'm lost and she's not looking for me.

Davy is also right about people like Cooley. Power is everything to them. They live and breathe it and they practise using and abusing it on little people like me. I go back over lunch. Cooley plying me with food and drink. *Plámás*ing me. The conversation and its subtle shifts of emphasis. Asking me about my business. The promise of easy money and a cushy life tempered with the implicit threat of *take it or I can make your life miserable*.

His country needs him, he reckons, with all the

belligerent arrogance of the egomaniac who figures he's born to greatness.

It's strange how the mind, when let run loose, can make connections, can dredge long-forgotten memories up to complement or illustrate an event or phenomenon of the day. I'm lying in bed and my thoughts are drifting back to when I was eleven or twelve years old and going to primary school. How our teachers used to line us up on the last Friday of every month and march us off to the local church for confession.

There was one priest we kids dreaded telling our little sins to.

Father Feeney.

Father Feeney didn't give a damn about run-of-the-mill sins like disobedience, petty theft or taking the Lord's name in vain. Such misdemeanours were incidental to him. He had his own priorities in the world of childhood waywardness. He was a specialist. He was into little-boy sex.

I was just starting to have wet dreams at the time and that was all Father Feeney was ever interested in hearing about. As soon as I got down on my knees in the darkness of the box and uttered my "bless me, Father," he'd hurriedly skim over the preliminaries and get right down to business.

"Did you have any bad thoughts?"

"Yes, Father."

"And?"

"And, Father?" I'd say, playing the innocent, though I knew damn well from bitter experience what he was after.

"And did your penis come erect? Did it get hard?"

"Yes, Father."

"Was it hot?"

"Yes, Father."

"And did anything come out of it? Was there any spillage?"

He made my flesh crawl. He had sex on the brain. He filled my vulnerable soul to the brim with guilt for my fantastic dreams. And he twisted all the goodness out of the sacrament of Confession. When I came out of the box after telling my sins to another priest, I always felt euphoric, like a great weight had been lifted from my shoulders and I was free of it forever. I felt liberated and serene. My soul had been cleansed.

When Feeney was finished with me, I felt contaminated. Dirty. He took that liberation and serenity, the happy grace of a good confession, and he shattered it into a million jagged edges of emotional shrapnel.

There were about fifty kids in my class at primary school. Normally, when we went to our monthly confessions, any priest but Feeney did the whole class in about three hours. He took twice as long. At least.

He was a pervert. Pulling his wire to the tune of a little boy's voice in the sacred, stealthy sanctuary of the confessional.

In itself, his perversion was his problem and his business. But he had the power. He was the master of the parish and he had us kids at his mercy. He had the power and it was his to use or abuse. He chose to abuse it. And us. He didn't have the right to do that.

Nobody does.

Feeney is a bishop now.

A Prince of the Church.

The swine.

9

Morning TV is bedlam with politicians of all stripes crawling all over each other to get a word in edgeways. It's feeding time at the zoo of ambition. There are interviews, profiles, retrospectives and debates. Propaganda dressed up as analysis. Reams and reams of bullshit. The pols would do anything short of telling the truth to get their faces on the box.

The talking heads are having a ball. They're all geared up to the excitement of the race. They're speeding. They've got an unnaturally intense buzz about them. It's as if they only come fully alive during elections, wars or natural disasters, and the rest of the time they're in semi-hibernation.

Waiting.

This is their meat and potatoes. Election time. It's their *raison d'être*. It's the oil for their engines.

The next four weeks will justify their existence for another four or five years, bar the odd hurricane, earthquake or the landing of an extraterrestrial spaceship on the Bog of Allen.

Between elections the scribes wistfully write books about the last election. Or the one before it. Or a mythical election that rumour has it took place in a suburb of Timbuktu at the turn of the last century.

The Gaffer is all over the box. He must have been up all night with his planners, advisers and spin doctors. But he's fresh as a daisy — waxing lyrical about peace in our time, Ireland eventually a nation once again and a permanent end to poverty and unemployment. He was wrong, apparently, about the election being a dogfight. According to the talking heads, it's not a close call at all. He's way ahead of the posse in the polls and it looks like the country is his to lose. But it's early days.

I slice a *croissant*, fill it with cheese and heat the sandwich in the microwave. Eating it with a cup of hot coffee, watching the old pro operate, I find myself half hoping Nuala will pull one of her stunts and blow him out of the water. I'm surprised at myself. At the vehemence of my distaste for the man. I thought I didn't care. I thought I reckoned that all politicians are much of a muchness. That one is as bad as the other. I thought it didn't matter which of them got crowned.

Now it seems to matter to me. Deep in my bones, I realise, I seriously want Cooley to lose. I don't like the man. I'm leery of him running the country. Something about him shivers my timbers.

I tell myself I'd probably feel the same way about the others if I'd had a conversation with them yesterday about finding their missing daughters at the onset of an election. If I'd been face to face with their hunger, their greed and their obsessive demagoguery.

But I'm not convinced.

I put on my black linen suit, a grey shirt and a muted silver tie. A pair of black Hush Puppies and grey socks. I've got an appointment to seal a deal with my supermarket manager today and I figure that a man who's so eminently lacking in imagination that he ends up spending his working life as a supermarket manager will indubitably expect a suit and tie.

I hit the road.

My first stop is the Temple Bar, where Nuala's film production company has its headquarters.

The Temple Bar is Dublin's Haight Ashbury for the new millennium. Except, instead of peace and love and marijuana, the spirit of free enterprise rules, with maybe a little quiet coke and Ecstasy on the side. Instead of degenerate dope dealers and panhandlers there are guys with briefcases and pony-tails. Instead of bombed-out bimbos there's up-and-coming fashion designers with tattoos on their shoulders and ankles and diamond studs in their belly buttons. Everybody dresses in black. The place is supercool and quietly throbbing with positive energy.

This is the stomping ground of the beautiful people. I have my eyes peeled for celebrities. Maybe I'll catch a glimpse of Sinead O'Connor. I have a recurring dream about Sinead. I'm in a bubble bath and she's sitting on a stool beside the bath. She has a two-day growth of hair on her head and she's bent over, scrubbing my back with the stubble. That's it. All of it. I swear.

There are plenty of eye-catching celebrity lookalikes and I could sit here all day watching this world go by, but, alas, there's no sign of the real thing.

I find the *Banba* Films logo on the heavy wooden door of a huge, square, red-brick building that looks like it used to be a warehouse. Inside the door a woman, wearing black jeans with holes in the knees and a black T-shirt with the logo *Meet Your Maker She's A Woman* on it in white, sits at a desk made of black glass and shaped like the shark in *Jaws*. The receptionist is thin as a rake and her hair is dyed snow-white. She looks like a Q-tip with Doc Martens on.

She looks me up and down. She must approve

because she smiles and this is a nice little boost to my ego. It's about time I got a lift.

"Hello," she says. "Can I help you?"

I tell her my business and she talks into a little Oscar statue that's really a telephone. Nice touch. Three cheers for good old Irish ingenuity. But it's probably made in Taiwan.

"You can go on up," she says, nodding at a set of stairs behind her that resemble the fire escapes in *West Side Story*.

Up the stairs I go. Under my breath I'm singing the *Maria* song from *West Side Story* and thinking what a shame it was that Natalie Wood had to fall into the water and die so young. She was a cracker.

At the top of the stairs there's what strongly resembles a revamped barn loft. It's all open-plan. The walls and the ceiling are painted peach and the sparse furniture is black. Carlos Santana supplies the background music. Yonder there's a bloke sprawled on a couch talking into a cellular phone. He gestures me over.

I go.

The guy is full of beans, all animated, full of enthusiasm, talking into the phone about a deal you'd be a fucking lunatic to turn your back on. He has a Dublin 4 accent — all aah's and no aaa's. He's in his late twenties or early thirties, with a pony-tail and granny glasses. He's wearing blue jeans, a black sports jacket and a peachy polo shirt that goes well with the walls and the ceiling.

It's far from the world of supermarket managers he does his business.

He throws shapes with his hands telling me to sit down. On the other side of the room there's a black armchair made of leather and steel tubes, but I figure we'd be shouting at each other. The couch is long enough to fit five and I'm heading for the far end when he kills his confab.

"Sorry about that," he says, nodding at the phone. "It's all go around here."

"Good for you."

He stands up and sticks out his hand.

"I'm DV MacEntee," he says.

We shake.

His face is open, friendly, generous.

Some people you like on first impression. You can't help it. There's something about them. They send out all the right signals. There's no interference, no static, no ready-made complications. No bullshit getting in the way of the good vibes. He's one of them. His aura is clean, I guess.

"What can I do for you?" he says.

"I'm a friend of Nuala Cooley's and I'm trying to find her," I say.

I figure it's smart to leave the Gaffer out of it for now.

"I'm a friend of Nuala's too and I don't know you," he says. "Who are you?"

He's being protective. Looking out for Nuala's welfare and safety. He doesn't trust me. It's in his eyes and his body movement. He goes up another two notches in my estimation.

"The name is Milo Devine."

His face lights up like a Christmas tree. He's obviously delighted to see me. And there's a flicker of relief there too.

I'm flattered. An approving smile from the Q-tip and a wide-eyed welcome from the yuppie. The day is shaping up.

"As I live and breathe," he says, "the legendary Milo Devine. I'm proud to make your acquaintance at last. Nuala has told me all about you. You're Ireland's last honest man, by her account. The renegade cop."

"Shucks," I say.

His eyes get a roguish twinkle in them.

"The Lone Ranger," he says.

The Lone Ranger. Jesus. That's what Nuala used to call me when we were having sex. She used to like to go on top, the better to facilitate her achieving orgasm. That suited me just fine because, being indolent by nature, I like to lie down. I also liked to look up at her. She'd be up there, riding the shite out of me and, knowing I had a fondness for old western movies and TV shows, she'd hum the *William Tell Overture* — the theme music from *The Lone Ranger* — and she'd roar at me, urging me to "Hi-Ho Silver Awaaay!" Sometimes I'd nearly miss the pleasure of the orgasm for laughing, but she'd always shut up and buck up just in the nick of time.

I didn't reckon on her gossiping about it. She must have been close to this guy.

I'm blushing.

"Jesus," I say.

DV MacEntee is chuckling. He pats a spot beside him on the couch.

"Come, sit down, Milo Devine. Nuala has given you a splendid reference. Would you like some coffee? Water, perhaps?"

There's a half dozen bottles of Ballygowan spring water on a little black glass table beside him. But I'm still happy with the aftertaste of my cheese *croissant* and coffee.

"No. I'm all right, thanks. Information is what I'm after."

He heaves a heavy, heartfelt sigh.

"Well, I'm glad you've finally arrived on the scene. I've been frantic. I can't find Nuala. She's just disappeared. I've checked everywhere and everyone I could think of. I don't know what to do. I've even thought of ringing that prick of a father of hers in Howth. But a policeman phoned looking for her and he said he was acting on behalf of the Gaffer. So I figure, well, at least the old man knows she's . . . away . . . and he's taking an interest."

"And you really have no idea where she is?"

"I haven't a clue."

"When did you last see her?"

He looks at his watch.

"This could take a while, right?"

I shrug.

"Maybe."

"I'm supposed to be at a shoot ten minutes ago. Can we talk on the way?"

"I don't see why not," I say. "I'll give you a lift, if you like."

"That would be grand," he says.

"Before we go, though, I'd like to take a look around her office, if that's okay?"

He laughs, looks around him, spreads his arms.

"Take a good look, Milo Devine. This is it. *Banba* Films is not the civil service. There's no bureaucracy. We're lean and mean, my man. We do our business on the hoof. Nuala's office is a cellular phone and a laptop. We have a hospitality room out the back downstairs for stroking clients. Otherwise, this is it."

Empty space. The new-age clutter is in cyberspace.

"I don't suppose she left her computer behind?"

He shakes his head.

"Right so. Let's go," I say.

He sticks his phone in his pocket, grabs a Ballygowan and off we go.

"What does the DV stand for?" I ask him on the way down the fire escape.

"Dominus Vobiscum," he says.

I look at him.

He chuckles.

"Joke," he says. "Though if it had occurred to my mother . . . it doesn't bear dwelling on. She was a great one for religion and held the saints in the height of esteem."

"Snap."

"Yeah. Ireland, right? The DV is for Dominic and Vincent. I'm called after Saint Dominic of Loyola and Vincent de Paul."

"A pair of holy terrors."

"Proper hellraisers."

"A lot to live up to?"

"I do my best."

In the car I ask him where we're going. The Liberties, he says. He's making a movie about the Easter Rising, revolving around the romance between the sickly rebel leader Joseph Plunkett and his sweetheart, Grace Gifford, who were married in Plunkett's prison cell just before he went out to face the firing squad.

"Sounds like a good one," I say.

"Oscar material, would you say, Milo?"

"You have my vote already. It's a marvellous story. Who's playing the lead? Daniel Day Lewis, I suppose?"

"No way, man. Daniel Day is *passé*."

"Really?"

He nods.

"Gabriel Byrne is playing the lead. He's co-producing the film with us."

We get back to Nuala.

The last time he saw her was the Friday before last. They finished up work in the office around four in the afternoon, had a couple of drinks in Peter's Pub and went their separate ways.

"I didn't hear from her over the weekend — there's no such thing as a day off in this business — but she didn't return any of my many messages. Then, when she didn't turn up for work on the Monday, I got worried. At first I thought she might be sick and I called over to her flat. There was no answer. Then the policeman, the Gaffer's man, phoned on the Tuesday and I got really anxious. I called everyone I could think of. Her friends, the pubs and restaurants she frequents, her gym. Her travel agent, even. No joy."

"Weird."

"Yes. It's not like Nuala at all. I'm worried, man."

"You obviously know her well enough to be more than her boss. I don't mean to be nosy, but are the two of you closer than just friends? I have to ask."

He laughs.

"We're just friends, Milo. I'm strictly a man's man, if you get my meaning. Here because I'm queer and queer because I'm here, as Brendan Behan liked to sing when he was in his cups."

He winks at me.

"Yikes," I say.

He chuckles.

"Do you feel safe?" he says, grinning lasciviously.

"I'll take my chances," I say.

He gets serious again.

"But Nuala and I were very close friends," he says. "Our relationship goes back a few years. We were at Trinity together. We met at the Film Society. She stood out as a pearl among swine. The arty crowd can be terrible drudges-cocky, snobby and pretentious. We're none of the above. We were kindred spirits and quickly became fast friends. She's a special kind of creature, is Nuala."

"Don't I know it."

"And another thing," he says. "I'm not her boss. We're partners. I started *Banba* on my own and quickly sussed that there are so many angles and considerations to this business I'd be overwhelmed on my own. I needed a partner. There was nobody else in the running as far as I was concerned and, fortunately, she jumped at the chance. She got her hands on a bit of money, bought in and we haven't looked back since. That was a year and a half ago. And we're doing well, Milo, if I may say so myself. We're doing very well."

"All the more reason for her not to just take off."

"She didn't just take off, Milo."

There's anguish on his face now and his eyes are damp.

"She didn't just take off. She wouldn't. She couldn't. It wasn't in her nature. Something has happened to her."

A shiver runs down my spine. Dread makes a fist and twists my intestines into a ball. For the first time since I got involved in this case, fear for Nuala makes its presence felt in my consciousness.

"I love her, Milo," DV says. "She's not just my business partner. She's one of nature's finest. And she's my best friend. You have to find her for me."

Then he takes the trouble to include me.

"For the two of us."

I like this guy.

"I'll do the best I can," I say. "But let's not start imagining things. Let's stick to what we know for the present and not jump ahead of ourselves."

He nods. Dries his eyes with a paper hankie.

"Has she been worried about anything?"

"Nothing she shared with me. But I did notice that over the past few months she's been, not obviously unhappy, but . . . less exuberant, if you know what I mean. There was no dramatic sea change in her personality, no mood swings or anything. She became somewhat subdued, is probably the best way of putting it."

"What about her love life?"

"She has no shortage of admirers. Never had. You know that. Plenty of dates. There's a lawyer fella who virtually haunts her."

"Stan O'Brien?"

"You know him?"

"I know him."

Stan the Man.

Poor Stan has been moonstruck over Nuala as far back as I can remember. His father is one of Cooley's apparatchiks. Stan would probably be the Gaffer's choice of a mate for his daughter. Such a merger would keep the family in the club. But it was never on the cards and pursuing it was a waste of Stan's time and energy. The chemistry was just never there for Nuala.

So Stan is still hanging in there. At least he deserves credit for persistence.

Or pity for self-delusion.

We're deep in the Liberties now and I park the

car down the road from where Gabriel Byrne is up on a soapbox, dressed in an Irish Republican Brotherhood uniform and a Sam Browne belt, delivering an oration to a crowd of scruffy, turn-of-the-century working-class Dubliners and a few top hats. The camera is rolling. Hollywood has come to the rebel Liberties.

We sit in the car for a while. DV is deep in thought.

"Mind you," he says, "recently I had the sense that maybe she met someone she wasn't comfortable talking about. Some mornings she'd come to work and she wouldn't bubble on about what she'd been up to last night. That was not like her. I didn't pry. I gave her some space, some time. But it crossed my mind once or twice that maybe she was seeing a married man and that was why she wasn't her usual perky self."

Bingo.

A lead. Something to get my teeth into.

A married man.

The director must have called cut. The crowd of extras loosens up and Gabriel Byrne gets down off his soapbox, takes his hat off and wipes his forehead with a hankie. We get out of the car and ramble towards the action.

"You have no idea," I say, "who the man could have been, I suppose?"

DV shakes his head.

"I haven't a clue."

"One last thing," I say. "Do you know where Nuala got the money to buy into *Banba*?"

"I have no idea. I never asked her. But there's never been any shortage of money in the Cooley family. I figured she had it in trust or something or else she asked the old man for it."

Gabriel Byrne spots DV and wanders over. DV introduces us. Gabriel Byrne shakes my hand.

"How's it goin', Milo?" says Gabriel Byrne.

"Grand, thanks, Gabriel," I say. "How's yourself?"

"Grand," says Gabriel Byrne.

I'm talking to Gabriel Byrne.

Pinch me and wake me up!

Then a woman dressed in black starts fussing with Gabriel Byrne's make-up and the camera crew converges on DV for a confab. It's time for me to be off. I take DV aside for a last word.

I like the man's style. I thank him for his trust. He appreciates it.

"I can see why Nuala holds you in high regard," he says. And I appreciate it.

We appreciate each other. Lovely.

He looks me up and down.

"Y'know, there's probably a movie in your story, Milo. The cops. The suicide. The attempted cover-up. The raw deal you got. That could make a great script."

"Do you think so?"

I'm thinking this could be the start of a beautiful friendship.

"Keep in touch, Milo," he says, "and let me know how you're doing. Or if I can help in any way."

"I will," I say.

Then he's swallowed up in a gaggle of moviemakers and I take a walk.

I'm scratching my head.

Gabriel Byrne is a cool dude. And a nice fella.

But Daniel Day Lewis.

Passé?

Fuck.

10

Spending the morning with DV has more or less finished off the job Davy started last night. I feel clean again. Rid of the lingering pollution absorbed throughout yesterday (and too many other yesterdays) spent with the heavy hitters and the low-lifes, who are often interchangeable.

DV has been a breath of fresh air. There's no vindictiveness about him. No ulterior motives. No heebie-jeebies. No shite. He's just an ordinary, smart young bloke with an open mind and a generous heart, outside the almighty loop of clambering potentates, doing the business, trying to make a life for himself.

In my business I spend too much of my time twisting my gut in the bad company of chancers, *sleeveens*, gombeen men and gangsters. Half a morning with DV has been refreshing.

But I'm sombre too. His anguish for Nuala is

infectious. Driving out of the Liberties, I'm more worried for her than I was when I started out from the *hacienda* this morning.

By now it's pushing noon and I have a date with the supermarket whizz kid at twelve-thirty, so I cruise on over to Bargain Billy's on the Malahide Road. Billy has six shops scattered round Dublin and he wants the security revamped in all of them. A pal of mine in his golf club put him onto me. This interview should be a doddle.

Billy would have second thoughts if he knew my pal is a conman by vocation and inclination. Leonard Longley is his name. Lenny the Loop, he's called in his fraternity of fly-by-nights. He pulls all sorts of stunts with bogus cheques and credit cards and other people's identities. And he plays a mean round of golf.

It takes all kinds to make the world go round.

Bargain Billy turns out to be a gobshite. A mini-fascist. I've met a few of them. They're guys who love guns and uniforms, but usually don't have the bottle or the wherewithal to get into the cops or the army, luckily for the rest of us. A lot of them become security guards. If he lived in the United States, Billy would spend his weekends in a forest or a swamp, dressed in camouflage gear and shooting live ammunition at defenceless animals and imaginary enemies. Some people take their manliness far too seriously.

"Do you carry a piece?" he says to me as he shows me around his shop.

"Now and then," I say, with a soft elbow in the ribs for dramatic effect. "It depends on the case."

He nods conspiratorially.

Lord, give me patience.

He's fascinated with the intrusiveness that sometimes comes with security work. He's turned on by the invasion of privacy, as are many people, so long as they're the perpetrator and not the victim — the watcher, not the watched. Billy loves the gadgets, the mechanics of the operations that enable us to delve into the nitty-gritty of other people's lives.

He'd give his eye-teeth, but not, alas, his money, to surreptitiously put microphones and surveillance cameras all over his supermarkets, in the loos especially and in the ladies' loo particularly — not in the interests of security, but rather to indulge his own depraved predilections.

I know Billy's form. He's a voyeur, a Peeping Tom in the rough. His kind is never subtle. They can't conceal their depravity. Lascivious is the word for it. He'd take the tapes home and start a collection to feed a habit that would evolve into God-knows-what form of base and deviant anti-social behaviour.

I have a brainwave. There's a security fair in the

Gresham Hotel on Saturday. I invite him along. He's chuffed at the notion. He'll live my job vicariously checking out the gear, we'll pick out some stuff for his shops and he'll be happy as a pig in dippity-doo-da.

I'll add the day to his bill as expenses.

He may be a gobshite, but his money still buys groceries and pays the rent. And he'll sing my praises maybe at his local chamber of commerce (and on the golf course) and put some more business my way.

I get out of Billy's at two o'clock and I'm feeling mighty peckish. I drive back into town and park the car at my office. I ramble over to Bewley's Café for lunch. Most of the business crowd is gone and I get a table to myself. I get bangers and mash with a killer wine sauce and a pot of tea.

I lap it up.

After I've eaten I give myself a half hour's rest and relaxation with the paper, which today is not a pastime conducive to distraction, because it's chock-full of chatter about the election.

All roads lead back to the Gaffer nowadays.

He has nearly all of page three to himself. There are loads of quotes from him. About how he's going to fix this, cure that, get rid of the other and rebuild the nation strong and free. It's a piece of fluff. Some desk-happy reporter rewriting Cooley's press releases.

The crossword is a safe haven.

11

When I get out of Bewley's the sky is dark and rain threatens. Nonetheless, I decide to take a chance on walking. I like a stroll after lunch when I'm in the city. I head for the Powerscourt Shopping Centre, where Cynthia Pilkington has her fake-fur shop. Cynthia is Nuala's best friend. At least she was up to about two years ago, which is as up to date as I am on Nuala's relationships, but they were thick as thieves as far back as I can remember and I'm guessing they still are. I'm hoping Nuala discussed her love life with Cynthia.

I take the scenic route.

Outside the Bank of Ireland, members of SPUC, the Society for the Protection of the Unborn Child, are walking in sacred circles, reciting decades of the rosary and holding up pictures of dead fetuses. I keep my head down.

Up past the pro-lifers, there's an aging hippie collecting signatures for a petition to legalise marijuana. His name is on the tip of my tongue – rhymes with Obi Wan Kanobe or something. He's been part of the furniture of Dublin streets for as far back as I can remember. I sign his petition for the umpteenth time. What the hell – you've got to admire his dedication and tenacity.

"Thanks, man," he says. "That's cool."

Cool.

That's me.

On the corner of College Street, across from the gate into Trinity, a pavement artist is doing the legendary Oisin's return from *Tír na nÓg* – the Land of Youth. Oisin has just fallen off his horse. The legend was that if he touched the ground outside *Tír na nÓg* he'd lose his perpetual youth and assume his true age. The picture depicts his rapid metamorphosis from gay young blade to decrepit old man to corpse. Some peasants gather around and look down on him with horror on their faces. The artist has deftly captured the transition.

This painter is one smart bucko. He's got a girlfriend there, dressed in the attire of the ancient Celts, reciting the legend of *Tír na nÓg* to a bunch of tourists. There's an Enya tape playing in the background. The tourists are enthralled, verging on hypnotised. They lap this stuff up.

There's one artist who'll never be driven to cutting off his ear.

I drop a fiver into the hat.

Shucks.

By the grace of the Gaffer I can afford to be extravagant.

Grafton Street is bustling for a Tuesday. There's a fair-sized crowd gathered around an acrobat in a top hat and tails, who's juggling daggers with his legs spread wide atop a unicycle and singing the Tom Jones song, *Delilah*.

A mime artist in white-face is having a stressful time getting out of the invisible box that apparently imprisons her.

A religious fanatic is walking around in circles swinging the catechism over her head, warning us all about the imminence of the apocalypse and urging us to repent and find a friend in Jesus.

Ireland's star is in the ascendancy on the world stage and Dublin is reaping the rewards. The city hums. It's the sexiest place in Europe, the pundits say. We're in with the in-crowd. Even the bloody Brits are coming over on day trips. It's as if the last remnants of de Valera's shroud of austerity have at last been cast off our shoulders to liberate the pagan Celtic soul and celebrate life in all its glory and splendour.

Our music is top of the pops. Our writers are

writing bestsellers. Our poets are garnering Nobel prizes. Our movies are winning Oscars. And our whizz kids are making so much money that Wall Street is calling us the Celtic Tiger. On top of all this there's the come-day, go-day, increasingly real possibility of peace forever after in the north – the crowning glory.

We're the tops.

The hucksters are making sure they get their piece of the pie. Here on Grafton Street, they've set up their portable stalls and they're flogging their jewelry, sunglasses, badges, leather gear, baseball caps and T-shirts. Their eyes are like windscreen wipers in the rain. They never rest. Swish, swish, swish. They perpetually sweep the street from one end to the other, forever on the lookout for an approaching copper. The traders are like the batteries – ever ready to fold up and scarper.

I spot Jamie Muldoon at his jewelry stall. He's gazing pensively up at the clouds. He looks like he's saying a prayer. I can read his mind. On the one hand he's hoping the rain will hold off so he can do a bit of business. On the other hand he's gumming for a pint and praying it will lash rain, so he can make a dash for the boozer and lower a few pints to soothe his rattled bones.

Jamie is a dreamer with a heart of gold and a monkey on his shoulder. He's an ex-junkie, if there is such a thing. He's off the smack three years now and he uses the booze to help himself stay clean. He's doing all right, I reckon. He's alive, for God's sake. A walk on the moon may be a giant step for mankind, but one more day off the powder for the likes of Jamie is a pure and simple glory. The monsters he's looked in the eye in his day would make quivering blubber of many of us.

His eyes come down from the sky and he spots me. He waves and calls across.

"How's she cuttin', Milo?"

"No use complaining."

"Happy hunting."

I give him the thumbs up.

The Powerscourt Centre is throbbing with energy, jam-packed with shoppers intent on living up to the demands of our new-found prosperity and the consumerism that goes with it. Dubliners were never better dressed and the byword is party, party, party.

Disposable income must be disposed of. Right? *Can't take it with you* may be the philosophy of the new millennium.

It's a brutal town to be poor in, with all the talk of prosperity, but a great place if you have the shekels. Like most places, I suppose. But this is my home town.

It's special.

12

The sign over Cynthia's shop says it all.

Falsey Furs – Wear Them With A Clear Conscience.

She's way ahead of her time, is Cynthia. Always has been. When she opened this place six years ago she handed the political purists of all shades a conundrum on a plate. Is it all right to wear something that looks like you're pretending you're wearing something that had life in it once?

The save-the-whalers didn't know which way to jump. Whether to applaud or denigrate. And the fur-lovers pondered whether they should be giving the finger to a business rival and spreading out the red carpet for a possible ally in the war for hearts and minds.

Caucus time.

And it was grist to Cynthia's mischievous mill.

She sees me coming in the door and her cherubic little white face sprouts a warm flush in the cheeks. She runs over to me, gives me a peck on the nose and a big hug. Her body is as generous and trusting as her optimistic temperament and she folds against me like tipsy jelly.

She smells of shampoo and health. She's wearing a black spandex dress that barely covers her arse. It looks like she's wearing coloured clingwrap. If she's got knickers on they're made of gossamer. She's not wearing a bra. I'm wearing an instant erection. I'm hopeless like that. Her dress hangs off one shoulder. As she cuddles me, I'm looking down at her bare shoulder. The skin is smooth and alabaster white, with a tattoo, a small set of puckered ruby lips, on the curve of her shoulder. I want to bite those ruby lips and suck them.

I want it bad.

It's always been that way for me with Cynthia.

When she and I and Nuala were together as a trio, all was fine. Nuala had a firm hand, if you'll pardon the expression, on most of my primal urges. Cynthia was just Cynthia. Nuala's friend. And great company.

But, if Nuala wasn't around and Cynthia was, the sexual current between us crackled like static in a storm. All I had to do was watch her take a sip of a drink, move her mouth in conversation, scratch her arse for heaven's sake, and I'd grow a bugle. If she licked her lips I'd practically have an orgasm.

Any man would. Except, I guess, for my

newfound friend DV MacEntee and his fellow travellers.

Cynthia is an extremely sexy lady.

She unwraps me, keeps a hold of my hand, takes a couple of dainty steps back, on tiptoes like a ballet dancer. She looks me over from head to toe. Her eyes twinkle and crinkle and flirt. She flutters her eyelashes.

"You're looking good, Milo," she says.

"You're not looking so bad yourself."

"Is that a gun in your pocket or are you happy to see me?" she says.

"You can be a shameless hussy, Cynthia, for a horse Protestant."

She squeezes my hand. Drops the act.

"You've been quite the stranger, Milo. And sadly missed. What's been keeping you away from us?"

I shrug.

"Life, I suppose."

"And is it life that brings you back to us?"

"You could say that. I'm looking for Nuala."

She closes her eyes and takes a few deep breaths. She's still holding my paw and she squeezes it tighter. People are starting to stare. Not that I care. They can stare all day long as far as I'm concerned. I'm happy where I am. She opens her eyes and relaxes her hold on my hand, but she doesn't let go.

"What a relief, Milo," she says. "You're my

knight in shining armour. I've been going up the wall worrying about her. I didn't know what to do. And here you are, Sir Lancelot himself."

I'm getting great receptions today.

"Here I am, Cynthia."

"Wait there for a sec," she says, "and we'll go for a walk."

She sashays away from me.

I try to be decent, to not be a sexist beast, to keep my eyes off her arse and her sturdy legs, but I'm fighting a losing battle. When the spirit is only half willing, the flesh will have its way. Her bottom is magnificent — a magnet for male eyeballs. I'm thinking I'd eat chips out of her knickers.

Hell, I'd eat her knickers.

Skid marks and all.

She has a quick chat with her help and sashays back. She links my arm and leads me out onto the street. My elbow presses softly into her tit. I'm the envy of every man we pass by and she knows it. She thrives on it.

I'm not exactly in tears about it either.

The rain is still holding off.

Jamie Muldoon will be raging.

We duck through a few lanes, out onto Grafton Street and up to St Stephen's Green. On the way we pick up a large sliced pan for the ducks.

The ducks in Stephen's Green must rank in the Top Ten list of the best-fed ducks in the Western hemisphere, but they've apparently been going through a dry spell, because they're mighty glad to see us. They probably haven't been fed for twenty seconds. In no time at all Cynthia has a big speckled grey fellow eating out of her hand and the others *quack-quack*ing jealously.

Nuala and Cynthia are still as tight as ever, Cynthia says, though in the last couple of months they haven't been seeing as much of each other as they used to. She's noticed little changes in Nuala.

"Nothing that you'd be overly worried about. Little things that would be normal in you or me, but just weren't Nuala's style, y'know?"

I nod.

"She seemed a bit subdued, for Nuala."

There's that word again. Subdued.

"That's exactly what DV said."

"Yeah. He and I talked about it after she went missing. Before that, neither of us felt it was important enough to be worried about. Everybody is entitled to their odd days, even cheery Nuala, right? She was less patient, less forbearing. For instance, you know Stan? The Lapdog, we used to call him?"

Stan the Man.

"Yeah."

"Well, he never gave up. He still fancies Nuala. Still phones her and turns up in the pub – by coincidence, *mar dhea*. Every couple of months she goes to the pictures or a play with him, does something with him just to humour him. He's been around so long he's part of the furniture. He's harmless – like a budgie you'd throw a cloth over when you want it to shut up and disappear. Well, recently, she started getting pissed off at him for calling her or showing up unannounced. She'd lose her temper, be rude even, which was definitely out of character. Life didn't seem to be so much of a laugh for her any more."

"Did it ever occur to you that maybe she was seeing a married man?"

She nods. The notion is not new to her.

"Yes. Well, there was something going on, for sure. But she stopped confiding in me. I was a bit ticked off with her about that. But, again, there was nothing solid that you could put your finger on. My friend Lorena said she was going through some kind of a catharsis."

"Lorena? I don't know her, do I?"

Cynthia shakes her head.

"She's a Yank," she says. "She's in the fake fur business over there. She's a Native American, a descendant of Geronimo or Crazy Horse or one of those famous war chiefs. Did you know that the

Indians are really pissed off at the European anti-fur crusaders, because they, the Indians, make their living hunting and trapping and are losing their livelihoods?"

"I think I read something about that."

"Things can sure get complicated. It's hard for people to know what's right these days. Anyway, Lorena was here for a couple of weeks back in June. She lives in New York now, but she grew up in California and you know what they're like there. Zen mad. And they're divils for therapy. If you have a headache in California, you don't take an aspirin, you go see a shrink. Lorena swears by it. She says she used to be a workaholic and therapy cured her. Mind you, she also said it cured her sex addiction, though you'd never know it by the way she was carrying on while she was here."

The large sliced pan is gone and the ducks are taking a hike across the water to more fertile pastures. They desert us for an old man with a brown bag full of crumbs on the other side of the pond.

"Aw, fickle ducks," she says. "Don't go."

Quack, quack, say the ducks.

"They must be males," she says to me. "They got what they wanted and they're off. "

"Is there a moral to this Lorena story?" I say.

"I'm just getting to it," she says. "Don't get your

knickers in a knot. Anyhow, I introduced Lorena to Nuala and the three of us went out drinking and dancing together a few times. Once I mentioned to Lorena that Nuala didn't seem to be herself lately and she said Nuala reminded her of someone well along in therapy and undergoing a catharsis."

"What's a catharsis?"

"A kind of a purging, or purification. Lorena said Nuala acted like she was going through a period of reflection in her life, getting ready to throw off a load of psychological baggage and enter into a new phase of being."

"This isn't California, Cynthia."

"I'm not finished, Milo. When I said we thought Nuala was maybe going out with a married man, Lorena, said yes, that could be it – it fit the bill nicely. The way it works, she said, is that a lot of people act out their unhappiness by cheating on their partners. At some stage they realise they're screwing up their lives and this leads them to therapy, to analyse their addictions, as Lorena put it. A milestone on the road to recovery, she called it. But, in English, what she was saying was, if Nuala was going out with a married man, maybe she got the guilts and decided it was time she took stock of her life and got rid of some of the rubbish in it. Now I'm finished."

"It makes sense," I say.

"I think so too," she says. "The only problem is, where's Nuala now?"

"And who's the man?"

"Right."

"You have no idea?"

"I haven't a clue."

The rain is starting to come down. A light drizzle.

"Come on," she says. "Let's head back. I've got a business to run."

She takes my arm again, holds onto it with both her hands and we ramble back towards her shop in the drizzle.

"Y'know, Milo," she says, "I always figured you and Nuala would get hitched."

"Really?" I'm surprised.

"Really. You made a great couple. Remember when I shared that flat with her at the back of Glasnevin graveyard?"

"Yeah. The crypt, we used to call it."

"And the weekends were *Tales from the Crypt*, if I remember correctly."

"Happy days."

"You used to stay over a lot and the walls were paper-thin."

"Ah Jesus, Cynthia."

"I used to listen to the two of you together at night. You were always laughing. I used to envy

Nuala. I used to lie there listening, thinking if two people could laugh so much together, enjoy each other's company so much in bed, they must be made for each other."

She gets a playful look in her eye.

"Then Nuala would go Hi-Ho Silver Awaaay!"

"Ah, Jesus Christ, Cynthia."

She pokes me in the belly with her elbow.

"Don't be shy, boy. You're repressed, Milo, y'know that? You need to learn to project yourself. To emote, as my friend Lorena says. She told me about this movement they have over in the States for men like you. They go into the woods for weekends and bang drums and howl at the moon to get in sync with their maleness. To tap into their inner selves. Maybe you should give that a go."

"I'll get right on it."

"Anyway, that's what I always remember when I think of the two of you at it next door. The laughter. It was magic. I thought you were really and truly in love."

I soften with the memories.

We walk the rest of the way in silence.

When I drop her off there's a pleasant drizzle still coming down and I decide to walk back to the office.

"Hey," she calls as I'm walking away.

I turn around. She's standing with her hands on

her hips and her chin in the air at the entrance to the Ilac Centre.

"Hey," she shouts again.

Everybody is looking at her. She doesn't give a fuck. She points a long white arm and an extended forefinger at me.

"Who was that masked man, *Kemo Sabay*?" she shouts.

I walk away shaking my head.

My face is hot.

I'm scarlet.

But laughing.

13

It's pushing on four o'clock when I get back to the office, wondering if everybody in the Dublin trendy set is privy to the details of my sex life. Angie calls me over to her desk in the lobby.

"That policeman was here looking for you again, Milo."

"McGonagle?"

"That's the one."

"Okay. I'll call him."

She squints askance at me.

"You're not in any trouble, are you?"

"No. It's just work."

"Good. But I don't think I like that man," she says.

"That makes two of us," I say.

"Three. Mister Hessnan upstairs asked me to ask you if we can expect this to be the way of the future — policemen trotting in and out of the building and prowling the corridors morning, noon and night. Those are his words."

I chuckle. Hessnan runs a customs clearance business on the third floor. I reckon he's a tad shady. Coppers make him nervous.

"Tell him to relax, Angie. It's just this case I'm working on. I should be finished in a week at most."

"I'll let him know. I'm sure he'll be relieved."

Though it may be a long week for him.

"I met Gabriel Byrne today, Angie."

"Gabriel Byrne the film star?"

"Yep."

"Oh, I love him. He's gorgeous. Did you shake his hand?"

"I did."

"Janey Mack. Which hand?"

I hold up the right one.

"Jesus. Can I smell it, Milo?"

I look at her. There's a twinkle in her eye. She's taking the mickey out of me.

"How come all the women I meet today are comics?" I ask her.

"You mean I'm not the only one? I'm raging." she says.

Her phone rings.

She answers it with one hand and shoos me away with the other.

I keep a fourteen-inch portable television in my office. I salvaged it from the office equipment of an ex-client who went belly-up financially and couldn't pay his bill. I turn it on and find some news. There's the Taoiseach's limo pulling up to the President's residence in the Phoenix Park earlier today. Our leader gets out and goes into *Aras an Uachtaráin* to ask our head of state to dissolve the Dáil. Okeydokey, says the Prez.

The bookies say the Gaffer is odds-on favourite to win the election.

I listen to my telephone messages.

There's one from Davy, saying he's put the word out and will get back to me when he hears something.

There's one from the guy with the dog who works the night shift for me down on the docks. He needs a night off on Friday. He's going to a wedding in the afternoon and won't be in a fit state for work later on, he reckons.

One from Bargain Billy, confirming he's okay for the security fair on Saturday and saying how much he's looking forward to it, it should be a rare oul' blast.

Another from a hustler selling office furniture.

Three from McGonagle.

I call around, find someone I kind of trust who wants a night's work on Friday at the right price. I call my man and tell him it's fixed, he can go to the wedding and get legless, with my blessing.

I call McGonagle. He answers with the static from his mobile phone. What's the panic, I ask him? He says huh? Where's the fire, I say? We just want a progress report, he says. We're in a rush y'know. I ask him what's with the *we*? Does he thinks he's fucking royalty, or what? I'm a gas man, he tells me. I ask him what's he doing, calling to my office, scaring off my customers? He was just passing by, he says. I tell him I don't need leaning on, I'm doing the business, he makes my neighbours nervous and I have my good name to consider. I'll call him, I say, when I have something to tell him. Okay, okay, he says, keep your hair on.

I hang up on him.

I make the call that's been on the back of my mind all day. To Maria. My chat with Davy last night helped me to put things in perspective. This morning I woke up with a decision made. No more messing about. No more running around on the end of a string. It's time to settle this once and for all.

Her phone rings and she answers it. She's on the night shift this week.

"Hello," she says.

It's Maria's voice I hear in my ear, but it's Nuala's face I'm looking at in my mind's eye.

"It's Milo," I say.

There's a little pause. A *difficult* little pause.

"How are you, Milo?" she says, trying to put friendly into her voice, but not quite making it.

"I need to talk to you," I say. My voice is flat, emotionless, won't take no for an answer. Real authoritative. In a pig's eye.

"Okay," she says.

She understands English.

"Lunch tomorrow?"

"I can't make it tomorrow."

"Thursday?"

"Okay."

Real chatty.

"I'll pick you up. One o'clock?"

"Okay."

I hang up.

I like neat endings. Everything tied up. No shite left over.

My heart is pounding. I'm sweaty. My hand is shaking.

Breaking up is hard to do.

The Gaffer is on the box again. Expounding. I turn him off.

I close the shop and go for a pint in Dwyer's. I wait out the rush-hour traffic. I finish the crossword.

14

I get home around eight, get into my sweats and put a tape on the deck. *Graceland*. I like the classics. I toast a corned beef and cheddar sandwich for my dinner, eat it with a can of tomato soup and wash it down with a cup of tea. Then I get out my little black book and I work the phone.

I call everyone I ever met who knows or used to know Nuala. I get loads of how's-it-goings and lots of long-time-no-sees, but no joy or consolation. Nobody has seen her lately. Nobody has the vaguest notion where she could be.

Stan O'Brien is not at home. I leave a message and my number.

For my *grand finale* I call Nuala's flat. No answer.

I get off the phone at tennish and treat myself to a bottle of Bass from the fridge. The dark is deepening outside. The days are getting shorter as we totter through September. *Graceland* has long ago spun itself out. At a whim I put on an oldie I haven't listened to in ages.

The Fureys & Davey Arthur.

Nuala is in my head. She loves the Fureys. She used to own this tape. The gritty Dublin voice of Finbar Furey fills the room. He's singing *Scarlet Ribbons.* Nuala had a fondness for that tune. Our song, she used to call it. In the old days, after evening sex and a smoke, we'd get up and have coffee or a drink. She'd put on *Scarlet Ribbons* and rest herself against me, all soft and comfy.

Then she'd pull me up standing and we'd have a waltz. More often than not we'd get lazy in the waltz, droop against each other and inevitably get horny again. And she'd laugh and coo and growl and lead me back to the bedroom.

Where we'd make more love and laughter.

I sit on my couch in the gathering dark, drink my bottle of Bass and listen to *Scarlet Ribbons.*

And I remember.

The good times.

I wake up on the sofa at two in the morning and I strip and crawl into bed. I fall back to sleep with *Scarlet Ribbons* playing in my head.

15

I wake up still thinking of Nuala.

It's seven a.m.

I call Stan O'Brien. I get his answering machine.

I call Nuala's place. No answer.

I take a hot shower. I make myself a poached egg, toast and a cup of tea for breakfast. I'm hoping to catch Stan in his office before he goes to court. He's probably on his way to work right now.

I'm on the road by eight, driving with one hand, a plastic cup full of tea with a lid on it in the other. I'm on the road, I hope, towards the hapless, indefatigable Stan, who willingly subjects himself to perpetual ridicule for the apparently hopeless love of a woman who, in every likelihood, will never reciprocate his feelings.

His office is over a boutique on Grafton Street. I get there at the same time as his help and she tells me he should arrive any minute. I sit in the waiting room and wait. She spoons coffee into a percolator.

Stan may be an *amadán* when it comes to matters of the heart, but he's doing all right in the law business. He's got a good name. He's popular with the subversives and that's a money spinner in this town. At least it has been. If the peace process takes and holds there's a horde of mouthpieces who'll be hurting. They'll perforce be changing their specialty when the guns are put away to rust. They'll all be chasing ambulances then. Or doing divorces. That's the new Ireland for you.

But Stan is not the worst of them. He has a social conscience too. Back in the bad old days, he did a lot of *pro bono* work for the poor and for victims of injustice. I asked him once how come he hadn't followed his father into politics. With the old man's clout and longstanding friendship with the Gaffer, the party machine would virtually guarantee Stan a seat in the Dáil. He told me it wasn't a question of him not being asked. But he said he'd seen the wheeling and dealing at first hand. He'd seen the compromises his father had to make. He'd stay where he could do something useful and still keep his integrity intact. Thanks, but no thanks, he said.

He's not short of the shekels. He owns a row of four Georgian houses in Rathmines and has them converted into flats and bedsitters for the students at University College. I hear he's patient about the rent. Even forgiving at times. That's a rarity in a landlord.

And a lawyer to boot.

He's in his late thirties, I figure, maybe on the cusp of forty, pot-bellied, going bald and still living with his mother.

A joke – how do you know Jesus Christ was an Irishman? Where else would a man in his thirties be living at home with his mother?!

I smell his aftershave before he breezes in the door. He follows the smell in. He's immaculate. His face is scrubbed so clean there's a shine off it. His starched white shirt gleams like an ad for Persil. Silver studs flash in the collar. You can see your face in his shoeshine. His three-piece pin-striped blue suit is soft and bouncy, just back from the cleaners. His red silk tie is conservatively striped.

He sees me and grins and sticks out his hand.

"Saints preserve us, if it isn't Milo Devine. Long time no see, Milo."

We shake.

"Too long, Stan," I say. "How are you?"

"I can't complain. Come on through to my office."

We go on through to his office. It's tasty. All solid mahogany and other dark woods. Comfortable black leather. There's a handsome, hand-carved Celtic

Cross on the window ledge. It's three feet high and has Portlaoise Prison inscribed on it. A token of appreciation from one of his subversive clients.

We sit.

He starts rooting through the papers in his briefcase.

"I don't want to rush you, Milo," he says. "But I'm up to my ears and I have to be in court at ten. What can I do for you?"

"I'm looking for Nuala Cooley," I say.

He looks up from his papers. He's grinning.

"Nuala, is it? Well, I haven't got her. I wish I did."

He doesn't know she's missing.

"How long is it since you've spoken to her?" I say.

The grin is fading.

"About two weeks. We had a bit of a tiff. Actually, we had a date and she stood me up, so I'm sulking. Not that it seems to be serving any useful purpose. Why are you asking, Milo?"

I tell him.

"Jesus," he says. "You don't think anything has happened to her, do you?"

"Nah. She's probably just larking about. You know Nuala. Still, I want to be sure."

"Of course you do. Don't we all? Jesus, I hope she's all right."

"When exactly did you last see her?"

"Nearly a month ago. She wasn't herself. She was

testy. Mean. That was a rare thing. New. She was never mean to me before. We have a kind of an understanding and our own way of going about things. One night I phoned her to ask her out and she told me to go fuck off with myself and hung up on me. I couldn't believe it. That wasn't the Nuala I've known most of my life. Then, on the Friday before last, she called to apologise. We made a date for the following Monday and she stood me up. I phoned her a few times, but I got no joy. I haven't seen her or heard from her since."

The woman from the waiting room comes in with two cups of coffee, cream and sugar on the side. We say thanks and she splits, quietly closing the door. I drop a little squirt of cream into my coffee. Stan shovels five spoons of sugar into his. My jaw drops.

"I have a sweet tooth," he says.

"I remember now," I say. "Have you any theory as to why she wasn't herself?"

"Well, to tell you the truth, I had the feeling that there was a new man in her life. I've been around her long enough. I can tell. This new guy wasn't very good for her. He made her miserable. And, with the way she wouldn't talk about it, I wondered if maybe he was married and that was the cause of her trouble."

So far it's unanimous. A married man.

"You have no idea who he could be, I suppose?"

"Nary a notion."

I take a slug of my coffee. It's delicious.

"Good coffee, Stan," I say.

"Colombian, I think," he says. "Mary outside gets it."

He's looking thoughtfully at me from under his bushy eyebrows.

"What?" I say.

"Milo, I know everybody thinks I'm bonkers mooning around after Nuala all these years. I know what people say about me. I know Cynthia Pilkington calls me the Lapdog."

I protest. I hold up my hands, palms facing him.

"That's none of my business, Stan. None of my business."

"I know, I know, but hear me out. I'd like you to understand."

I surrender with my hands.

"I love her, Milo. It's as simple as that. I love her with my very bones. I can't imagine my life without her in it. I know I'm pretty low on her list of . . . *paramours*, for want of a better word. But over the years I've watched the others come and go, including you, if you don't mind me saying so. I figure I'll just hang in there. If she doesn't meet someone, maybe I'll get her by default, so to speak. And then I'd grow on her. At least I'd have her."

Poor Stan.

Beneath that tight-arsed, pinstriped veneer, desire and passion pump through a hungry heart and soul.

"I gave myself till I'm forty before I give her up and settle for less," he says, "I'm thirty-eight. Two years to go."

Lawyers. So logical, even in quiet desperation.

Who can fathom the breed?

"Well, Stan," I say, "there's a certain logic in what you're saying, I suppose."

"She's one in a million, Milo."

"I know she is."

"Don't you think she's worth the wait?"

"I suppose it depends on what might be passing you by while you spend your life waiting."

His face says he'd trade his very soul for just a piece of Nuala Cooley.

I polish off the last of my Colombian coffee and stand.

"I tell you all this, Milo," he says, "because I want you to know how much I care. I want you to keep me informed of your progress."

"No problem."

"And if there's anything I can do to help, a phone call will suffice."

"Thanks, Stan."

Outside his office I ask Mary where she gets the coffee.

"I brought a sack of it back from Guatemala with me," she says.

"Stan says it's Colombian."

She shakes her head.

"Guatemalan," she says.

"It's great stuff."

She smiles and nods.

"Fresh too. Straight from the factory."

"I couldn't get it in Bewley's so?"

"I'm afraid not, Mister Devine."

"Call me Milo. Guatemala, huh? They used to shoot their dissidents for sport there, didn't they? Not much in the news these days, though. It's a funny place to go for your holidays."

She shakes her head.

"It was volunteer work. I was teaching the kids to read and helping to build a schoolhouse up in the mountains."

She's sixty if she's a day. Some people will just inspire and amaze you.

"Fair play to you, Mary," I say. "Next time you're over, maybe you'll bring me back a sack of that coffee?"

"Maybe I will," she says.

I'm on her mailing list now, I know. I'll be getting begging letters looking for donations to lofty, do-good enterprises in the developing world.

That's all right.

16

I tinker over to my office, mulling over Stan the Man, his passion and his incredible patience, about his receptionist Mary and the old adage that there's nowt so queer as folk.

The phone is ringing as I get in the door. It's DV looking for news. No news, I hope, is good news, I tell him. Likewise, he says.

I hang up and instantly the phone is ringing again. I answer to the less than dulcet tone of McGonagle.

"How's it going, Milo?" he says.

"How's it going yourself. What's the rumpus?"

"No rumpus, Milo. Any news?"

"I've got a couple of leads. Nothing substantial. I told you, didn't I — when I have some solid news I'll call you."

"I know you will, Milo. But the Gaffer likes to

keep the pot on the boil, so to speak. He's anxious, you understand?"

"I understand. But I'm not a pot and I don't need to be kept on the boil, thanks very much."

"He's doing well in the polls. What do you think of that?"

"God help us all."

"Ah, Milo, you're a card. I'll say goodbye, so. You'll be in touch?"

"I'll be in touch, McGonagle."

Cheerio.

Prick.

Davy calls. Word has come back to him. The scuttlebutt has it that Nuala and the Gaffer never really saw eye to eye and things were always pretty cool between them. Nothing new in that, says I. But over the past few months, says Davy, the temperature of their animosity has bubbled over its boiling point. There were shouting matches in his office at the Dáil, an icy atmosphere at family gatherings. She was conspicuously absent from public functions.

The Cooley father and daughter were patently at ardent loggerheads.

"Thanks, Davy," I say.

"So, how's progress?" he says.

"It's early days, but a picture is forming, I think."

"Good. I have to go. I've got a class. Be seeing you."

"*Adios* for now."
"Be careful, Milo."
"Right."

It's time to check out Nuala's flat. I should have done it first thing yesterday, but I wasn't really taking all this too seriously at the beginning.

Now I am.

A bad feeling is growing, like lockjaw, in my bones.

Her castle is a semi-detached, three-bedroom house in Glasnevin. She likes Glasnevin. Always did. When we were an item, sometimes she liked to walk in the graveyard. It made her feel peaceful, she said. And she loved to explore the headstones. She got great delight out of finding the grave of someone famous. I have a photo of the two of us standing by the grave of Jim Larkin, the great trade unionist and leader of the workers during the infamous lockout of 1913. Larkin is one of my heroes.

On my way out of town I stop and pick up lunch at a Chinese takeaway. Spring rolls, shrimp chow mein and pork fried rice. And a bottle of Ballygowan to wash it all down.

I pull into a housing estate, park and put the nosebag on. It's the quiet, early afternoon, before the kids get out of school to kick up a racket. In a back garden across the road from me, a couple of housewives natter over the fence. Next door, a woman hangs out the washing while a nipper swings out of her apron. Yonder, two middle-aged men hold up a corner wall, smoking, looking at the ground, with their shoulders sagging. On the dole, most likely – victims, perhaps, of the less salubrious decades that preceded the awakening of the Celtic Tiger. Out of work so long they don't know how to go about looking for it.

I remember mitching from school when I was a kid and feeling this quiet time of the day. Normally I'd never see it, because when I was off, so were all the other kids and there was a different quality to the hour. The streets were full of noise. But, when I mitched and I was on my own, the quiet was so silent I could hear it.

It was downright spooky, sometimes.

Nuala's house is at the back of the graveyard, just a few streets away from the old flat where Cynthia Pilkington listened in on Nuala and me making love. It's one of a block of square, pretty, red-brick buildings set in a *cul de sac*. The street is one of those occasional oases for yuppie childless couples who plant themselves in a community out of some near-dormant but still beating tribal instinct and then work, eat, drink and live in the city.

I knock on the door.

No answer. Surprise, surprise.

The lock is a breeze to pick and I'm in already. The hallway is cramped. I can't spread my elbows. Maximum utilisation of space. You have to admire the economic ingenuity of architects.

If you're not Milo Devine, who likes his space.

There's a pile of post on the floor at the door. Magazines, bills, a postcard from Florida from someone who calls himself Dirk.

Jesus, Nuala.

Dirk!

Sounds like the name of a porno movie star.

Coats and hats are hanging in the hall. A cacophony of shapes and colours full of her in-your-face character. A loud and sassy red raincoat with a floppy hat to match. A silk jacket that resembles the skin of a leopard. A pair of dark green Doc Martens. A yellow brolly with black polka dots. Wellington boots to match. Two black velvet gloves on the floor waiting to be picked up.

The items of apparel in the hall. They're full of life.

A sitting-room off to the side. Bookcases, a telly and a CD player, random stacks of discs. Sinead O'Connor, Michelle Shocked, Roy Orbison, David Bowie, Tracy Chapman, the Cranberries. Loads of Mary Black, Christy Moore and the Furey Brothers.

There's the battered, flowery sofa I recognize from her old flat. A magazine on it. *Vanity Fair*. Sitting open on an article about the latest Hollywood brat-pack.

Two framed pictures on opposite walls. A print of *The Lady of Shalott* and a poster advertising a James Bond movie. Nuala always had the hots for Pierce Brosnan.

A coffee table with a lonesome book on it. An old one. A dog-eared copy of Tolkien's *Lord of the Rings*. I remember reading it way back when. The book is enjoying a comeback now that they've made a movie of it.

A wickerwork white rocking-chair beside a knitting-basket. She must have taken up knitting. A forlorn ball of red wool has rolled under the telly. A cat would have a field day.

A dying bowl of geraniums dehydrate on the window ledge.

Into the kitchen.

Fridge, stove, cookbooks, microwave. Dirty dishes in the sink. A small, four-seater oak table with an empty, tea-stained cup and saucer on it and a side plate with the crust of a piece of Hovis bread. Not a heel. Nuala always ate the heels first. Never shared them. Matching chairs. Four of them. One of them has a cookbook on it, opened to a recipe for jerk chicken.

I feel like I'm walking around the *Marie Celeste*.

I fill a glass with water from the tap and go give a drink to the geraniums. They suck it down. I put the glass back in the sink.

A bedroom. The spare one. Full of boxes full of books and junk and house-moving stuff. She's still in the process of unpacking.

The bathroom. Painted a cheerful shade of royal blue. And a sky-blue shower curtain with black pictures on it of matchstick men and women with halos. It's a lively room. Vintage Nuala. I like it.

Toothpaste, toothbrush still there. Likewise soap, shampoo, conditioner, perfume. Bubble bath, moisturiser, a basketful of creams and gels and the like from the BodyShop.

Under the sink a cupboard full of toilet paper, tampons, shaving cream, disposable razors, cotton wool. And an overnight bag containing all the requisite gear for a week in the sun or a dirty weekend — miniature bottles and parcels of all of the above.

A ghost walks over my grave.

The other bedroom. Hers. I'm in the door and the smell of her is all over me, the nearly forgotten essences of Nuala bursting out of my subconscious memory, filling my senses as if it was only yesterday we thrived and throbbed together.

The rest of the house could nearly be anybody's,

but this bedroom is quintessentially hers by virtue of the air that I breathe and the ethereal character of Nuala that's in it.

There's socks and knickers, stockings, casually strewn around the floor. That's the Nuala I know. Tidiness, what's that? *Frankly my dear, I don't give a damn.* A king-sized bed with a cream-coloured duvet and satin sheets.

Satin sheets.

Hmmm.

Nuala, Nuala, Nuala, if you weren't missing and I wasn't worried about you, I'd hop into that bed there, wrap myself in the satin and linger in the hope that you'll be home soon to join me.

It's far from satin sheets I was reared.

But you're missing, love.

And we're missing you.

The dressing-table is full of make-up stuff and photographs in frames. There's a picture of her with her mother on the lawn of *Saoirse*. Pictures of herself and her sister and brother, both of whom long ago went to the States.

There's not hide nor hair of the Gaffer.

Facing her bed, facing her when she sleeps, because I remember she sleeps on her right side, there's a framed picture of Nuala and me.

It cuts me to the quick.

My heart does a lurch and my eyes go damp.

Like it was yesterday, I remember the picture being taken, though it was many, many moons ago. I'm skinny in it. One Easter weekend we rented a cottage in Dingle. The picture was taken in front of the building David Lean reportedly used as the schoolhouse in the movie, *Ryan's Daughter*.

Nuala asked an old tinker passing by to take the snap. The man had no teeth and a bit of a hump on his back. The foam was mighty that day on the sea.

Nuala.

Nuala, darling, where are you?

I take the picture, frame and all. I put it in my pocket.

On the other side of the bed there's a little table with a jug of dusty water on it and a glass. And a book. By Roddy Doyle. *The Woman Who Walked Into Doors*. With a bookmark between pages sixty-eight and sixty-nine.

Now the shits are truly up me.

She left everything behind.

Nuala is not off gallivanting.

I fear.

Beneath the book there's a little drawer. In it four packets of condoms. And a dildo. I don't remember that.

Attagirl, Nuala.

Safe sex.

Back downstairs to the hall. At the foot of the

stairs there's a little table with a phone on it and a little black book. One of those leather and bronze ones where you press a button, the lid pops up and there's your A-to-Z of acquaintances, cronies and friends and their phone numbers.

I stick the book in my pocket with the picture.

I stand there.

No Nuala. No clues. And no laptop computer.

Outside, through the hall door, in the distance, an ambulance beepaws.

Inside here, it's silent and still as the graveyard down the road.

On a whim I trot back up the stairs, nip into her bedroom. I lift a pair of her black silk panties off the floor and I put them in my pocket beside the picture and the book.

It's a souvenir. Call me impulsive.

And I'm out of there.

17

I dawdle and drive in a roundabout way to the office.

I pass quiet streets and quiet houses full of secrets. Secrets maybe never to be revealed. The buildings enclosing all the answers, all the history, and giving nothing away.

I'm morose. And detached. I feel like an outsider. Like all the real business of life is going on in the quiet houses and others two or three streets away, or just over the next horizon, and I'm petering around on the edge, trying to feel my way back, my umbilical cord to the rest of civilisation prematurely cut.

I give myself a little shake.

Lose the fantasies, Milo my man.

There's work to be done.

Back in the office I brew up some coffee. I stand the

picture of Nuala and me on my desk and I stare at it awhile, remembering.

I pop the little black book open on A. I leave the panties in my pocket. Angie might walk in and if she copped me fondling a pair of woman's panties she'd give me no peace for a month of Sundays.

I check out the black book and I work the phone. About half the names are familiar. I call them first, the ones I haven't called already. No joy. Nobody has seen her since she's been gone. I make a note of the names who don't answer the ring. I'll try them later. Then I start on the strangers.

I'm down to the W's before I get a possible break. Jack Walton, his name is. He has two phone numbers. Nuala has printed a little 'w' in front of one of them, for work, a little 'h' in front of the other, for home. I check my watch. It's three minutes to five. Almost clocking-off time. I try the 'w'. The female voice that answers has the patient, singsong lilt of someone who answers the phone for a living.

"Doctor Walton's office. Can I help you?"

Another bloody doctor. Are all the women I know hanging out with medical practitioners all of a sudden?

"Doctor Walton, please," I say.

"Doctor Walton is out of the office today," she chants. "May I take a message?"

"When will he be back?" I say.

"I can't say. The doctor is out sick."

The doctor is sick. That's kinda funny haha in an oxymoronish way.

I go fishing.

"How long has he been sick?" I say.

There's a pause on the line. The soprano is doing her job. I'm getting personal and she's protecting his privacy.

I ad-lib.

"Jack is an old school friend," I say. "I'm home from New York for a short holiday and I'm hoping to get together with him before I go back. I'm going back tomorrow."

She loosens up.

"Oh dear," she says. "Well, Doctor Walton hasn't been in since the Friday before last."

Alarm bells go off in my head.

Eureka.

The Friday before last.

Him and Nuala.

This is it. It's gotta be.

"Do you have his home number, sir?"

"Yes, I do. Thank you very much."

"My pleasure."

I hang up. There's the trace of a shake in my hand and my heart is skipping along. The trail is heating up. I can feel the fire in my belly.

I call Jack Walton at home. Thirteen times the phone rings before I hang up. I call the soprano back, sing her the blues, that I'm really anxious to talk about old times with Jack the Lad.

"There is one possibility," she says. "He's supposed to speak at a public function at Liberty Hall tonight at eight. He called and instructed me to cancel all his medical appointments for this week, but he hasn't pulled out of his speech, so he may be planning to go ahead with it."

"Liberty Hall at eight?"

"Yes, sir."

"You're a great help. Indulge me just once more please. I haven't heard from Jack for ages. Did he ever get married?"

She hesitates. Decides it's okay, I'm kosher.

"He did, but it ended sadly. He married a lovely woman from your part of the world. A Yank. But it didn't work out. They're separated now. She's gone back to the States."

I shake my head into the phone.

"That's tragic. Any kids?"

"No kids. No, sir."

"When did she leave?"

"Just a few months ago."

"Poor Jack. Ma'am, you're a star. From the bottom of my heart, I thank you."

"My pleasure."

I hang up.
Yowzah!

I ramble out and score a paper, take it back to the office. Angie is gone home. The Gaffer is on the front page again, a self-satisfied grin creasing his countenance. He's still way ahead in the polls.

I skip on through to the what's-on page. There it is. Liberty Hall at eight. A public meeting on prison reform. *REHABILITATE THE PRISONS*. There are three speakers. A Labour Party MP who is prominent in the Prisoners' Rights Organisation. A lefty senator from Dublin Four, the Oz of Irish liberals. And Doctor Jack Walton, the noted psychiatrist.

Nuala's new paramour is a shrink.

I check the time. The day is flying away. It's getting on towards six and the meeting is at eight. I may as well relax and stay in town.

I turn on the telly for *The News*. Hunger is rampant in the developing world, another French fascist wins a by-election to parliament and the peace process in the North takes another wary, faltering step forward. Item number four is the Gaffer lording it over his manor. He's entertaining the talking heads in the kitchen where he fed me. He's sitting at the table, looking sage and confiding in them that he's guardedly optimistic about winning the election.

His wife is beside him. She's lending her support, presumably, but she may as well be a ventriloquist's dummy with a grin stitched onto her face for all she contributes. She looks a bit spaced out. Like she's taken one too many Valiums. Life can't be easy for her, with all her children scattered and a man like him to manage, and all in the public eye.

I kill the telly, go for a stroll. I stop off at a chipper for some smoked cod and chips. I eat on a bench in Stephen's Green.

I have the Green to myself, except for a few vagrants and a teenage couple snogging up against the railings. They're eating each other's face, he's got one hand up her skirt and pumping, she's got his buns cupped in her hands, one of her fingers sticking up his arse through his trousers.

God be with the days.

Back in the office I brew up some tea to wash down the grub.

I make the last of the phone calls.

Nothing stirring.

18

Liberty Hall is a midget skyscraper perched on the bank of the Liffey. It's the Buckingham Palace, the Mecca, the Jerusalem of the Irish trade union movement. James Connolly rallied his Irish Citizens' Army there for the Easter Rising. It was a different building then. The old one burned down during the Civil War, but the spirit of struggle was passed on.

It's got a noble history and it's a popular venue for people with causes.

Tonight it's the turn of the prison activists and they're calling, according to the leaflets, for an overhaul of the custodial system. The jails, they say, are nowadays just steel and cement containment cells and the people who run them have completely abandoned the principle of rehabilitation.

It's an old, old tune and a desolate lost cause, I fear, for ordinary, decent criminals, as the Brits used to call them. You have to be a subversive these days to get a fair shake from the jailers. And there's not many subversives left in the prisons, thanks to the Good Friday Agreement.

It's ten to eight and the punters are straggling in. I lean against a telephone pole and eyeball the goings-on.

There's a left-wing circus of sorts outside the door. All the regulars are out tonight. Greenpeace, the Prisoners' Rights Organisation, the Irish Council for Civil Liberties, Sinn Féin, the Sisters for Justice, a slew of Trots of various persuasions, Marxists, Marxist-Leninists (the Stalin is silent) and a flock of *Hare Krishna* chanters to add a lustre of the surreal to the proceedings. To get to the door you have to walk a gauntlet of paper sellers and leaflet distributors.

The usual.

There's a cruiser ostentatiously parked half up on the footpath outside the entrance to Liberty Hall. It's aggressive surveillance. I spot Sweaty Finnegan behind the wheel and I'm not surprised. Aggro is his middle name.

Sweaty is a hard-nosed git of the old school. A crony of McGonagle's. Picture the fat, corrupt, racist Yankee state trooper caricatured in a thousand Hollywood movies, give him a Galway brogue and you've got Sweaty Finnegan. He's the kind of jumped-up petty tyrant that gives policing a bad name. Wouldn't be out of place in the old KGB or putting the boot to homeless kids on the streets of Rio de Janeiro.

His roving eye lands on me and gets a flinty glint in it. He'd like to have my guts for garters. He mutters something to his partner, gets out of the car and rolls over to me. He's wearing a rumpled blue business suit gone shiny in the worn spots, a white shirt with a grimy collar and a tattered woollen tie that's been out of fashion since the 1980's.

His right hand holds the ever-present hankie he uses to wipe off the sweat. There's something wrong with his glands or his pores. They're like taps and the perspiration rolls off him in buckets. A massive gut hangs over his belt and I'm thinking it must be decades since Sweaty got a glimpse of his dick that wasn't in the mirror.

"Lo and behold, it's Milo Devine," he says.

"Sweaty," I say.

"Smile when you call me that," he says.

I smile. Sweetly. I blow him a kiss.

He hawks up a greener and spits. The glob hits the dust between my feet and settles there like a tired snail having a nap.

"You're a classy guy, Sweaty," I say.

"What's the story, Milo?" he says. "What are you doing here? Are you going into politics?"

"Just checking out the scenery. Like yourself."

"I'm looking for subversives. What are you looking for?"

"You wouldn't know a subversive if one jumped up and bit you on the arse," I say.

Finnegan and I took the gloves off years ago.

"Fuck you, Devine," he says.

"I see you've been going to charm school," I say.

He scowls, gets up close, pokes me with his gut, sticks his face in mine. His breath reeks of stale beer, bad breath and tobacco.

"I'd like to do you, Devine," he says. "Just give me an excuse."

I poke his belly with a finger. It's like jabbing jelly.

"You're going soft," I say. "Why don't you come and see me sometime? Take off the badge and leave the protection at home, Sweaty. We'll go a few rounds and I'll make shite of you."

"I'll get you my own way, Devine."

The punters and the paper-sellers are all going inside. A few of them are looking in our direction. I move away from Finnegan.

"Nice talking to you," I say.

He glowers.

I'll be watching my back.

Sweaty is a malicious bastard.

And dangerous.

He is a cop, after all.

Inside the lobby the paper-sellers are packing away their gear. In the Sinn Féin corner I spy Christy Craven. He's an inner city councillor. One of the best. Full of principle and piss and vinegar. If things go according to plan up north, if the guns go west for good and Sinn Féin becomes respectable, I wouldn't be surprised to see him sitting in cabinet in the Dáil.

Times change. And people too. Sometimes. Who'd ever have dreamed, ten years ago even, that the Shinners would be leading the charge towards peace in our time and an Ireland free of guns?

Christy and I grew up together. We robbed orchards, mitched from school together and shared illicit cigarettes as kids. His nickname was Gollier in tribute to the munificent texture of his saliva and the tremendous distance he could spit it.

I joined the cops and he moved up north to man the barricades. He did two years on an arms charge in the early eighties. Since then, as far as I know, he's concentrated on the political end of things. Like all the Shinners nowadays, with the Provos going respectable, he's wearing a natty suit. This is the first time I've ever seen him with a tie on. His neck is red from the chafing of the collar he's obviously still not used to.

I say hello and we shake.

"Are you going into politics, Milo?" he says.

"Finnegan asked me the same thing."

He snorts.

"That bollix," he says. "I wouldn't piss on him if he was on fire."

"You're still in the thick of things anyway," I say.

He grins.

"You know me. No home but the struggle. What are you doing here, Milo? This carry-on is hardly your cup of tea."

"I'm working. I need to have a word with this Jack Walton fellow."

"Well, you're out of luck. He's a no-show."

Fuck.

"The organisers are chasing their arses looking for a last-minute replacement," he says. "They've been trying to call Walton for days, apparently, but they can't track him down."

He sees I'm pissed off.

"What do you want with Walton anyway?" he says.

"It's a long story," I say. "Do you want to go for a pint?"

"Twist my arm," he says.

"Mulligan's?"

He nods.

"After the meeting. You're buying?" he says.

Gollier is a full-time activist. Never has any money. Despite the suit and tie.

"Okay," I say.

19

I sit through the meeting. No Jack Walton. A radical priest takes his place and waxes lyrical about injustice, compassion and how a society stands or falls on how it treats its outcasts. Ireland is sadly lacking in the just society department, he says.

I hear all about suicide, drugs and AIDS in the nick, about Open University, conjugal rights and sub-standard grub, about fighting the good fight and keeping hope alive.

I put a fiver in the collection box and I'm relieved when it's all over.

Afterwards I walk with Gollier across the bridge at Tara Street. I feel Finnegan's eyes bore into my back. Him wishing they were bullets and wondering what I'm up to with Gollier. I can visualize the cogs turning in his head. Ever so slowly.

Mulligan's is renowned for the creamy quality of its Guinness. I get the drinks in.

"Down the hatch," I say.

"May your soul be in Heaven half an hour before the devil knows you're dead," says Gollier.

For the first pint he and I mull over old times. He was fond of my da, who was one of his mentors in the Republican movement. They shared the same subversive faith and the two of them would talk politics and history into the early hours of the morning. Halfway through the second pint we get down to business.

I tell him who I'm looking for. He minds his manners, doesn't ask who's paying me.

Walton is a Dublin 4 Utopian, he says. A small 'l' liberal – for egalitarianism, divorce on demand and the woman's right to choose. In the eighties he supported liberation struggles in the likes of Nicaragua, El Salvador and Guatemala. He was big in the anti-apartheid movement. But he ran, and runs, bitter cold when it comes to Irish bombs in Manchester or coppers getting shot in Belfast. As did, and do, most of us.

That's a sore point with Gollier. He has little patience with Irish liberals, who have no problem supporting freedom fighters in Africa or South America, but spit on the IRA. They're all gas and no bottle, he says.

I keep my head down.

But that's all changing now, he says, with the peace process picking up steam again, and a permanent end to the troubles looming into sight on the horizon.

Fingers crossed, I say.

And down to business.

He can safely say, he says, that Walton keeps his distance from the murky side of Irish politics, but he'll put the word out. If Walton pops up anywhere around the country, he'll be told. He'll give me a bell.

"Thanks," I say, as the barman calls last drinks. I get us two more and we chat.

Driving home I ponder my night and the peculiarly Irish incongruity of it.

On the one hand there's Christy Craven, the subversive. Often maligned by the establishment and the population at large for his erstwhile embrace of the Armalite, he's one of the most honest, most altruistic, noblest men I've ever met. In a normal place he'd be a mainstream leader, a pillar of strength and decency.

On the other hand there's Finnegan, the cop. The guardian of peace and democracy. And he's a vindictive, malicious guttersnipe of a man, a schoolyard bully come to fruition and bordering on the psychotic. We should lock him up and throw the key away.

They both have nicknames.

Gollier gave up spitting when he was twelve. And Sweaty went from bad to worse.

What a country.

Everything is inside out.

But the times are changing.

We hope and pray.

At home I check my messages. There's one from Davy Mullen. No news. He's just saying hello, checking in. One from McGonagle, saying what's the *craic*, how am I doing, call him before the turn of the century.

Diddly-squat else.

I try Jack Walton's home again.

Nada.

Déjà vu.

I hit the sack.

20

Morning breaks with a chill in the air and a hint of winter on the wind.

I poach a few eggs, heat up some chili, pop a couple of slices of bread in the toaster. One on top of the other and they're a breakfast to waken the taste buds. I make a pot of tea and eat listening to *The News* on the radio.

The Gaffer has reached his peak in the polls, the newscaster says, and the election is his to lose. He's on his plateau of popularity now and he can hang on up there and keep his opponents at bay for as long as his little heart desires. Or he can screw up and come tumbling down in a landslide of his own making. The smart money is not on the latter. Cooley is not known for his mistakes.

After grub I have a shower, get into Levis, a sweat-shirt, a pair of Doc Martens and a parka. I'm going rural today. Walton's place is beyond Dublin, at the foot of the Wicklow Mountains.

The phone rings.

McGonagle.

"I hear you're taking up the cudgel for prison reform," he says.

"News travels fast," I say.

"I ran into Sweaty Finnegan this morning."

"You were up early."

"Clean living, Milo. What on earth did you say to Sweaty? He's out of sorts with you."

"The man is a Neanderthal, McGonagle. It's a wonder he walks upright. You'd better keep him away from me."

"Don't worry about Sweaty. He's all bark and no bite. How goes the hunt?"

"I'm getting closer. I can feel it. Did you know that Nuala was hanging around with Jack Walton?"

"The left-wing head doctor?"

"Yeah."

"No."

"Well, she was. And there's no sign of him either. Not since the same day Nuala was last seen."

"Well, isn't that curious, now? A fortnight of fornication is it, do you think?"

The sophisticate McGonagle. To the manor born. We wish. No wonder women are pissed off at us men. He has a wife and four kids. I wonder if the wife ever had an orgasm. I'll ask him when this is all over. Because she did with me once, I'll say, it lasted ages. Probably her first and last, I'll say. Then I'll run for cover.

"I'm getting a bad feeling about this, McGonagle."

"Well, let's take things one step at a time. What's next on your agenda?"

"I'm going down to Wicklow to check out Walton's place."

"It's a nice day for a drive. Not for walking, though. There's a bit of a cut in the air."

"I don't plan on walking to Wicklow."

"I was just remarking on the day that's in it."

"I'll talk to you later," I say.

"Righto," he says.

Wanker.

I call Walton's number on the off-chance. Nothing doing.

It's a quarter past nine. I find a coffee shop and kill an hour with the crossword. I'm allowing myself an hour to drive down, an hour to poke around and another hour for the return drive. That should have me back in Dublin just in time for lunch and confrontation with Maria. I call Angie at the office, tell her my plans for the morning.

"A drive in the country, is it?" she says. "Very nice. It's well for some, I must say."

"It's work," I say.

"Have a nice day," she says.
"You should be working in McDonald's," I say.
"They'd probably pay better," she says.

I can't win.

I fetch my car keys from yesterday's jacket. Nuala's panties are still there. I put them in my parka pocket.

For luck.

The temperature is a bit razor-bladish, but the sun is out and McGonagle is right about one thing – it's a lovely day for a drive.

The morning traffic is almost history and I dawdle through the city at an easy canter. Out on the south I stick to the coast and take the scenic route. I leave the city and the suburbs behind and I'm into the quiet and the chirrup of the country.

I'm a city boy, born and bred and committed, but driving through the sticks I'm thinking I don't do this often enough. Already my head is clearing out and my bones are settling easy. Bog therapy.

Walton's place is an isolated bungalow on a couple of acres nestled in the shade of the hills. It cost a pretty penny here, I reckon. Separating the house from the road there's a white picket fence Tom Sawyer would have given his eye-teeth for.

I park beside the fence and eyeball the place. It

looks deserted. There's a smokeless chimney. The birds have all the noise to themselves. The doc's shingle hangs on the gate. Built onto the house, what used to be a garage is now a workplace of sorts. A black sign edged with gold on the door calls it the surgery.

I go to the front door, ring the bell. The chime plays the first few bars of the theme music from the movie, *Titanic*. There's no answer.

This is a lifeless house. I can feel it in my skin.

I remember well the sound of doorbells ringing through empty homes.

When I was a kid I used to collect money door to door on Friday nights for the weekly football pools. I got paid on a commission basis. It was slave labour. If the client wasn't in on the Friday I'd have to come back on Saturday. I became an expert on the texture and timbre of doorbells ringing and how lonely they sound if the house is empty.

Nobody comes to the door.

I go for walkies.

There's another bell on the surgery door. It just rings. *Ciúnas*. Quiet. No reply. There's a handle on the door, low at my waist where the lock is. I turn the handle. It moves. The door is unlocked. I don't realise it till I'm looking back on it later, but I've stopped breathing. The hairs move and bristle on the nape of my neck. My bowels tighten.

I have a bad, bad feeling about this place.
I push the door.
It's ajar now.
My nose is full of warm metal. The odour of a room full of wet pennies. I know the smell well. It's blood. Hot blood. Something sinks at the pit of my stomach. My bones grow cold. I want to go away. Far away. I push the door again. It swings open. Wide. There's a narrow corridor in front of me with a door at the end of it which I reckon goes into the main house. Halfway down the corridor, on my right, there's another door hanging open. It goes, I reckon, into the clinic.

My feet are made of lead and I'm walking in slow motion, but my senses have an edge to them. It's the danger rush. The tips of my fingers are tingling. I can see, hear and smell better, more lucidly.

I'm in the corridor. I'm fighting the urge to close my eyes. Absurd though it is, I'm thinking of the movies. An old classic. *Apocalypse Now.* Robert Duvall in his cowboy hat saying he loves the smell of napalm in the morning.

Shit.
I reach the door.
I go in.
It's a waiting room. Empty of animate stuff. There's a sofa, chairs, a coffee table, magazines. *Time,*

Newsweek, Tidbits, Woman's Way. The RTE Guide. No muzak, I think. Funny how the mind works, what it thinks of. Crazy.

Fuck.

All over me that primitive, feral, unmistakable stench of blood. Pervasive.

And another door ajar across the room.

My journey is not over yet.

A cigarette I'd love right now. I haven't smoked for thirteen years. I should go find a shop, I say to myself, get some smokes and come back. In about a year.

Fuck this for a game of cowboys.

I'm gliding across the carpet. Onwards and downwards in my heart towards the pit, scared shitless.

I'm in the door. I'm in the surgery.

Aaaah.

It's bad.

It's a nightmare.

There's blood all over the place.

Wall-to-wall books, a gorgeous rosewood desk with an easy chair behind it, both adjacent to a black leather couch and an armchair to match. That's all. Except that sitting on the easy chair is the man I presume to be Jack Walton, with the top half of his head blown off and his brains and blood splattered on the wall and the window behind him.

And on the couch is Nuala, with a hole in her heart not beating any more, blood dripping off her on to the floor.

They're both tied up with rope.

Walton's arms are tied around the chair behind him. His feet are bound together.

Nuala's hands are also tied behind her back. But her legs are free. Spread wide. One of them rests on the couch, the other hangs languorously towards the carpet. The position is grotesquely lewd. Her white woollen skirt, now red-stained, has ridden up till it's almost around her waist. I notice she still has her panties on. Black silk. Just like the ones in my pocket. Deep inside my shock and horror, a voice says be thankful for small mercies. At least she wasn't raped. Apparently.

There's white noise inside my head. Which feels like it's going to burst.

God.

I puke.

There's a tiny bathroom on the other side of the room. I pick my way over Nuala's leg, my hand on my gagging mouth. I'm dribbling vomit. I puke my ring up. I barf eggs and toast and chili and what feels like my stomach lining into the toilet. I grab a ream of toilet paper, blow snot and puke into it. I turn on the tap, splash water on my face, have a gargle. I swallow some. I cough and splutter some more.

I look at the white ceiling, close my eyes and hold my breath for thirty counting seconds. One elephant, two elephants . . . the noise abates a trifle in my head.

I go back.

They're still there.

Dead as doornails.

Nothing surer.

I make sure anyway. There's a job to be done, no matter what.

I move over to Nuala, lean down to her, touch her throat with my forefinger where the vein would pulse if . . .

She's still warm. But that's all. She's dead. Nuala is stone dead.

I straighten. Walton is next to check.

And I get whacked.

A thump in my shoulder sends me flying, spinning. My face hits the wall, I hear a pop and shattering glass — I'm not sure of the sequence — and I land on Nuala. She's warm and soft and bloody. Dead.

I jump up, recoiling, disgusted. My shoulder is going mad with fire and pain.

I've been shot.

Fuck.

I've been shot.

Another pop.

I hit the deck. I'm looking at Nuala's death mask. I turn away.

The shots are coming from outside the window.

"*Ha, ha, ha, ha, ha,*" I hear.

Laughter. Some mad bastard is laughing out there.

Another pop. Dust and plaster confetti spill on me.

This scumbag wasted Nuala. And now he wants to add my scalp to his collection. I gotta get out of here.

"*Ha, ha, ha, ha, ha,*" at the window.

Jesus.

I crawl out the door and into the corridor. I get up and make a beeline for the door that doesn't go outside. As I run I'm reciting a mantra, a prayer. Please God, let the door be open. *Please God let the door be open.*

I reach it and it is.

Thank Christ.

I'm into the main house. The sitting-room. Armchairs and telly and ornaments and shit, but fuck them, I'm through them, through the door on the other side and out into the back garden.

Nothing but fields. Up front in my head, I'm checking out the lie of the land, but the top of my mind at the back is still saying a prayer and I'm a breath away from panic. I squeeze my shot-up shoulder with my good hand and the pain is ferocious. But it kills the prayer and the panic.

I look again.

I never noticed before how the land in the country is laid out so tidily. As far as the eye can see the meadows are hedged off in rectangles a geometry teacher would fantasise about. And each field seems to have a texture and colour all of its own.

Any second now I'm going to launch into a chorus of *The Forty Shades Of Green* and that mad fucker behind me will blow a hole a yard wide in my back and it will be curtains for poor Milo.

I get another grip on myself.

In the field to my left there's a bunch of haystacks.

At the bottom of the garden there's a ditch.

I must clock sixty miles an hour hurtling down the garden. I dive headlong into the ditch. Into six inches of muck.

Fuck.

I'm glad I wore my jeans today. My linens would be destroyed.

I scuttle along the ditch to where I reckon the haystacks must be. I pick up stray rocks as I move. Weapons. Rocks against a shooter.

Milo and Goliath. Where's my slingshot, Tonto? Different show, *Kemo Sabay*. I think I'm delirious.

"Milo," I hear.

The fucker knows who I am.

"Miiiilo."

It's a casual, sing-song, crazy-but-ever-so-smart voice. Like Jack Nicholson in *The Shining*. Coming to get you. *Honey, I'm home and you're dead meat.*

And I know it.

Jesus.

I know it.

Godammit – I know it.

It's McGonagle.

Momentarily, relief floods over me. I start to stand up.

I'm halfway up when reality kicks my delusions away. I behold the truth and I freeze. I peek up over the side of the ditch. The haystacks are a couple of feet to my right. The house is to my left.

He's standing at the back door. Large as life.

McGonagle.

With a shooter in his hand the length of half his arm. The gun is the size of something Wyatt Earp would carry. It's hanging down by his side.

Fucking McGonagle is the killer, the mad bastard.

"Miiiilo," he lilts, dragging it out in his crazy mad hatter, Jack Nicholson voice. Make my day, he doesn't say.

Yet.

He scans the lie of the land. Eyeballs the haystacks, the ditch.

He moves. Walks towards the ditch. He does a little whirligig of a dance to cover all directions, to see everything around him as he goes, much like British soldiers used to do on the telly when they were on patrol on the Falls Road or the cowboy country of Armagh.

I sidle down the ditch till I'm behind the nearest haystack. I climb out and crawl behind the stack. I drop to my belly and watch the ditch through the grass.

He gets to the ditch. He's about eight feet away from me. He's chuckling to himself. *Chuckling*. The guy is fucking loony tunes. He does his little dance. I'm up on my knees. He looks into the ditch, down towards my end. I'm standing. He does another little dance, looks back in the ditch. Down the other way. His back is to me.

I make my move.

I'm the hurler in the ditch.

I'm the master bowler.

I wind myself up and pitch my biggest brick. Full force. Crack, the brick says when it smacks the back of McGonagle's noggin. *Howzat*! Ugh, goes McGonagle. And he does a header into the ditch. Alas, he takes his gun with him.

I run like fuck.

I'm going like the clappers. My legs are pumping up and down like pistons. I'm the Fastest Man on Earth. I'm the Supertrain. I'm Arkle's ghost. I'm Mister Coyote, Hurricane Hilda and the Six Million Dollar Man, all rolled up into one supersonic sprinter.

I am the fucking wind, man, and I'm blowing.

To my car out front, thanking Christ I took the keys with me and praying to the same Jesus that McGonagle didn't have the foresight to disable the motor. I hit the side of the house and there's a pop. A bullet ploughs a furrow at my feet.

Fuckin' hell in a handbasket.

I hear McGonagle roar. He's not lilting any more.

Up your bum.

I don't look back.

I'm out the gate, my keys in my hand. The blood is pumping in my ears. I'm in the car, the key's in the lock. I'm turning the key. Sweat is pouring off me. Pop goes the weasel again — another roar — and the back window disintegrates. I'm showered with little glass nuggets. And the engine starts. There's a *phtinnnggg* as the bullet ricochets somewhere and we're into gear and away.

Jesus, help me, God.

I get a hurried glimpse of McGonagle in the rear-view mirror, standing crouched in the middle of the road, his legs spread, the shooter clutched in both hands, thinks he's Arnold Fucking Schwarzenegger, lining up for a shot, but I'm zipping round the corner, onto the main road and up to the ton in seconds flat.

My motor is no slouch in the acceleration department.

Praise the Lord.

No Chitty Chitty Bang Bang this.

I don't look back.

I drive like a maniac.

Ten minutes and I'm on the Dublin Road.

And I'm fucking and blinding and crying, fucking and blinding and bawling my eyes out. My fists are whacking the steering wheel and salt water streams down my face, splashing onto my lap. At least I haven't wet myself, I'm thinking while I'm crying. I was afraid enough.

But then I realise I'm not crying for myself or for my fear. I'm crying my heart out for Nuala. My Nuala. My sweet, sweet precious, splendid Nuala, all dead and gone and wasted in her prime.

The bastard murdered Nuala.

The bastard murdered my Nuala.

I'll get him for this.

I look in the rear-view mirror.

I'll get him.

No hot pursuit.
The bastard.
McGonagle must have hidden his car out of sight. He'll have had to go and fetch it. By then I'm long gone.
Just watch me.

21

I sob my grief out for two or three minutes. That does the job and calms me. It's time now to think of practical things. The pain comes back to me. There's blood still dripping out of the hole in my shoulder, rolling down my skin inside my shirt. It's sticky on my belly.

The fucker shot me.

I'm losing blood.

And I'm in trouble.

I've been set up nicely, I reckon.

McGonagle was all set to blow me away and have me take the rap for wasting Nuala and the doc.

But first things first. Gotta get sorted out. Gotta get my war wound fixed.

Where do you go when you're physically hurting?

To a doctor.

Or a nurse.

Maria.
Yes.

Keeping just under the speed limit, I drive into Dun Laoghaire. It's a picturesque, lively suburban seaside town with fishing boats and yachts parked scenically in the harbour.

I reckon if McGonagle has done his homework, and if I want to stay alive I should presume he has, the word is out on me already and the long arm of the law is reaching out for me.

I have to ditch the car.

I find a street of quiet semi-detached houses just off the seafront and I park the motor outside number forty-two. I have a raincoat on the back seat and my gym bag in the boot. I fetch them both and take a hike along the sea front.

I find a public toilet and lock myself in a cubicle. I flush the loo for fresh, clean water. I take off my parka and my shirt, tear the bloodless side of the shirt into strips. The bleeding has slowed down in my shoulder. I use toilet paper and the water in the bowl to clean the blood off me. I clog up the wound with some shirt and tie my snot-rag there with some more.

There's a sweatsuit in my gym bag. I dry myself off with the pants and put on the top. I put on the raincoat. There's a patch of blood on my jeans, but you wouldn't know what it is. It could be anything. And anyway the raincoat will cover it.

I empty my parka pockets. Wallet, money, car keys, odds and ends.

Nuala's panties. My eyes let loose the waterworks again. I stop them. Gather myself. I put the panties and stuff in my raincoat pocket. I stuff my parka and the reddened remains of my shirt in the gym bag.

Outside the cubicle, I check myself out in one of the mirrors over the sinks. Dots and dashes of blood on my face and neck. I wash them off. I look okay, considering I'm supposed to be ringing the bell on the pearly gates just about now. I hit the road. I dump the gym bag in a rubbish bin.

I'm on the lam.

Jesus.

It's a far cry from an illustrious career in the cops.

Here I am, all grown up. I'm single, childless, gunshot in the shoulder and on the fucking lam in Dun Laoghaire.

Can't wait for my next school reunion.

I check my watch. It's twenty past one. Already. Maria will reckon I stood her up.

A chilly gust blows along the boardwalk, picking up the spray from the sea and sprinkling it on my face. The salt tastes good — pure and fresh — in my mouth. A middle-aged man and a priest are out for a bracing walk with their dogs. They smile and nod as they pass me by.

Out on the sand some kids, skiving off from school no doubt, skim rocks along the ocean. Their voices carry, disjointed, on the wind. "Nice one, Cyril," I hear, and "Ya lucky cunt."

Pensioners and courting couples on the benches. The young ones huddle up to each other to keep out the weather. The old ones button up their coats, turn up their collars.

The normality, the everydayness of it, calms me, eases my anguish, slows my galloping anxiety down to manageable proportions. My blood pressure must be up through the roof.

I make a beeline for the DART. I pay my fare and hop a train to the city. I get off at Connolly Station and catch a bus to Fairview. I hoof it over to Maria's.

Doctor Kildare's car is parked outside her door.
Fuck.
I'm losing blood. I can't fart around all day waiting for him to go.
I take a chance.
Ring the bell.

She opens the door.
Her jaw drops.

"Jesus, Milo," she says.

Nice to see you too.

"Hi," I say. Sometimes I have a way with words.

"We were just watching you on the telly."

"You know the story, so."

"What are you doing here?"

Céad míle fáilte. A hundred thousand welcomes.

A friend in need indeed.

A couple of months ago every second day or so this woman moaned and groaned, slithered and shook and, on occasion farted, goddammit, while I licked chocolate-mint yogurt out of her vagina.

Now it's what are you doing here?

Jesus.

But I need her.

"I've been shot," I say. "I need your help."

"You should be in hospital."

"For fuck's sake, Maria, I can't go to a hospital. I'd be nicked."

"Jesus."

"Can I come in please?"

"Huh?"

"Can I come in?"

"I suppose so," she says.

With all the warm hospitality of the Ebola virus.

She moves aside and in I go. She sticks her head out the door. Looks up and down the street.

"I haven't been followed," I say.

"I hope not," she says.

"Don't worry."

"That's easy for you to say."

Christ.

In the sitting-room Doctor Kildare sits on the sofa, his feet up on a coffee table, watching telly with a pair of Levis on and his shirt hanging out. His feet are bare. He looks up as I come in and his eyes turn into saucers.

"Jesus Christ," he says.

"Milo Devine," I say.

"Very funny," says Maria.

Doctor Kildare looks at Maria, at me, back at Maria. There are question marks on his eyeballs. She shrugs her shoulders.

I take off my coat and sit down beside him.

"What's on the box?" I say.

"Ha, ha, ha," spits Maria.

"You are," says the doc. "You just missed a news flash. It was all about you."

"Fancy that," I say.

"You're in deep shit, man," he says. The doctor doesn't mince his words.

He's gotten over the initial shock and there's actually what sounds like a note of compassion in his voice. He surprises me. The first impression is good. Despite myself, I'm rising to this bloke.

I can't say likewise for Maria.

"Whatever made you come here?" she says.

God.

"Your expertise," I say. "I told you. I need your help."

I take off my sweat-shirt.

"Ouch," I say, as I stretch the wound.

Doctor Kildare's training kicks in. He goes into surgery mode. He takes off my makeshift bandage with the business-like, deft touch of the professional. Checks out the hole in my shoulder.

Maria just stands there.

"In and out the back," he says. "Clean enough. At least the bullet's not in there. My bag is in the car. I'll go and get it."

He puts on his shoes and socks, tucks his shirt in.

He moves to stand up.

I look at him. He looks back. He's no fool, this fellow. He speaks the eyeball lingo, knows what I'm saying. He nods slightly, reassuring me.

"I'll be right back," he says.

"I'll put on the kettle," says Maria.

"Have you any whiskey in the house?" I say.

"Give him tea," says Doctor Kildare on his way to the door. "He's probably in shock."

"I'd really prefer a drop of whiskey," I say.

"Tea," he says.

The voice of authority.

The door slams behind him.
She puts on the kettle.

Doctor Kildare jabs me with a needle, cleans out the wound, stitches it up. He puts a bandage on me.

Maria gives me a cup of tea. Kind of. She puts it down on the coffee table with a clatter. No fig rolls or cucumber sandwiches.

"Thanks," I say to the doc.

"You should get some rest," he says.

"He can't stay here," says Maria.

"I'm in the bloody room here, Maria. Talk to me, not about me," I say.

The woman is really pissing me off. If there's anything that's guaranteed to make my blood boil, it's somebody talking about me in the third person when I'm sitting right in front of them. I've always hated that.

Another news flash comes up on the telly. The screen is full of a ten-year-old picture of me. It was taken after my police training in Templemore. It's a leaner, keener, younger me, but I'm eminently recognisable.

I'm wanted for questioning, the talking head says, about the murder of well-known psychiatrist Doctor Jack Walton and Nuala Cooley, daughter of the Leader of the Opposition and possibly our future Taoiseach.

There's a picture of the Gaffer, then some footage of Walton's house, with the cops huffing and puffing outside, the forensics people crawling and picking, cameras flashing, citizens rubbernecking.

A suspected crime of passion, says the talking head, more on the six o'clock news. There's a phone number at the bottom of the screen for Seán Citizen to call if he has any info for the cops.

Soon there will be a reward.

"Jesus," says Maria. The Lord's name is being taken in vain a lot around here this afternoon.

"What are you going to do?" says Doctor Kildare.

"Fix things, I hope," I say.

I look at him.

"I didn't do it, you know," I say.

He shrugs.

"Okay," he says.

"I'll be out of your hair as soon as I can," I say to Maria. "I'll have to make a phone call."

Doctor Kildare looks at his watch.

"I have to be off," he says. "Duty calls."

His departure is awkward. Maria is too embarrassed to give him a hug in front of me. He's a smart lad. He busses her on the cheek. He turns to me.

"Look after that shoulder," he says.

I stick out my hand. He shakes it.

"Many thanks," I say.

He nods and he's off.

22

All the warmth goes with him.

A thermometer would crack, the air is so chilly between me and Maria. We're worse than strangers. She's busy inspecting the carpet.

"Can I use your phone?" I say.

"You know where it is."

"Thanks very much."

She goes into the kitchen, clatters some dishes around.

I call Davy Mullen.

"Hello," he says.

"It's me," I say.

"Aha," he says. "So it is. *Conas tá tú?*" How are you?

"I'm in trouble, Davy."

"Not at all, Milo. You're a celebrity. A TV star."

"You watch too much television," I say.

"So my wife keeps telling me. Are you all right?"

"So far, so good."

"Where are you?" he says.

I tell him.

He dwells on that for a while.

"Can you trust that woman?" he says.

I ponder that. Maria is still making cranky noise in the kitchen. Trust her? Not for much more than this, I reckon. It's time I hit the road. But I do trust Doctor Kildare. Funnily enough, I trust him more than I do Maria.

"I think I'm secure for now," I say, "but the sooner I get out of here the better."

"Okay," he says. "I'll come and get you in a few hours. After dark. What's the address?"

I tell him.

"Sit tight," he says.

"Thanks," I say.

I hang up the phone.

Maria comes in from the kitchen.

"A friend is coming to pick me up," I say.

"Right," she says.

"In a while," I say.

"Right," she says.

"You should be in sales," I say.

"What?" she says.

"You're so chatty," I say.

She sniffs.

But I'm coming down now. With a rush.

The couch is soft. The adrenaline is all pumped out of me. I'm emotionally whacked.

I crash.

When I awake it's getting dark outside. Inside the room is gloomy. Maria has pulled the curtains. She hasn't turned on the light. She's sitting on the armchair. The coffee table is between us. It may as well be the Berlin Wall.

She's sucking on a cigarette. The ashtray is full of butts.

"I thought you gave up smoking," I say.

"I started again," she says.

"Not on my account, I hope."

"Figure it out, Milo."

She's laying on the guilts. One of her many talents. She's probably been sitting there chain-smoking since I crashed out, willing me to wake up so I could see I've driven her back into the narcotic arms of Lady Nicotine.

Spare me.

I change tack.

"What time is it?" I say.

"It's after eight."

I've been out for more than three hours.

I missed *The News*.

"I missed *The News*," I say.

She snorts.

"Big deal," she says.

God, give me patience.

"Any chance of a cup of tea?" I say.

"This is not a hotel," she says.

"What did I ever do to you to make you so hostile?" I say.

There's a knock on the door.

Just as well. I feel like wringing the bitch's neck.

I slip into the kitchen.

The bitch opens the door.

It's Davy. I come out of the kitchen. He spots me from the doorway. He nods at Maria.

"Are you right?" he says to me.

"Right as rain," I say.

I pull on my sweatshirt and my raincoat. He throws me a hat. I look at it. It's one of those tweedy ones with a floppy brim all round. The kind the country squire wears. It will hide most of the top of my face.

"Donegal tweed," I say. "Tasty. But it doesn't go with my raincoat."

"Very funny," he says. "Some comedian you are. You'll be the star of the show in the Christmas concert in Portlaoise Prison. Come on."

I put on the hat, pull up my collar and go on.

"Thanks for your help," I say to Maria on my way out. My voice is lacking gravitas.

She looks like a million dollars and she's a crackerjack of a she-devil in the sack, but when the chips are down her feet are made of crumbling clay. If I may mix my metaphors.

Arrivederci, Maria.

The door slams behind me.

Davy squints at me.

"I suppose a ride was out of the question?" he says.

23

There's a bright red Mercedes parked at the kerb.

"Where did you get that?" I say.

"It's a loaner," he says, "My yoke is getting a service."

"Inconspicuous," I say.

Davy taps his temple with a finger.

"Nobody's going to be looking for you in a scarlet Merc, Milo."

He has a point.

"True for you," I say.

And the windows are tinted so you can't see into the car.

The inside smells of leather. The upholstery is new. The colour of blood. Appropriate.

"Where are we off to?" I say.

"Not too far," he says. "I found you a safe house."

He drives me up the Howth Road. Takes a right on Castle Avenue and pulls up outside a semi-dilapidated Georgian four-storey building fighting off the fading of its glory with roses round the garden and vines crawling over the walls. He leads me around the side to a flat with its own entrance on the main floor. The accommodation is pretty basic. Self-contained, the landlords call it in the ads.

There are three rooms. Kind of. A sitting-room, a bedroom and a cupboard for a kitchen all carved out of what probably used to be a rich man's parlour. The bathroom is through a door into the main house and down the hall. I'll be sharing it with the occupants of three other bedsitters on the same floor, Davy says.

My new home.

The sitting-room has a single tattered sofa with an armchair to match and a huge, awkward, antiquated television in a corner, the likes of which you might see in reruns of shows like *I Love Lucy* or *The Honeymooners.* Ekco is the brand name. Probably a subsidiary of the communications corporation that published the first printing of *The Ten Commandments.*

The telly is perched on a sagging, yellowish art deco coffee table, beneath which the floor is sagging from the weight. The furniture looks like the previous occupant abandoned it in relief when he finally found a job after a lifetime on the dole. The carpet has been worn down to thread.

The kitchen is off the sitting-room and if you close the door you don't have room to move. There's a cooker and a sink with a press over it and a small cupboard below it. The pantry. There's a little plastic table and a battered chair for sit-down meals. Movie props they look like. Something the Joad family would have on the back of the pick-up truck in *The Grapes of Wrath*.

The night is dark.

Davy flicks the light switch. Nothing happens. There's an electricity meter low on the wall beside the door. Davy puts in a punt piece and the room lights up. He roots through his change and puts the rest of his punts on top of the meter.

"In case you run out," he says.

"Thanks," I say.

The place smells mustily of damp. Davy pulls out a four-bar electric heater from behind the telly. He plugs it in. The dial in the electricity meter starts flying round, doing ninety miles an hour at least. I'll be needing all those punts.

"Home sweet home," Davy says.

I grunt.

He reassures me.

"It won't be for long."

I grunt again. I'm not in the best of form.

"It could be worse," he says. "It could be Mountjoy Jail."

I grunt again.

"It's nearly nine o'clock," he says. "Time for *The News*."

I turn on the telly. It flickers slowly, asthmatically, into life. It bleeps and splutters and starts warming up. I flop onto the bed. I'm completely exhausted. Knackered.

Davy has a couple of bags of stuff with him. He empties them onto the table. There's a bag of suicide wings. Cans of draught Guinness. Two pint glasses. A couple of bottles of Black Bush.

"I've lately developed a taste for Crested Ten," I say.

He waves a fist at me, spread-eagles the fingers.

"Go on," he says. "Bite the hand that feeds you."

I grin. He's playing a stormer.

"You're very well versed at this kind of thing," I say.

He winks.

"You're a dark horse, Davy Mullen," I say.

The last item out of the bag is a pair of pyjamas. I usually sleep *au naturel*, but I look at the bed, at the geriatric, hand-me-down blankets. You never know what's been living in there. Jammies are a good idea.

"Great," I say.

Davy finds some plates in the press over the sink, gives them a wipe with his sleeve, puts the wings on them and bungs them in the oven, turns it on.

"I think a few scoops are in order," he says.

He pours us out a Guinness each, locates a couple of grimy wine glasses in the press, wipes the dust out of them with his finger and rinses them under the tap. He pours the Black Bush. He splashes himself a civilised dose, fills my glass to the brim.

He brings me my drinks.

"*Sláinte,*" he says.

I look at the measure of booze in the glass.

"Are you trying to take advantage of me, Davy?"

"I'm driving," he says. "Can't be too careful."

He gets his drinks and settles down on the sofa.

The telly splutters into life. The picture is black and white. There was probably no such thing as colour TV when this set was manufactured. The ads are on before *The News*.

I drink. The whiskey burns its way down to my belly. I close my eyes and savour it. Blessed relief. I needed that. I know now how a junkie feels when he finally gets his elusive fix.

The day recedes and exhaustion sets in. I relax.

"Who owns this gaff?" I say.

"I do," he says.

"You?"

"Yep. It's an investment."

"So, you're a landlord, on top of everything else? You're full of surprises, Mister Mullen."

"My accountant tells me diversification is the key to financial longevity. Don't have your finger in just the one pie, he says."

Judging by the looks of the room it's been a while since anybody lived here.

"Why isn't it rented?" I say.

Davy shrugs.

"It's on the market."

"It looks like a safe house to me," I say.

Davy chuckles.

"Don't tell me you're a Provo, Davy," I say. "Not after all these years of us knowing each other. And me assuming you were way up there above the fray."

"You're letting your imagination run away with you, Milo. You've had a rough day. You've been set up and you're paranoid. Don't invent intrigue where there is none, old son."

"If you say so."

"I do."

"Right, so."

The News comes on.

I'm the top story.

Milo Devine and the Demagogue's Daughter

The talking heads have found their Nirvana. Political murder in the middle of an election is grist to their mill. They'll be guzzling and repeating this story like pigs at a bottomless trough.

We watch the stiffs being carted into ambulances. One of those stiffs is my Nuala. The camera shifts to the scene outside the morgue. There's coppers and suits all over the place. The Gaffer comes out. He's just after identifying the body. He's rubbing his eyes. His handlers steer him into his limo. McGonagle is right behind him. He gets into the driving seat. A reporter sticks a mike through the window, holds it up to McGonagle's mouth.

It seems to be a crime of passion, says the lying, two-faced bastard, in the clipped, unnatural vernacular coppers are prone to using. The police are actively seeking a man who had a prior relationship with Miss Cooley and who apparently had trouble accepting it when she finished said relationship, he says.

That's me he's talking about.

The scumbag.

He makes it sound like my relationship with Nuala was recent. Smooth bastard. I realise that his story makes eminent sense to bystanders. To potential members of the jury.

I'm in scalding water.

The camera shifts again. The same ten-year-old picture of me they used the last time fills the screen.

Police are looking for this man, says the talking head. Milo Devine is his name, he says.

And murder is his game.

"Jesus," says I.

"That's not a very flattering likeness," says Davy.

I grunt.

"You'll have to get yourself an agent," he says.

"Ha ha," I say.

The talking head is outside my office building now. Angie is shooing him away and trying to close the door. What can you tell us about Milo Devine, the talking head demands. They don't broadcast Angie's answer. But I can read her lips.

"Fuck off," she says.

That's my girl.

But the talking head doesn't give a shite. It's all milk and honey to him. He stands in front of the building and does a wrap. He gives a brief précis of my career in the cops and my departure from the force. The script is maliciously spun to elicit sensation. He makes it sound as if my life since then has been lived somehow beyond the fringes of regular society.

"Poxy lowlife reporters," I say.

The gist of the message is that I'm shady.

He doesn't say anything specific. His language is well chosen and careful. But he manages to leave the impression that since I left the cops I've been going around with a chip on my shoulder that ultimately drove me to murder.

He's doing a number on me. Inferring a scenario in which a psycho under pressure finally cracks, goes around the bend, wreaks havoc and leaves mayhem in his wake. And the psycho's moniker is Milo Devine.

He doesn't seem to give a damn that it's my life he's turning upside-down. That it's my good name he's nailing to the crucifix. On scant evidence. On the word of a crooked cop.

And the whole world is watching.

"Fucking hell," I say, when *The News* goes on to something trivial, like thousands of Africans dying from hunger.

"The media juggernaut is in motion," says Davy.

Both my glasses are empty. Davy fills them. He fetches the suicide wings.

"What did you do to deserve this?" he says.

"I'm up Shit Creek without a paddle," I say.

"You have a paddle, Milo," says Davy. "You've got friends."

I'm touched.

"I think I'm going to cry," I say.

"Don't worry," he says. "We'll find a way out of this. We'll get the bastards. Now, tell me all that happened."

We eat the wings and I tell him.

When I finish he's topping up my whiskey glass again. I rinse my sticky fingers under the tap.

One of the whiskey bottles is dead. That was quick.

My thoughts are swimming.

I'm feeling around on the bed for the channel changer. I'm a good two minutes at it before I realise I'm not at home and this television set came off the production line long before remote control was a twinkle in Mister Mitsubishi's eye.

"So, McGonagle must be the killer," says Davy.

"Must be," I say.

"But why?"

"Search me."

"That's the key, Milo. When we know why, we know everything. The whole kit'n'caboodle."

I knock back my whiskey, drain my glass of Guinness. I get up and go to the telly. I have some difficulty putting one foot in front of the other. I turn the knob and search for another channel.

"At least I have more than one channel," I say.

"We aim to please," says Davy.

I find a movie. *Goodbye, Mister Chips*. The old Robert Donat version.

"Magic," I say.

It's one of my favourites.

"I love this film," I say.

"It's a good one," says Davy.

"A classic."

Mister Chips climbs a mountain in the mist and meets his lovely wife-to-be.

I pour myself another Black Bush. I wave the bottle at Davy, lift my eyebrows. He shakes his head. I fill a glass with Guinness. The head fizzes over. A lot of it lands on the table. I make my wobbly way back to the bed.

"Do you remember when Snooks gave me a box in the head?" I say.

Mister Chips has reminded me of my school days. I'm getting into nostalgia mode. Snooks taught us English in fifth year.

"Yes," says Davy.

"He thought I was standing up to him. I wasn't. I was just showing off."

"I know."

"He said, 'By Jesus boy, don't raise your fist to me'. I must've really hurt his feelings."

"Nah," says Davy. He's rolling a joint.

"I was really fond of Snooks, y'know."

"I know."

Chippings' wife is dying. I might be crying.

"Poor Mister Chips," I say.

The booze is doing the talking. Drink — you put a thief in your mouth to steal away your tongue. Mattie Ross said that to Rooster Cogburn in *True Grit*. The Duke got his Oscar for that one. Not before his time.

Davy lights up the joint, passes it over to me.

The grass creams me.

Davy lets me smoke nearly all of it. I wash it down with my Guinness. I can barely find my mouth with the glass.

"Right," says Davy. "It's time to hit the sack."

He helps me out of my clothes.

"The Duke is dead," I say. "The Big C got him in the end."

"He had a good innings," says Davy.

He gets me into the pyjamas.

"Long live the Duke."

Davy tucks me in.

"They never had any kids," I say.

"Who?" he says.

"Mister and Mrs Chips."

"Right."

"What day is today?"

"Thursday."

"Is that all?"

"It's a slow week, eh?"

"Remember," I say, "when we were in school and you nicked your old man's car and drove it up my street?"

"No," he says.

"You gave all the kids a run around the block."

"Did I?"

"I loved you for that."

"Thanks," he says.

He turns off the telly and the light. He says goodnight.

"Don't go out," he says. "I'll be here first thing in the morning."

And he leaves me.

My brain is floating on a sea of giddy tranquillity. But I'm physically wrecked and emotionally exhausted. Sleep is rushing at me and I'm not complaining.

But . . .

I feel in the dark at the foot of the bed for where I dropped my raincoat. I'm all drunken, doped-up thumbs. Eventually I feel out the appropriate pocket and my fingers find Nuala's panties. I take them out, put them under the pillow, hold them there in my hand.

Embracing sleep, I'm remembering a poem.

> *She lived unknown, and few could know*
> *When Lucy ceased to be;*
> *But she is in her grave, and, oh,*
> *The difference to me.*

It says.

24

I wake from the sleep of the just. I'm bursting for a piss.

I do it in the sink.

I'm an animal. And itchy.

Yuch.

Strange grimy beds are the pits.

I'm grubby from the ancient blankets. I need a shower. Badly. I hate dirt. Loathe it. To the point of being phobic, almost. Now look at me. I give the sink a good rinse, look in the cupboard under it for toiletries. There's half a bar of Fairy Soap. No shampoo.

My watch says it's a quarter to ten.

I open the door, peek into the hall. The place is quiet as the grave. Everybody is at work, I guess.

Flatland.

I search my flat. Nary a towel to be found.

I'll dry off with my jammies.

I trot down the hall to the bathroom, turn on the shower.

The water's freezing.

There's another one of those meters stuck in the wall. You have to pay to get the water hot. Pay-as-you-go is the order of the day in flatland.

I fetch one of Davy's punts and bung it into the slot.

I make some tea and drink it while the water heats up.

I do a little soft-shoe-shuffle in the shower to keep the bandage dry on my shoulder, but nonetheless the hot water is refreshing. Cleansing. Restorative. Worth the wait and the punt.

When I'm finished Davy is waiting for me in my room. There's a pile of bags on the table and the floor. He's been shopping.

"Top of the morning, Milo," he says.

"Hello, Davy," I say.

I nod at the bags.

"You've been busy."

"Just a few odds and ends to make life easier for you."

He's emptying the odds and ends onto the kitchen table. Food. Eggs, bread, tins of beans and the like.

Tea and coffee. Milk. There's socks and knickers, T-shirts, jeans, a denim shirt. A surplus army jacket. Toiletries: soap, shampoo, conditioner. Shaving cream, brush, disposable razors. Two towels. I jumped the gun with my shower.

"Where's my cologne?" I say.

"Cologne my arse," says Davy.

He puts scissors on the table. Hair clippers. Brown hair dye. My natural colour is black, with a few sad old streaks of grey.

A pair of John Lennon granny glasses with regular glass in the lenses instead of prescription. There's a light blue tint to them.

"I raided the drama society's storehouse," he says. "We're going to do a makeover on you."

I'm impressed. Again.

"You're playing a stormer, Davy," I say.

I put my hand on his shoulder.

"I'm going to owe you plenty after this," I say.

He looks me in the eye. The band should be playing *He ain't heavy, he's my brother*.

"You'll owe me nothing, Milo," he says. "*Nada. Rien*. Let's just do the business. Right?"

I grin. Buddies in bad times.

"Right," I say.

I make a pot of tea. Davy has already eaten, he says. I boil a couple of eggs, make some toast. I wish I had a few spoonfuls of chili.

I polish off my spiceless breakfast.

Davy sits me at the kitchen sink and goes to work on my hair. He shears my lovely locks.

When he's finished with me my head looks like Kevin Costner's in *The Bodyguard*. Mousy brown hair clipped tight to the skull. I could pass for a marine. Or a skinhead. Fortunately, nowadays it's cool to be bald.

With the glasses on I barely recognise myself.

I look intelligent.

We get down to business.

"Now," says Davy, "you have three choices, Milo. You can take a hike. Leave the country. I can get you a passport. A new name. New identity. No sweat. Probably a green card for the States at the right price. You could start a new life."

"How come you can manage all this?" I say.

"You know what they say – it's not what you know, it's who you know. So, do you want a new life?"

"No thanks. I kind of like this one. At least I used to."

"Right. Option number two – give yourself up and take your chances with the law."

"I'm against that."

"That's wise. They'd bury you."

"Deep in the well."

"Yep. You wouldn't stand a prayer."

"Maybe I should fly the coop, after all."

He shakes his head.

"The scoop, as I read it, is this," he says. "McGonagle set you up. He set the trap and you walked into it. That's all we know. We don't know why he did it, but we agree that it's safe for us to assume for now that he killed Nuala and Walton and planned to bump you off and put the blame on you. Right?"

"It was ambush city, man."

"Correct me if I'm wrong. He was waiting for you out at Walton's place?"

"He left the bloody door open for me."

"How did he know you'd be going out there yesterday morning?"

"I told him, for fuck's sake. He phoned me in the early morning. Just checking in with me, he said he was."

"He could have phoned from Walton's place?"

"Could have."

"What we don't know is why he did it or if he's on his own in this."

"Or where Archie Cooley figures in it all."

"Right."

"Even Archie Cooley wouldn't waste his own daughter, though. Would he?"

"The notion chills the bones."

"You're telling me."

"But he did hire you to find her."

"It was McGonagle's idea. I think."

"Okay. Let's say for the sake of argument that McGonagle set both you and Cooley up. He did a great job of it too. He had it all worked out. It's classic psychobabble stuff. You were the jealous lover. Plus, hypothetically, you've been going around with a chip on your maladjusted shoulder ever since you were run off the police force. Finally, your sick mind couldn't take the pressures any more. You cracked. You kidnapped Nuala and her new paramour. You held them hostage in Walton's house for nearly a fortnight."

I flinch.

"Finally you killed them."

"Jesus. It almost makes sense."

"He's a crafty bugger, that McGonagle. The rest of it is easy. He makes out that it was your idea that you help find Cooley's daughter. He met you in a pub, say, and, you being an old friend of Nuala's, he told you the story and you planted the idea in his head. Of course you planned the entire encounter, cute and cunning headcase that you are. McGonagle realises that in retrospect. Eventually, our hero smelled a rat. He followed you and caught you just after the act of murder. But he made one mistake. He slipped up before the final curtain and let you get away. You're supposed to be pushing up the daisies right now, Milo."

"But what's it all about?"

Davy shakes his head.

"I haven't a clue. That's what we have to find out."

"Just how are we supposed to do that?"

"We need a plan," he says.

"We need a miracle."

"Come on, Milo. Work with me. You're the detective."

"You're doing all right so far."

"Right. All we can do at the moment is guess at the whys and the wherefores. We have no hard facts besides McGonagle and a couple of corpses. Knowledge is the power. We need information."

"Agreed."

"So, what I think is this. Since McGonagle is the key, I say we should concentrate on him, watch him and see what he gets up to in the next few days. We'll haunt the bastard and see what we come up with."

"I suppose."

"It's all we can do."

"You're right. He's the only lead we have."

"And we may as well be doing something. Better that than sit here on our arses waiting for the sky to fall in."

"And letting the trail go cold."

"So, are we agreed? We go after McGonagle?"

"Okay."

"All right, so. We'll need a surveillance team. Drivers. I have a few people in mind."

"Me too."

He stands up. All business.

"Let's do it. Round up the usual suspects, my friend. I'll go see my people. We'll all gather here tonight and put our heads together. There's a public phone in the hall. I don't know if it's secure. Best to leave nothing to chance till this is over. I'd go out to make phone calls if I was you."

"Okay."

"I probably don't have to tell you this," he says, "but I'll say it anyway. You're a marked man, Milo. There's those in the polis, with long and bitter memories, who'd blow you away as soon as they'd look at you. They'd be playing right into McGonagle's hands. One thing is for sure. He wants you dead and voiceless. And one or two of the others could be in on this with him, whatever this is."

I nod.

"Sweaty Finnegan, for instance," I say.

"He's no fan of yours," he says. "You be careful out there, *amigo*."

"*Si, señor.*"

"Eight o'clock tonight?"

"Eight o'clock."

Davy takes a hike. I drink another cup of tea. I clean my teeth, shave myself in the sink and get dressed. The Levis and the denim shirt. My own Doc Martens. The John Lennon granny glasses. I throw on the army jacket, look at myself in the mirror. Not bad. But who the fuck is it?

25

I take a walk.

The day is bright and dry with a bit of a nip in the air. The streets are quiet. A few occasional cars on the road. An empty bus whizzes by. It's eleven-thirty a.m. and all is well. For some.

I ramble along the Howth Road, looking for a phone box.

The traffic-lights ahead of me are red. A cruiser sits there. Cops on the prowl, waiting for the green light. Walking towards them on the empty street, in my mind's eye I'm a thousand feet tall and ten feet wide, a giant dressed in diagonal stripes with a ball and chain attached to my leg and a wanted poster pinned to my chest.

In my head Johnny Cash is singing. *Wanted Man*.

I fight the urge to drop my eyes, to look away

and act guilty. The light goes green. I keep my head up and walk. The cruiser cruises by. I start breathing again. My make-up job has faced the test. And passed with honours.

Johnny Cash changes his tune. *Let There Be Peace In The Valley.* I hum along.

I feel better already.

Outside a pub, The Beachcomber, I find a public phone. I put in the money and dial the number for the Burke twins. Jake and John-Joe. They flog cars and run a limo service in the city. I use them now and then when I need some discreet surveillance done. They're the best. Virtually undetectable.

Jake is another ex-cop. He was a London bobby for ten years. Then he made a killing on the horses. There was a whiff of scandal about it. Something his superiors took a dim view of. The fix was in, was the general assumption. But it couldn't be proved. Jake took his profits and came back to Dublin. Opened up the business with his brother.

Never looked back.

They're thick as thieves, the brothers.

John-Joe was a small-time pickpocket and scam artist before Jake came back across the water. I saved his neck once when I was on the force. He was facing a murder charge. Somebody mugged a Yankee tourist behind the Gresham Hotel. Only, the trouble was the mugger tapped the tourist in a soft spot on the wrong side of the head and the tourist snuffed it. The Gresham was right in the heart of John-Joe's stomping ground. His area of expertise was in scamming the tourists. He was arrested and charged on circumstantial evidence.

I knew John-Joe's *modus operandi*. He was a conman and a pickpocket. He wasn't into violence. You wouldn't find him whacking and mugging tourists in back alleys. That wasn't his style. I also knew that on the scale of naughty-to-psychotic bad guys he was somewhere around roguish and the last thing he'd want to do is bump somebody off. If he knocked somebody out in the course of his business he'd call an ambulance.

I had faith in him. It paid off.

I did a little extra-curricular snooping and found the real killer. A homeless junkie. There was still a bit of the Catholic upbringing lingering around his ruined psyche. I got a guilt-ridden confession out of him. No sweat.

John-Joe never forgot. Neither did his family. We're all the best of pals now. His mother still counts me in her prayers. I don't add up the bills, but the Burkes reckon they owe me big time.

John-Joe answers.

"It's me," I say.

"So it is," he says.

I rattle off the number printed on the public

phone, tell him to run out and call me. Can't be too careful.

There's no one else waiting for the phone. I hang it up, stay where I am. In two minutes it rings.

"John-Joe?" I say.

"Milo. What's the story, man?"

"You've heard about my predicament, I presume?"

"Who hasn't? You're famous."

"I need a helping hand."

"You've got it, mate."

"You and Jake. All right?"

"No problem."

I give him the time, the address and I bid him *adieu*.

I stroll through Clontarf to the seashore. I find another public phone. I call Billy Cartwright. He's a mechanic, but his real passion is stock-car racing. He's the best fast driver in Dublin. If Jake and John-Joe are the essence of discretion, Billy is speed incarnate. The man for the moment when the object of your surveillance catches onto you and floors it.

Next to stock-car racing, fishing is the love of his life. I fish too. That's how we met. In the middle of the night, poaching salmon on the Shannon. Each of us shat a plank, thinking the other was the bailiff. We then got stoned and bonded, as the new men say.

We've been friends ever since. He's done the

odd job for me. Nothing untoward, though. Billy is strictly on the up and up.

He picks up the phone.

"Hello," he says.

"Don't say my name," I say.

Billy is a straight arrow. He's unversed in the nefarious ways of the underworld. But he's quick on the uptake. He pauses.

"Okay," he says.

I do the routine again. I give him my number, tell him to go out and call me. I figure if anybody's phone is safe it's Billy's, but we're playing for big stakes here. My neck.

The phone rings. I answer it.

"Jesus, Milo, are you all right?" he says.

"Sure I am," I say. "I just need some help."

"No problem."

"Your driving skills."

"Okay."

"Thanks."

I tell him the time and the place. He'll be there, he says.

"Make sure you're not followed," I say.

"Right," he says.

I believe him. A cruise missile couldn't keep up with Billy when he puts the boot down.

The business is done.

I walk. Along the seafront.

The tide is coming in. A cold breeze full of salt and seaweed blows in from the Irish Sea. Down on the sand at the water there's a young couple with a toddler and a dog. The father throws a stick out to sea and the mutt rips out after it. The toddler wants to follow the dog, but the mother has him on a leash. The dog runs back with the stick. The toddler claps, delighted. The mother laughs. Her laughter breaks on the breeze, comes across to me in pieces.

All of a sudden Nuala Cooley is all over me. Her face in my head. Her perfume fills my nose. I can almost feel her skin on mine. She had my picture on her bedside. Facing her as she went to sleep and slept. Her panties are under my pillow.

I'm tasting salt and it's not off the sea breeze.

I was in love and I didn't even know it. Bloody Milo. Fucking gobshite. Milo the Oblivious. Posthumously in love. Typical. Fucking typical. Oh, Nuala. My heart is clamped in pain.

I find another phone.

I reach out and touch. I'm breaking the rules, but fuck it, I need to.

I call Cynthia. At work. She answers the phone herself.

"It's me, Milo," I say.

"God Almighty," she says.

"No. Milo." I laugh, but it's hollow. Weak.

"Where are you?" she says.

"I'm safe."

"How are you?"

"Surviving."

She waits.

"Cynthia, I didn't do it."

"I know that," she says.

"Do you?"

"Yes, Milo. I do."

"Thanks," I say.

"Do you need anything? Can I help?"

"No. Everything is under control. I'll be in touch."

"You do that."

"See ya."

"Take care."

I hang up. I feel better for that little chat.

I'm passing a church. I go in.

It's deserted. That's how I like my churches. All to myself.

I light a candle for Nuala. I sit and smell the suggestion of incense in the air. I let the time pass. I let myself go quiet inside. I empty my head.

And I rest.

26

Time just flies when you're having fun.

I come back to the land of the living and it's three o'clock. Outside the church the weather is a drizzle. I walk.

I'm composed now.

Quiet.

And getting mad.

I'm in no hurry back to the safe house. I take the roundabout way back. Through Saint Anne's Park, past Mount Everest standing proud, my discarded cherry adding lustre to its aura, at least for me. I wonder if Cecilia Duffy, my cherry-picker, remembers. I wonder if she was sitting all cosy last night, watching telly with the hubby and kids and my face filled the screen. I wonder if she blurted, "Janey mack, that's Milo Devine. One day, many moons ago, he lost his cherry to me at the foot of

Mount Everest, the tallest tree in Saint Anne's Park."

At a supermarket I pick up some French bread, butter and the makings of a chili. There's an off-licence in the back. I score some more whiskey, some beer for the lads and a bottle of *Beaujolais* '96. That was a good year for *Beaujolais*. That and every year before and since. Guess what. I'm no connoisseur. I just know what I like.

I go for a pint. Back in the Beachcomber. There's a gang of men clustered at the bar. They're sitting on stools, nursing their pints. All except one guy, who is dressed in a blue suit and a white shirt with the collar open. He's standing, belly up to the bar, with a pint in one hand and a whiskey in the other.

"What the fuck. I'm on my holliers," he says as I come in.

I sit up on a stool at the other end of the bar. I order a Guinness. A television hums quietly on a shelf over the barman's head.

The man in the suit has the floor. He nods at me, acknowledging my presence. I nod back to be civil. Return to my pint. Cheers, but now leave me in peace, is the message. Blue Suit talks to the room.

"Where will we go for our holidays, says the

wife? Where else, says I, but the local, the Beachcomber Bar? Ah, could we not go somewhere nice, says she? All right so, says I, we'll go to the lounge."

That gets a laugh.

"You're a gas man."

"Bleedin' incorrigible."

"Did you hear the one about the saxophonist in the céilí band?" says Blue Suit.

"Ask me bollix."

"Would you ever fuck off."

"A saxophonist in a céilí band — that's absurd, that is."

"There was this sax player, you see," says Blue Suit, "and all his life he loved the blues. He lived for the blues. But his trouble was, he was a poxy saxophonist. He was thrown out of more blues bands than I've had hot dinners."

The room goes into a hush. This is a serious joke. A long one.

"Well, one day his car broke down when he was drivin' through the Burren in County Clare, which, as everybody knows, is smack dab in the heartland of traditional Irish music."

"Aye."

"True enough."

"We know that. Go on, for fuck's sake."

"The car can't be fixed till the morning, so yer

man has to stay the night in this one-horse town, with only a room over the pub for lodgings, which suits him just fine, 'cos he's a bit of a dipso as well as a poxy sax player."

"A bit like yourself, eh?"

"Now, now."

"I mean the bit about him being a poxy sax player."

"Yaboya."

"There's a session on in the pub that night and it's the first time yer man ever really listened to the traditional music. Well, he falls head over heels in love with it. And, drivin' back to Dublin, doesn't he decide, well, fuck it, he'll form his own traditional music band. Which he does. And they quickly become famous as the only traditional band with a saxophone player in it."

Over the barman's head, *The News* begins on the telly. I can barely hear the sound. It's something about the peace process. The pictures show Stan's father, Ned O'Brien, the Gaffer's right-hand man and the party chief whip, strolling around West Belfast with Gerry Adams. Time was — not so long ago either — when it would have been political suicide to be filmed on walkabout with Gerry Adams in the heartland of the Provos. But we live in interesting times, as the Chinese say.

Tell me about it.

"Next," says Blue Suit, "what do you know, but isn't yer man approached by an agent to do a tour of Irish America. Fuckin' ace, says he, I will. So, off he goes to the land of the free and the home of the brave."

Somebody hums *The Halls of Montezuma*.

The Gaffer appears on the screen. It's a still shot. I catch Nuala's name. The camera cuts to a copper giving his story. An update on the investigation.

"So the lads are performin' in this Irish pub in Boston. They're doin' *Dublin In The Rare Old Times* and it's time for yer man's sax solo. He steps up to centre stage and he's giving it the business, pouring his fuckin' heart and soul into the sax, and out of the corner of his eye he spots this fella sittin' at a table in the audience, bawlin' his bleedin' eyes out. He's fuckin' roarin' cryin'. And he's black as the ace of spades."

My face comes up on the television. I was half expecting it, but still I almost drop my pint. I have a surreptitious scope of the gathering at the bar. A couple of them are half looking at the telly while they're listening to the joke. Nobody looks at me, though.

Touch wood.

"So yer man is really affected by this," says Blue Suit. "He reckons he must be movin' the black fella to tears with his music. The man must be from Dublin, he reckons, and the song is making him homesick. But he figures the black fella looks like he's around the same age as himself and if he was from Dublin, well, him being black an' all, he thinks he would have known about him, Dublin being such a fiercely white city when he was growin' up – back in the days when people wanted to get out of Ireland, not get into it – when the Irish were the refugees. He's a bit mystified. But he's bleedin' gratified and he gives the sax an extra little belt for the black fella's sake and the black fella just breaks down and collapses onto the table in huge, gut-wrenchin' sobs. His shoulders are quiverin' in unmerciful grief."

A telephone number shows on the screen beneath the picture of me. I can almost read the newscaster's lips – "If you can help the police locate this man, call this number." At least nobody in the bar is taking down the number.

"Well, after the gig, yer man picks his moment and goes over to the black fella. He says, pardon me, but I couldn't help noticin' that you got very upset while I was playin' my sax solo. Are you from Dublin, he says? And the black fella looks up at him. He's still wipin' his eyes, the tears still leakin' out of them. No man, he says, I'm a saxophone player."

My face leaves the screen. The boys at the bar break their hearts laughing. I'm safe. For now.

I finish my pint. I get up to go. Blue Suit nods at me.

"That was a good one," I say.

Back to base.

27

I find a battered old pot under the sink, give it a good wash. I turn on the television. While it's warming up I open the *Beaujolais* and pour myself a glass. I put my chili makings on the table. When *The News* comes on I'm chopping up green peppers.

I'm the top story now. The talking heads are at the Gaffer's place. A close-up of the ritual wreath hanging on the front door. Inside, in the kitchen, Cooley grief-stricken at the table.

McGonagle hovering in the background.

He bears no malice, says Cooley. The man is clearly unbalanced. That's me he's talking about. Unbalanced. A shiver goes through me. Cooley engages the camera with his eyeballs. He urges me to give myself up and get help. His wife is under sedation, he says. The strain is too much for her. She's taken to her bed.

We'll never get over this, he says.

The talking heads are sombre, their voices uncharacteristically soft in the midst of all this grief.

Is Mister Cooley still in the running, the talking heads ask, for Taoiseach?

He can't say, he says, for a few days. Until after the funeral at least. The family comes first, y'know, he says.

The talking head does his wrap. The country is behind Mister Cooley, he says. It occurs to me that, with the sympathy vote, the chances are that Cooley may, if he decides to stay in the running, get the biggest majority the country has seen since the days of de Valera.

I chop the garlic.

Another talking head is listening to a spokesman for the investigation team. Harry Kilfedder. I remember him. I didn't know him well. He was a middle-of-the-roader. Kept his head down and his nose clean. Obviously it paid off in the long run. He got promoted. He's Inspector Kilfedder now on the telly.

There was no evidence of sexual abuse, he says.

They're seeking Mr Milo Devine to help them with their inquiries, he says. It definitely looks like a crime of passion. This is the man we're looking for, he says. He shows the talking heads a picture.

The camera zooms. Locks on me and Nuala in Dingle. My arm loose around her shoulder. The pair of us beaming, happy as pigs in shite.

I know what the punters watching this are thinking. They're thinking what they think nine times out of ten when your run-of-the-mill serial murderer is nicked and his face appears on the box.

He looks so normal. That's what they think.

Normal.

Just like me.

It's the picture I found in her house. The picture she faced in her sleep. The picture I left on the desk in my office.

I groan.

Exhibit A.

I chop the onions.

The coppers have their minds made up. I'm the prime suspect. There are no tangential investigations going on. I'm their man and they're coming after me and only me. If I slip up and they nab me, I'd have to get the trial moved to Timbuktu to sit before a jury of my peers — twelve good men or women — who aren't already convinced of my guilt.

My goose is cooked.

I put a punt in the meter and go to work on the chili.

My belly is full. I'm drinking tea and eating dessert

– a buttered bread crust with Tabasco sauce on it – when Davy arrives at a quarter to eight.

There are two guys with him. Big lads with the looks of old soldiers about them. There's prosperity written all over them. They wear made-to-measure suits that scream success. Silk ties that look like they belong in an art gallery. Soft leather shoes with shines on them you can see your face in.

"Say hello to Tom and Henry," says Davy.

We shake hands and say hello.

Henry has a plummy English accent. He talks like the upper-class twits always spoke in the old Ealing Brothers comedy films. There's nothing ostensibly twittish about him, though. He's built like a tank and looks like the Kinsale giant dressed in a fancy suit. His black eyes are deadly. They seem to cut through you like lasers.

His manner is perfectly pleasant, but to the discerning eye civilisation is just skin deep on him. I know his type. The man is danger on legs. In other ages, guys like him did their time and learned their trade in national service, then went off to join the Foreign Legion for a more adventurous kind of soldiering. Or they advertised in *Soldier of Fortune* magazine and hired out their guns and services to tinpot armies in Africa or South America. Nowadays, they go into the private security business.

Tom is the junior in this relationship. He defers

to Henry with his manner. Like his partner, he fills his clothes like a superhero, but, unlike Henry, he doesn't exude menace. He's less elemental. He talks in a sanitised vernacular like a middle-Ireland, middle-class Mr Spock. No colloquialisms. No bad habits. You'd never guess where he comes from. He'd walk into a job as a broadcaster on RTE.

I wouldn't want to get on the bad side of either of them.

And I wonder where on earth and under what circumstances Davy crossed paths with the likes of them.

Tom and Henry are in corporate security, says Davy, and they're also old friends whom he'd trust with his life. Which is reassuring for me to hear since he's trusting them with mine.

"Thanks for coming," I say.

I offer them drinks. Henry has a beer. Tom is happy as he is.

We sit and make small talk.

The bell rings.

It's the Burkes. They're dressed identically. Black leather jackets, white T-shirts, black jeans and black boots.

"Howya, Milo."

"Howya, Milo."

"Hello, lads."

Introductions all round.

The bell rings again.
Billy Cartwright.
Introductions again.

The beer is popped, the smokes are lit and everybody looks at the floor. Davy takes control. He tells my story. The real story, not the one on the telly. He lays out the lie of the land.

The first thing, he says, is trust.

"Milo has been set up," he says.

"Set up," says Jake.

"Set up," says John-Joe.

They're very close.

"Milo is all right in my book," says Jake.

"Sound as a bell," says John-Joe.

Billy Cartwright nods.

Tom and Henry look me up and down. Then they look at Davy.

"If you say so," says Henry.

"I say so," says Davy.

Henry nods.

Tom shrugs. Henry is the boss.

We have a quorum.

I look around at them. I'm charmed. There's an Irish word, *meitheal*, which means a group pulling together to get a job done. This is my *meitheal* and I'm finding out who my friends are.

"The score is this," says Davy. "This McGonagle

bugger is the key to the puzzle. And he's the only lead we have. So we haunt him. We're his shadow, the only difference being he can see his shadow and he can't see us. Right, lads?"

Right all round.

"We'll be a boil on his arse," says Jake.

"A pimple on his prick," says John-Joe.

"And he won't know a dickybird," says Jake.

"Nary a whisper," says John-Joe.

Billy Cartwright looks around at everybody. Bemusement is stark on his face. He's out of his depth. I catch his eye, smile, reassure him. I hope.

"If nobody has any objections," says Davy, "I'll ask Henry to take the floor."

Nobody has any objections. Henry nods at Davy.

"We'll need three cars for starters," he says.

"Consider it done," says Jake.

"No problemo," says John-Joe.

"Spotlessly clean," says Henry. "We don't want to get stopped for unpaid tickets or outstanding warrants."

"They'll be clean as a whistle," says Jake.

"Spring-cleaned with Flash," says John-Joe.

Billy looks at me again. I smile again. His frown says he wishes he'd gone fishing.

"Let me get this straight," he says. "We're going to be following the policeman who's driving

Archie Cooley, who is a big shot, being the Leader of the Opposition and maybe the next Taoiseach?"

Henry nods.

"Technically, we'll be following his driver," he says. "But, yes, that will mean that a lot of the time we'll be following Cooley."

"I don't mean to be finicky," he says, "but won't the Special Branch be minding him? And watching out for terrorists or the like doing exactly what we're planning on doing?"

"Given the political climate and the ongoing peace process," says Henry, "we don't think there's any reason for the police to be excessively vigilant. We expect them to be relaxed."

"But we'll be careful," says Tom. "For example, we'll be changing cars frequently."

"And Tom and I can supply more staff if necessary," says Henry.

"There's seven of us. That should be plenty to be going on with," says Jake.

"Loads," says John-Joe.

There are worry lines around Billy's eyes, but he nods his acquiescence. He's a game little fucker.

"There will be five of you on stakeout," says Davy. "You're the experts. Just do what you do. I'll be the co-ordinator. And Milo will stay here. I don't think he should be exposed to the extent that he's following peelers around."

"Agreed," says Henry.

"Roger," says Tom.

Everyone nods.

"You can have a lie-in, Milo," says John-Joe.

"I'll keep you up-to-date on developments," Davy says to me.

"Okay," I say.

"It's the weekend," says Billy.

"So?" says Davy.

"Well, won't everyone be taking the weekend off?" says Billy

"There's an election on," says Davy.

"So what?" says Billy.

"So," says Davy, "it's all systems go for the politicians and their staff. For them, there's no such thing as time off or weekends. They'll be working all the hours God sends them."

"Oh," says Billy.

"Don't you read the papers?" says John-Joe.

"Not much," says Billy.

"You must watch telly."

"Only the football."

"When was the last time you voted?" says Jake.

"I always vote," says Billy. "It's my duty as a citizen."

"Who do you vote for?" says John-Joe.

"Well, I'm in the Gaffer's constituency. I always vote for him."

"Me too," says John-Joe.
"And me," says Jake.

The lads work out a rota for tomorrow. Eight-hour shifts around the clock. There will be two cars on McGonagle, one of them sitting outside his house at five in the morning. Tom and Henry will take the first shift. Billy will be on stand-by in case a fresh face or car is warranted. After eight hours Jake and John-Joe will relieve Tom and Henry. Every shift change entails a new car.

Very slick. Billy is goggle-eyed at the boldness of the venture. At the audacity of the very idea of running surveillance on the omnipotent Archie Cooley.

Henry has a bag at his feet. He reaches down and takes out seven mobile phones. He hands them out. Davy's mobile will be headquarters, he says, and he gives out the number. Memorise it, he says. Like we're in *Mission Impossible*. The watchers will phone in a report every two hours. Henry spots the half-empty bottle of wine on the counter beside the sink. Milo's code name, he says, is Beaujolais.

Jake picks McGonagle's code name.

"Blue Nun," he says.

"It works for me," I say.

We relax.

I distribute the drink. Tom takes tap water. Billy

Cartwright sinks a double whiskey. Jack stands up and proposes a toast.

"To the vindication of Milo Devine," he says.

"Our pal," says John-Joe.

"I'll drink to that," I say.

"And to truth, justice and the Irish way," says Jack.

We stand and knock the booze back. Sit down again.

It's time for me to say a few words.

"I want to thank you all for sticking your necks out," I say.

They go *pshaw*.

"No, I mean it," I say. "And I want you to watch your backs out there. Our enemies have the power and they won't flinch at using it. They make the law. They wear the uniforms They carry the badges."

"Badges," snorts Jack.

"Badges," snorts John-Joe.

I see it coming. They speak in unison.

"We don't need no steenking badges," they say.

After a bit of a drink Davy hustles them all out the door, tells them to get a good night's sleep – he wants everybody on the ball for Operation Beaujolais tomorrow. He sits with me awhile.

"What's the story with Tom and Henry?" I say.

"How do you know a couple of up-market SAS types like that?"

Through his older brother, Ben, he says. Davy comes from a family of high achievers. Ben is a big shot in the corporate world. Fortune 500 material. He's the Chief Executive Officer of a New York-based multinational, Greenglobe Inc. Though he's based in the States, he keeps a house in Ireland and he's a regular feature in the society columns of the national newspapers.

Twenty years ago or so, when kidnapping corporate big shots was the flavour of the fund-raising month with the paramilitaries, the cops told Ben they'd heard there was a plot to hijack him. Greenglobe hired a corporate security firm to mind him. Along came Tom and Henry. They were Ben's guardian angels for a few years. They actually foiled one kidnap attempt. Ben got chummy with them and Davy met the lads at family gatherings. Relationships evolved from there.

Luckily for me.

Davy says he has a big day ahead of him tomorrow. He takes a hike. He hugs me at the door. Think positive and keep your chin up, he says. He'll give me a ring in the morning.

I make a pot of tea. I'll be going easy on the

booze for the next few days. I'll need all my faculties about me, I reckon. I watch the box. *Law & Order is* on. It seems appropriate, somehow.

I hit the sack early. As I begin to drift off to sleep, Nuala appears in my mind's eye. She's sitting, with her back against the chimney, on the roof of a thatched cottage on the side of a rocky hillside that looks like Connemara. She's wearing a fleece against the cold and her hair is dancing on the breeze. She has a gang of people with her. They're all sitting around on the roof, looking half asleep, as if they're not long out of bed. I recognise the Corrs and U2. And Paul McCartney with a guitar. It's a windy day. The Edge has to hold his cowboy hat on his head. I can hear the waves crashing against the shore beyond. They're all singing. I can just about hear the words of the song over the breeze. It's a sentimental old Irish ballad – *I'll Take You Home Again, Kathleen.*

> *I will take you back, Kathleen*
> *To where your heart will know no pain*
> *And when the fields are fresh and green,*
> *I'll take you to your home, Kathleen.*

Lovely.

28

All the next day I feel like I'm Nero fiddling as Rome burns. I twiddle my thumbs and scratch my arse while the boys in the cars launch Operation Beaujolais. I hate sitting on the sidelines. I like to be at the centre of the action. In the know. In control. Lying low is not my style. I'm antsy.

To kill some time, I ramble down to the local supermarket. I buy a dozen eggs, some sausage meat and breadcrumbs. Back in the flat I make Scotch eggs while I watch the telly.

The election rules the TV roost again. The Gaffer is conspicuous by his absence. He's still in mourning. But his spirit hovers relentlessly over all the doings of the day. Physically, his place is amply filled by his crony, Ted Greeley.

Ted is the party whip and second in command. He's the fixer. The tidier-upper. He's the man who throws salt on the ice of Cooley's slippery slope to political fortune. He gladhandles the press and tidies the mess. Thirty odd years ago, he hitched his wagon to Cooley's and, if he's known for one outstanding characteristic, it's his unblinking faith in the Gaffer. Through thick and thin, through fire and water, through good, bad, great and disastrous, he has stood unflinching in his loyalty by his master's side.

Now he's doing it again. Ted is hot on the campaign trail. He pontificates at a breakfast meeting of the Chamber of Commerce. He turns the first shovel of dirt at the site of a new shopping centre. He meets a delegation of peace activists from Derry. A little girl reads him an essay she wrote about her father being murdered by Loyalist death squads. He tut-tuts and hugs her. Makes all the right noises. Wipes a tear from his eye with his hankie. He visits a pub, a school and a day-care centre.

All before noon.

He dodges the question of whether the Gaffer is in the running or not, but assures the nation that there's no better man for the job and the party's loss would be the country's affliction. The times call for the sure hand of a true leader. And that man is Archie Cooley. It's our destiny. No less.

He says.

He eats lunch in the Mansion House with the

Lord Mayor of Dublin. Then he hops in a chopper and heads for the country.

I have a bowl of chili and some toasted garlic bread for my lunch. I overdo it on the garlic. I don't have to worry about the smell on my breath. It's not as if I'm doing a lot of socialising.

Davy calls on the mobile and fills me in on Operation Beaujolais. The boys are in hot pursuit and so far undetected. The Gaffer is having a relatively quiet day of it. He paid a visit to the Garda barracks in Harcourt Street, headquarters of Nuala's murder investigation. He dropped in at the party offices for an hour. Had an early lunch with sundry political honchos at Buswell's Hotel and headed for home.

He gave McGonagle the rest of the day off.

Jake and John-Joe took over the watch at one o'clock and they're hot on the bastard's trail. They'll stick to McGonagle like limpets, says Davy.

I go for a walk. Pick up *The Irish Times*. I try to read. Can't concentrate. I rack my brains. I dredge the undergrowth of my subconscious for a clue. For an insight. For a flash of inspiration into the circumstances of my predicament. The whys and the wherefores. The burning question – what the hell is going on?

I come up empty. Mystified. My ignorance is far from bliss.

I watch *The Simpsons* on the box. That Homer is a howl.

Fuck this for a game of cowboys.

Davy drops by around seven. Henry arrives close behind him. He's carrying an envelope. Eight and a half by eleven. I make a pot of tea. We sit. Henry empties the envelope. There are two pages of computer printouts and some photos. The printouts consist of a sequential list of the pitstops McGonagle made throughout the day and the times he made them. If he stopped the car at a red light, the time and the length of the stop are entered on the list.

"He did nothing untoward all morning," says Henry. "It was all Archie Cooley's agenda – political stuff and business pertaining to the funeral."

Nuala's funeral. It's scheduled for Monday, says Henry. The coffin is being taken to the church as we speak. I watched some of it on the telly earlier. It was too painful. I had to turn it off.

"The day got interesting," Henry says, "when your lads took over and Cooley gave McGonagle time off. First he went to Garda HQ. He was in there for about an hour. Then he drove to a brothel on Parnell Square, where he spent the rest of the afternoon."

"A knocking shop?" I say.

"That's a great job he has," says Davy.

"The sign over the door says the place is a health spa and lists massage, acupuncture and aromatherapy as a few of the services rendered, but every Dubliner and his dog knows that the most commonly administered treatment is a blow-job or a hand-shandy."

"Patricia's Place," I say.

"Yes," says Henry.

Davy looks at me with his eyebrows raised.

"Have you been keeping secrets from me?" he says.

"It's a popular after-hours spot for the lads in Special Branch," I say. "It has been for years. Ever since I can remember. And not just for the sex. There's a bar there too. It's a place for the lads to go after the pubs close and unwind with other cops. Aunty Patricia, the Copper's Comfort, they call the lady of the house."

"You're full of surprises," says Davy.

"McGonagle left the place with this man," says Henry. He hands us each a photograph.

"Nice photo," I say.

"Digital camera," he says.

"You should see their office," says Davy. "It's like Microsoft headquarters."

"Really?" I say.

I'm humbled. I'm ruefully thinking of my

walkie-talkies and my Polaroid Instamatic. I thought I was going high-tech when Angie showed me how to access the internet on the computer.

"This man and McGonagle went for drinks together in Mooney's Long Bar," says Henry. "While John-Joe shadowed them in the bar, Jake brought the camera over to the office. I hooked it up to the computer and out popped the picture."

I'm jealous.

"Very slick," I say.

Henry nods.

"In the bar," he says, "the subjects seated themselves away from the din and held a huddled conversation. John-Joe couldn't discern what they were talking about, but he got close enough to hear that the new bloke was a fellow countryman of mine."

I look at Henry, raise my eyebrows.

"He had an English accent," he says.

Bells go off in my head.

My mind leaps frantically to half-arsed speculation. Espionage. Smoke and mirrors. Betrayal. Deception. Skullduggery. MI5 or MI6 shenanigans. McGonagle working for the Brits? Passing over intelligence? The access he must have to classified information! The mind boggles. Is perfidious Albion at the root of my misfortune? Is McGonagle enriching himself? Betraying the nation for the infamous forty pieces of Saxon silver? Could Nuala have discovered this? Is this why she was murdered?

"A spy?" I say.

Davy puts the kibosh on my fantasies.

"I know this man," he says.

"Huh?" I say. Erudite as ever.

"I've met this man at parties," he says. "He's no undercover agent. Not nowadays, anyway. Sure, he's a Brit. And maybe he is a secret agent, but he's on the up and up. He's out of the closet, so to speak. His name is Watson. Miles Watson."

"What does he do?" I say.

"His field of expertise is counter-terrorism. His job? He's a liaison officer at the British Embassy. It's his business to establish and maintain relations with the Gardaí. Twenty years ago spy would have been the right word to describe him. He'd have been working under cover. But the times have changed. Nowadays, at least at Watson's level, the British and Irish governments and police forces have excellent working relationships. The Brits don't need spies to get access to the contents of most Garda files on the paramilitaries. They only have to ask."

"So, what's he doing cosying up to McGonagle?"

He shrugs.

"Maybe they're comparing notes on what a great ride they both just had. Or they could be just having a pint and a chinwag. That's no longer regarded as fraternising with the enemy, you know. These days the Brits are our partners. Believe you me, if McGonagle was working under the table for one of their intelligence agencies, he wouldn't be dealing with this man. And they certainly wouldn't be making contact in the likes of Patricia's Place or the Long Bar on a busy Saturday afternoon."

"I guess not," I say.

"Pity about that. I rather hoped we had something," says Henry.

"Back to the drawing-board," says Davy.

The dejection shows on my face when I walk them to the door.

"Cheer up, Milo," says Davy. "It's early days. We'll get the bastard yet."

I hit the sack restless. Partly, it's because of the do-nothing day I had, which didn't exactly prepare me to sleep the sleep of the just or to drift with exhaustion into blissful oblivion. I'm not exactly worn out from over-use.

But, beyond all that, there's a niggling feeling in the back of my mind that I'm overlooking something. That a vital snippet of information has traversed my consciousness at some point during the day and I've let it slip unidentified through the nether regions of my awareness.

A tenet of working in the intelligence/security

business is cover all your angles. Don't take shortcuts. Have eyes in the back of your head. Forget nothing. Dismiss nothing. Every shred of information, however unimportant ostensibly, is relevant. It all goes into the files. Into the mix.

I close my eyes and set my thoughts free. I let my mind go drifting. If all the layers of consciousness relax and float and mingle, maybe my errant thought, my will o' the wisp of a suspicion of a notion, will re-emerge. In slow mental motion, I drift back over the day. The boredom. The anxiety. The frustration. The anger.

Nero fiddles. Rome burns. Milo watches telly. Ted Greeley wipes the grease off a pole. *Lunch*. I can taste the garlic. Milo stinks. *The Irish Times*. Can't concentrate. *The Simpsons*. Homer is a howl. Milo grins. *Operation Beaujolais*. Milo grins. Nuala's body goes to the church. Milo weeps. Upper-class agents with English accents. Yuppie high-tech ex-SAS men selling security. Milo resents. Knocking shops. Branch men in brothels. *Cops in coitus*. Shooting the breeze. Milo is jealous. The Copper's Comfort. Talking the talk. *Aunty Patricia*. Milo reaches. *Patricia's Place. Patricia. Patricia's Place. Patricia.* Milo stretches. *Patricia's Place. Patricia.* Milo strains.

Patricia's Place. Patricia.

Milo touches.

The light bulb pops. It bursts. Milo roars. *Bang!*

Splat! Kerpow! Revelation surges through the layers of my consciousness like a rocket blasting through the ozone layer.

Slabash!

This must be what it's like to be born again. To find Jesus.

Jesus.

Fucking Patricia's Place. Patricia. *Fucking Patricia*. Fucking Aunty Patricia. Listening. Her girls. *Listening*. While the coppers shoot the breeze. While they let it all hang out. They talk the talk.

The girls listen.

Ah, yes.

I remember it well.

When I worked in Special Branch, there was nothing Patricia didn't know. She and her girls were privy to the works. All the loose talk, the unleashed frustration, the station-house gossip, the word on the street. There was no such thing as security, as guarded tongues, as *loose lips sink ships* in Patricia's Place. That was where the guys wound down. Where they felt safe and hung loose. Tongues wagged incessantly. Patricia was trusted implicitly. And as for her girls — well, they were part of the furniture.

But they weren't deaf. Though you'd never know it from the way the coppers blabbed. The girls listened. They couldn't help it.

If there's anything out there, if there's a morsel of gossip floating around that can shed a shred of light on my plight, the chances are I'll find it in Patricia's Place. Aunty Patricia, the Copper's Comfort, will know the score.

She and I used to be friends.

Way back when.

There's good stuff up my nose. It's the sweet smell of success.

I say a little prayer of thanks to Jesus. I roll over, move my hand under the pillow. I rest it in Nuala's panties.

I go to sleep.

29

I'm up at the crack of dawn. The chapel bells are ringing. It's Sunday morning. I'm hyped up, raring to go, but it's a mite early to be paying a visit to a knocking shop on a Sunday morning.

They'll all be out at church. *Ha ha.*

I make a pot of tea. Grill a few slices of toast. I listen to the radio. They're singing a Mass in the Pro-Cathedral. It seems to suit the morning. The operatic solemnity fills the flat, creating an atmosphere of pendulant melodrama that's peculiarly appropriate for the sense of anticipation expanding in my breast. Some deep breathing relaxes me.

Sometimes, when you get a good hunch, the process verges on the mystical. It's like ESP. You can feel the certainty, the rightness, the *truth* of it in the marrow of your bones. Your skin tingles a tad with extra-curricular electricity. You get the scent of the hunt in your nose. The hunch envelopes you. You become more than yourself. The force of the hunch turns you and points you in a singular direction. And you have to go with the flow. It would be sacrilege – just *wrong* – to fight it.

That's the way I am this morning.

And it sure feels good. It feels promising.

Optimistic.

Hopeful.

For a change.

I take a shower and dress for the day. I put on a pair of new jockeys that Davy brought me. New undies are a tonic. I wear my jeans, a new T-shirt and a new pair of socks. My Doc Martens. I carry my army jacket over my arm. I don't forget my specs.

I hit the streets.

It's almost eleven, still early in prostitute time. So, to kill an hour or so, I shun public transport and walk.

The good weather has the populace out early. They ramble in their Sunday finery to services at the Catholic church in Killester or the Protestant one just down the road in Raheny. I'm going against the tide, heading for the city. Occasionally, young men in ones and twos, bedraggled, silent and seedy, pass me with their heads down, making their weary way home, their bodies and minds near buckling under the after-effects of their Saturday night on the town.

I set a leisurely pace for myself. I stroll. The sun feels good on my face. I take strength from it. With the ringing of the church bells fading in the distance, I set my sights on the city and, in contrast to the bells and the good folks abroad with the holy spirit, the incongruous prospect of spending the afternoon of the Sabbath in a whorehouse.

The inner city is dead as a doornail. Like any big town, Dublin is a place of many faces. Up in the north inner city you can tour the remains of its conspiratorial side. During the seventies and the early eighties, Parnell Square and its environs housed a hotbed of political fervour. It was the geographical hub around which revolutionary fervour in the twenty-six counties revolved.

Dilapidated, neglected by the city fathers, and located close to a couple of Dublin slums, the cost of property was cheaper here than in other more illustrious parts of the city. The rents were cheap. The place was a magnet for subversive groups of varying degrees of radicalism along the spectrum of militant Irish nationalism.

The common assumption was that even the public phones were tapped.

The Provos still have their offices here. The Irish Republican Socialist Party owned a house nearby.

A plethora of conspiratorial organisations born and bred out of the country's troubles hung their shingles here.

Communists. Trotskyites. Neo-Trotskyites. Marxists. Marxist-Leninists. True-Blue Marxist-Leninists. Stalinists. Anarchists. Socialist Republicans. Republican Socialists. Fenians, Whiteboys, Pikemen and Minutemen. Official IRA. Provisional IRA. Old IRA and New IRA. Just Plain Gunmen. They all came here to set up shop. They flocked here in droves to ferment mayhem and plot conspiracy. More *ists* and *isms* than you could shake a stick at and each of them, at one time or another, occupied a dilapidated office in one or other of the crumbling Victorian edifices that dominated this particular section of Dublin.

Most of the offices have closed since the Berlin Wall came down. Some of the groups became respectable along the way and entered constitutional politics. Others simply vanished. In the 90's, the property boom put an end to the cheap rents and the north inner city has gradually been moving upscale. But, on a clear day, if you close your eyes and sniff the ambience, the unmistakable whiff of cordite still lingers.

If these walls could talk they'd keep us intrigued for aeons.

Amidst all the skulduggery and subversion, all

the clannishness and conspiracy, life goes on. Revolutions come and go, philosophies sink and philosophies swim, upheavals heave and ho, the times, they change, the earth moves and the oldest profession ever just carries on regardless.

Patricia's Place is located in the basement and first floor of a four-storey building a few doors down from the place that used to house the Dublin headquarters of People's Democracy before they voted themselves out of existence and joined Sinn Féin en masse. The third floor is the premises of a property developer and on the fourth there's a women's advice centre.

The vagaries of life make for strange bedfellows.

The door into the brothel is down a few steps to what used to be the tradesmen's entrance to a rich man's mansion. I ring the bell. Soft shoes shuffle on the other side of the door. They stop. Silence. I'm aware of the fact that someone is probably in the process of looking me over through the peephole. I stand there, trying to appear nonchalant.

Whoever eyeballs me apparently decides that I'm harmless. The door opens. Patricia stands there. Large as life. Just as I remember. She's a hefty, big-boned woman with curly red hair and freckles. She's dog-rough. She did some time back in her prime, before she found her feet with this place.

Grievous bodily harm, I believe. She knows how to look after herself. She's no stereotypical whore with a heart of gold. She knows life is a bitch. Her horizons are firmly fixed on the profit margin. But she's a straight dealer. On the level. She keeps an eye out for her regulars and she'd cut your heart out and eat it if you tried to hurt one of her girls.

She's wearing a beige kimono and black slippers and she smokes a cigarette.

"Yes?" she says.

She coughs.

"Those things will kill you," I say.

She grunts. She's not amused.

"You're up early for a Sunday," she says.

"The early bird catches the worm."

"A philosopher, huh?"

"More a fisherman."

She looks me over. Sizes me up. Her eyes glide over my left hand, taking in the fact that I don't wear a wedding band. That I'm not some Desperate Dan after telling his wife he's off out to Mass and Communion and scooting up to the whorehouse for a quickie.

"We're closed," she says. "It's Sunday morning, for God's sake."

"I thought this place never closed."

"It's not a bloody bus station, Mister."

"I'm not looking for a bus."

"We don't do Mass either."

"Still the hussy with the lip. You haven't changed a bit, Pat."

This is the banter Patricia and I constantly inflicted on each other in the old days. I slide back into it real easy. The hussy with the lip was the moniker I teased her with. The turn of the phrase has struck a chord in her memory. She stiffens. She glares hard into my eyes.

"Do I know you?"

I look behind her into the hall. There's a door ajar yonder, with a haze of cigarette smoke wafting through the doorway. I hear the sound of muffled conversation. I take a step towards the doorway. She steps back. She's wary. It's a dodgy, treacherous racket she's in. I could be a headcase on the rampage for all she knows. She can't let her guard down. Ever. She points a warning finger at my chest.

"Try any funny business here and you're dead meat, Mister. I swear."

"It's me, Patricia. Milo Devine."

She sucks on her cigarette and squints at me through the smoke.

"What?" she says.

"It's Milo. Milo Devine."

She looks me up and down again.

"No, you're not."

I stand solid.

"I am."

Her eyes scrutinise my face, searching for familiar features. Gradually, recognition dawns on her. She darts a look back over her shoulder.

"Mother of God," she whispers. "There's three branch men and two detectives in the back, just off the night shift. And not a one of them, as far as I know, is any great fan of yours, Milo. What the fuck are you doing here?"

"I need a word."

She glances back over her shoulder again. All clear. So far.

"Lamb of Jesus. You'll get me arrested. Get in out of that."

"Thanks, Pat."

She hustles me in off the doorstep, softly closes the door and ushers me into the room to the right of the entrance. The Blue Room, says a sign in the shape of a heart on the door. Talk about tacky! The walls are powder blue and the furniture is painted in varying shades of aquamarine. There's massage table, a dressing-table with a rake of creams and potions on it. A chair, a closet and a four-poster bed with navy blue satin sheets and pillows. A mirror on the ceiling.

"You've had the decorators in since my last visit," I say.

"The place needed a bit of class."

"Who's your interior designer? Dame Edna?"

"Liberace's ghost."

"It's a bit cheesy, even for a whorehouse, isn't it, Patricia?"

"You should see the Red Room."

"I don't think my eyeballs could stand the shock."

She laughs.

"How are you keeping, Pat?" I say.

"Surviving. But – no offence Milo – let's bypass the chitchat. You tell me, please, what madness possessed you to come visiting here when all the coppers in Christendom are after your arse and five of them are sitting in the next room."

"I need a little chat, Pat."

"You'll get the both of us locked up, you thick prick."

I sit on the chair.

"I really need your help," I say.

She studies me.

"You look wrecked, Milo."

"I've had a bad week."

"You resemble a man at the end of his tether."

I grin crookedly.

"It's nothing a life sentence in Mountjoy Jail won't fix."

"I heard about your trouble. What am I saying?

The whole world and his uncle have heard about it."

She moves behind me, puts her hands on my neck and gently, but firmly, kneads the muscles.

"God, you're tense."

"The stock market has been erratic. I'm worried about my investments."

She chuckles.

"Always the kidder, Milo. Well, I'm glad you haven't lost your sense of humour. I always liked that about you. Now, what can I do for you?"

"I didn't kill Nuala Cooley, Pat."

"I never figured you for a killer. Certainly not a murderer of women."

"I think Joe McGonagle did it."

Her stands stop. Momentarily. And start again.

"Do I need to hear this?" she says.

"I think so. You might be able to help me."

She sighs her resignation.

I tell her my story. I've just finished the bit where I escape from McGonagle when a man with a thick Kerry accent calls to Pat from the other room.

"I'd better go," she says.

"All right."

"I'll be back in a few minutes."

She stops at the door. Looks at me reassuringly.

"Don't worry," she says. "I'll say nothing."

"I know."

She goes.

Five minutes pass. Then there's a soft knock on wood and the door opens. A woman comes in and closed the door behind her. She's a looker. Jet-black hair cut short, parted on the side and swept flat over her head like a man's. Milky white skin. Prominent cheekbones. Full, shiny red lips and multi-fathomed hazel eyes. She's wearing a powder blue kimono that goes with the room. Black silk slippers.

"I'm Pam," she says.

"Hello, Pam."

"Patricia sent me."

"For what?"

"She said you needed a massage."

"That's not really necessary."

"I always do what the boss tells me."

"That sound like a sensible policy."

She takes me by the hand and leads me over to the massage table. She unbuttons my jacket and shirt and takes them off . She tells me to take off my pants. I do as I'm told. She lies me down on my belly. I rest my chin on my arms. I hear her splashing lotion on her hands. She starts at the side of my head, right behind my eyeballs. In five seconds flat I'm limp. My body feels like melting snow. Slowly, gorgeously, she works her way down to the soles of my feet. She kneads and rubs and pokes at the stress and strain and grief of the past few miserable days. Her fingers push and suck and force the accumulated tension out through the pores of my skin

"Aaah," I say.

After fifteen minutes I'm so languorous I can't even manage a moan or a groan.

She turns me over on my back and does the front. She does the works again. From the roots of my hair down to the balls of my feet. And then my toes, one by one. I don't know if it's a phenomenon associated with the therapy or if I just feel so good I'm a tad hysterical, but as she works through my toes a voice in my head recites a nursery rhyme from my childhood – *this little piggy went to market, this little piggy stayed at home* . . .

She eases down my undies, takes my balls in the palm of her hand, rubs them together and lightly strokes the shaft of my prick. My flute goes *boing* and stands at attention. Her fingers feel like silk. I'm drowning in blissful relief. She lazily, skilfully tosses me off. I die and go to Heaven. I'm in deep, deep tranquillity, twenty thousand leagues under the glee, and when I ejaculate it's like the one last, singular scrap of garbage, of hypertension, of badness, taking its leave of my happily surrendered body.

I feel like a new man.

"Lordy, lordy," I say.

"Was that all right?" she says.

"Play it again, Pam," I say.

She chuckles. "Really?" she says.

"No. Thanks. I feel great. Honest."

She wipes my prick clean with a Handy Andy.

"Can I do anything else for you?" she says.

"Marry me."

"Are you rich?"

"With your gifted hands, you'd never have to worry about money."

"You wouldn't live off immoral earnings, would you?"

"There was nothing immoral about what you just did for me, Pam. That was truly a religious experience."

"You were in a bad way. Your body was rigid with stress."

"Not any more, thanks to you. I feel like I've turned into rubber."

"I'll leave you in peace, so, and let you relax."

"Thanks."

"You're welcome."

She departs. I lie there, floating on my newfound sea of serenity.

I doze.

It seems like a lifetime later when Patricia comes back, but my watch says it's only twenty minutes.

"How's the man?" she says.

"Fresh as a daisy," I say.

I get up and put on my clothes.

"You look much better," she says.

"That rubdown was a tonic."

"You needed it. You looked like shit."

"How much do I owe you?"

"It's on the house. For old times' sake."

"Thanks. You're a lifesaver."

"It's Sunday. I'm feeling charitable."

She opens the door and ushers me out.

"The polis are all gone to their homes or to Mass. You'd better make tracks before more of them turn up."

"I was hoping you and I could have a bit of a chat."

"There's no need for that."

She has her hand on the lock of the front door. She pauses. I look her in the eye. Her eyeballs widen infinitesimally. She whispers.

"The Cooley girl and the man who was killed . . ." she says.

"Yeah?"

"The papers say they were an item."

"Yeah."

"What if they weren't?"

"What do you mean?"

"What if they weren't an item?"

"I don't follow you."

"The man — what was his name?"

"Walton."

"Yeah. What did Walton do?"

"He got killed."

"But what did he do? Think, Milo. What did he work at?"

"He was a doctor."

"What kind of a doctor."

"A psychiatrist."

"Right."

I'm perplexed.

"So what?"

"So, how did they meet?"

"I'm fucked if I know."

She groans. She's exasperated.

"So what would the Cooley girl be doing with him if they weren't star-crossed lovers? If they weren't involved personally?"

I think hard. Finally, I get it.

"She'd be his patient? He'd be treating her?"

Patricia nods. She opens the door.

"Away with you, Milo," she says.

I'm flabbergasted.

"Are you sure?" I say.

She nods.

"The whisper doing the rounds is that the Cooley girl had a mental problem. I don't know what it was. Nobody seems to know. She was seeing the doctor on a professional basis."

"That puts a whole new complexion on things."

Patricia tilts her head at the street.

"Pardon me if I don't gossip on the doorstep," she says.

"Okay."

"So long, Milo."

"Thanks, Pat. For everything," I say, as I step out of the bawdy house.

"Good luck," she says.

The door closes.

I need a think. And a drink would be nice. And some grub. The rubdown has given me an appetite. I make my way down O'Connell Street, over the bridge and up Fleet Street to the Palace Bar. I order a pint and a ploughman's lunch. I pay for them and go sit in a corner, away from the hubbub at the bar.

That's quite the scoop Pat gave me. If it's on the up and up. Which it probably is. I have no good reason to think it wouldn't be. No reason to suspect that Pat would pull a fast one on me. She's an old pal. I more or less trust her. And I trust her judgement. She's smart. She has clarity of vision. If she says Nuala was seeing the Walton fella professionally, well, that is in all likelihood the way it was.

I'm a dope. An idiot. A *schmuck*. I missed the

ball completely on this one. The signs were all there. The man was a shrink after all. And there was Cynthia's American friend Lorena's analysis of catharsis. And the change in Nuala's psychology. The signs were there, but I missed them because I was too close to the subject. Too familiar. I couldn't see the forest for the trees.

I jumped to the conclusion that Nuala and Walton were tight romantically. So did Cynthia and DV MacEntee. Why wouldn't we? It would never occur to any of us who knew her that Nuala Cooley would be undergoing treatment by a psychiatrist.

She was always the chirpy one. Always quick with a smile. Quick to crack a joke. The picture of mental health. Why would Nuala need to see a shrink?

Who knows?

The shrink knows.

Knew.

Why? What was going on in Nuala's life?

Stop the lights. I haven't a clue. But the question gives me a sense of direction. It's a fresh angle. A new lead. Hope.

There's just the one question to be answered now.

The big one.

Why was Nuala seeing the shrink?

30

I demolish my pint and the ploughman's lunch. Then I hop on a bus and go back to the flat. I put my feet up and ponder.

I'm still pondering and none the wiser when Davy phones in around eight. He's been out for the day with his family. A drive to Newgrange to see the ancient burial mound. He's just off the phone from Henry, who reports that McGonagle has also been doing the family thing. He attended eleven o'clock Mass with his wife and teenage daughter. Painted the front of his house in the afternoon. White. Pottered about in the garden. Took his wife down to the local lounge for a few drinks in the evening. Then home sweet home. And lights out.

Life in the suburbs.

Normality.

"What did you do with your day?" says Davy.

"I spent the afternoon in a brothel."

"Let me guess. Patricia's Place?"

"Yep."

"Are you any the better for it?"

"I shed a few wrinkles and crinkles."

He chuckles.

"Good for you. And did you find out anything?"

I tell him. He whistles.

"That's interesting," he says.

"This could be the key to the case, my friend."

"Why? Do you think she was killed because she knew a secret? A secret McGonagle was afraid she'd share with her shrink?"

"And she may have already spilled the beans to Walton. That would explain why McGonagle killed him too."

"Presuming, of course, that McGonagle is the killer."

"Of course."

"What on earth could Nuala know about him that would be so volatile as to drive him to murder?"

"I haven't a clue. But I plan to find out."

"I can tell by the sound of your voice you have something in mind."

"I need to get a look at Walton's file on Nuala."

"That makes sense."

"I plan on paying a visit to his office tomorrow."

"Is that wise?"

"It's the hand we've been dealt."

He thinks.

"I suppose you're right," he says.

"I'll need some ID for cover."

"That's Henry's department. I'll call him. What do you want to be?"

"A copper."

He pretends to be shocked.

"Don't tell me you'd actually impersonate a police officer?"

"Just this once."

"Righto. I'll see to the ID."

"Great."

"You'll need a new name. What will we call you?"

James Larkin springs to mind. Defender of the working class. Tilter at windmills. "Jim Larkin," I say.

"I'll get back to you in the morning," says Davy.

"Grand."

He pauses.

"Are you all right, Milo? I'll come over if you like and we'll go for a pint."

"No. I'm fine. Honest. You stay with your family."

"You sound much better this evening."

"I had a good day today."

"The first in a long time, eh?"

"You've been reading my tea-leaves."

"See you tomorrow."
"Good night."

It's still early. I take a walk. I head down to the sea front again, to the Bull Wall and out onto the single-lane boardwalk that juts out into the Irish Sea. The tide is in and the sea is choppy and playful. The incoming breeze is cool and carries a whisper of the encroaching winter.

At the end of the boardwalk there's a statue of *Stella Maris*, the Mother of God and spiritual minder of mariners, in luminous virgin white, a beacon of light in the darkness. She majestically presides over the dark expanse of water that stretches from here across to Liverpool. High up over the waves, she stands on her pedestal, arms extended in a ready embrace, a long-standing fountain of comfort and assurance to homecoming or departing sailors.

The statue stirs a memory of a hymn I used to sing in the school choir. I close my eyes and try to recall the chorus in my head.

Lah di dah dah,
Star of the Sea,
Pray for the Wanderer,
Pray for Me.

The incoming wind bears the salt of the sea. It

tastes clean and fresh in my mouth. All of a sudden I go warm all over. The heat starts on the inside and emanates out, to the tips of my fingers even. *Stella Maris* holds me in a hug. She whispers at me. There's a new day dawning, she says, and with it comes Hope.

With a capital H.

The voice of *Stella Maris* talks to me through the sound of the sea.

Ere you shall fade, ere you shall die,
My Dark Rosaleen!
My own Rosaleen!
The Judgement Hour must first be nigh,
Ere you can fade, ere you can die,
My Dark Rosaleen!

"It's a great country, this, *Stella*," I say. "Everyone's a poet."

She grins. Winks.

"There's a new day dawning, Milo."

She says.

I walk softly back to the safe house.

I go to bed.

I sleep like a baby.

31

I'm awake at eight. I'm full of vim and vigour, almost heady with my sense of purpose. I've got important stuff to do today. Destiny is dancing on the wind. I feel it in my bones.

Breakfast is scrambled eggs and Tabasco on buttered toast. I need to do some grocery shopping. This larder lacks imagination. What I'd really like for my breakfast this morning is smoked salmon on crusty brown bread. And my good name back.

I turn on the telly. The Gaffer, as usual, hogs the morning news. They're burying Nuala today. The TV crews are all set up inside and outside the church. It's early yet, but already the crowds are beginning to converge. Hundreds of them. The big shots are out in force, looking sanctimonious and stricken. Hogging the limelight. Nuala would puke.

I should be there. I should be carrying the coffin.

'Nuff said of that, for now.

Cooley's opponent, the current Taoiseach, must be doing his nut. Because of Nuala's death, the Gaffer is getting all the media attention. His handlers have announced that he'll be holding a press conference at his home tomorrow afternoon. The speculation is that he's going to announce he's still in the race.

The fucker is a shoo-in.

I'm item number two on the journalistic agenda. The police are investigating a number of reports of sightings, a uniform tells a reporter. Now I'm a UFO. We're confident in our ultimate success, the uniform says. The country is sealed up tight, he says. It's one of the biggest manhunts in the history of policing in Ireland, he says. He asks the public to please remain vigilant, to keep their eyes peeled. But on no account are they to attempt to detain me themselves. Leave that to the proper, trained authorities, he says.

I should be perceived as being armed and extremely dangerous, he says.

Davy calls to say he's talked to Henry and arranged false ID for me.

Five minutes later the bell rings and a motorbike courier is standing at the front door with a package for James Larkin. I sign for it, take it inside and open it. I pull out a laminated identity card, authorising Mr James Larkin to act as a member of the Garda Síochána. It's a ringer for the real thing. There's a picture of me in it. It looks like the one the cops have given to the media. My head cut out of the snap of Nuala and me in Dingle. Henry has doctored the image on his computer so that it resembles the current me.

Isn't technology grand.

Sound man, Henry.

I take a bus into the city. I don't linger. I set a brisk pace for myself. Walton does his business on the ground floor of a modern five-storey office complex on Dame Street. The building is mostly glass. It's called the *Brosna* Health Centre and the sign on the door lists a pharmacy and a plethora of medical practitioners. There's an orthopaedic surgeon, a paediatric surgeon, a plastic surgeon, a dental surgeon, a neurologist, a cardiologist, an immunologist, an acupuncturist, an obstetrician, a dietician and an optician.

An aromatherapist.

And a shrink.

Inside, the bits that aren't made of glass are decorated vividly, almost gaily, in airy bright greens, reds and yellows. To cheer up the manic depressives? There are rubber plants all over the place.

A receptionist rules the roost from her desk in the foyer. She's a twentyish, good-looking woman with hazel saucers for eyes, long black hair and a friendly smile, which she beams at me. There's a name tag on the lapel of her starched white coat. *Sandra*, it says.

"Can I help you?" she says.

I recognise the sing-song voice I spoke to on the phone in what seems like an eternity ago. In fact, it's been only a week.

I flash my ID and her face goes serious.

"Are you a guard?"

"Yes."

"Is this about Doctor Walton?"

"Yes."

"I thought you lads were finished with us."

"There's a few things we have to double-check."

She nods.

"Are you any closer to catching your man, Devine?"

"We'll catch him. Don't you worry."

"He should get his neck stretched."

I should keep my mouth shut, but I can't resist it.

"You know, technically he's innocent until a jury finds him guilty."

Her eyebrows arch.

"That's not what your lot were saying last week.

They had him hung, drawn and quartered. We have him dead to rights, I believe their words were."

I change the subject.

"How long have you worked here, Sandra?"

"About six years. Since I left school."

"You thought highly of Doctor Walton, I gather?"

Her face softens.

"He was the best. I was very fond of him. Everyone here was. And his patients thought the world of him."

I nod sympathetically.

"He was a fine man," she says.

"How did he first come into contact with Nuala Cooley?"

"She phoned and made an appointment. About six months ago, it was. If my memory serves me right, her general practitioner recommended Doctor Walton. The details will be in her file."

"Then she was a patient? They weren't involved romantically?"

She shakes her head.

"I know what the police and the papers are saying. But they're wrong. Doctor Walton was a very conscientious person. He wouldn't mess about with a patient. That's unethical. He wasn't that kind of man."

"Ms Cooley was an attractive woman."

She nods.

"And he was a handsome man," she says. "They would have made a lovely couple. And they were getting very close. But, even if Doctor Walton was falling for her, he wouldn't have done anything about it. Certainly not before he was finished treating her."

"Did you tell this to the Gardaí who were here last week?"

"Yes. But they didn't pay any attention. They were laughing up their sleeves."

"What do you mean when you say Doctor Walton and Ms Cooley were getting very close?"

"Well, it's common enough. When a doctor and his patient go deep into therapy, they form a special bond, a closeness. It's only natural. And they were seeing a lot of each other. In the last few weeks she was taking two sessions a week. Three some weeks. My sense was that her therapy was working, that they were making some kind of breakthrough."

"This would add an intensity to the relationship?"

"Oh, yes. Very much so."

"So, to the outer world, they could look like two people infatuated with each other?"

"I suppose so."

"Maybe that's why her friends thought she was romantically involved – if she hadn't told them she was seeing a psychiatrist?"

"Could be."

She's no dimwit and she begins to grasp the implications.

"So," she says, "if this guy Devine killed them because he was jealous of them being lovers and they weren't really lovers at all . . . Jesus . . . the waste!"

I nod.

"I need to take a look around his office." I say.

"Again?"

"I want to check the doctor's file on Nuala — Ms Cooley."

She gives me a funny look. She reaches behind her, where there's a board on the wall full of hooks with keys hanging on them. She finds the appropriate room number, takes two keys off the hook and hands them to me. She nods her head backwards.

"Room number eight on the main floor just past the pharmacy," she says. "The big key fits the door. The little one the filing cabinet."

"Thanks," I say and I walk away. I feel her eyes on my back. I can almost hear her thinking. Wondering.

You can tell by the furniture and accoutrements in his consulting room that Doc Walton was the kind of guy who went to trouble to put his patients at their ease. And he had a sense of humour. The walls are full of framed cartoons slagging shrinks. A poster with a picture on it of Freud in a straightjacket. Another that says insanity is just a state of mind. There's a telly. Comics. *Mad Magazine.* Comfortable chairs. A sideboard with a coffee machine and cups on it. A bookcase along the wall to my left.

At the end of the bookcase there's another door. In I go. The room is the size of a cupboard. There's a desk with a computer on it. A swivel-chair behind the desk. And a four-drawer filing cabinet.

The top drawer is marked A to E. I get out in the key and put it in the lock, but I don't need to turn it. The cabinet is open. I flip through the A's, the B's and the C's to Cooley, Nuala. I take out the file folder. I hold my breath. And open the folder.

The big zip.

Nada.

The folder is empty.

I go through the rest of the files, all of them, with a fine tooth comb, on the off chance that maybe Nuala's records got misfiled.

Nothing.

I turn on the computer and open the menu. I click onto Cooley, Nuala. Guess what?

It's been washed.

Not even her address is left.

Somebody has sanitised the Nuala Cooley story.

Sandra raises her eyebrows when I tell her the news.

"No," she says.

"Yes," I say.

"Are you sure?"

"Do you want to have a look?"

There's always the chance that she may know about some cubby-hole with the confidential files of VIP's in it, or some trick of the computer trade that could produce results. I'm reaching, but you never know. Leave no stone unturned is my motto.

"Come on," she says.

She leads me back to Walton's office and does her business with the files and the computer. No joy.

"That's very strange," she says, after she's had a good gander around the doc's office. She scratches her head. "Why would Doctor Walton erase his files?"

"Maybe he didn't."

Her eyebrows arch again. Her face is getting lots of exercise today.

"What do you mean?"

"Maybe someone else erased them."

"Nobody has been in here since the doctor's

death but the Gardaí," she says. She looks at me. Holds the connection. "And the Gardaí would have no reason to be taking the files. Would they?"

"They'd have to give you a receipt for anything they were taking."

"Nobody gave me anything."

"You haven't had any break-ins?"

"No."

"How many times were the police here, Sandra?"

She thinks.

"Twice. One guy came on his own on the day of the murder and the next day two more plainclothes men came around and asked the same questions again. When did I last see Doctor Walton? Did he have any enemies? That kind of thing. And they talked to the other doctors in the building. That was it."

"Did they go into the surgery?"

"Not the second pair. The first one did."

"On his own?"

"Yeah."

"What did he look like?"

"Why?" she says.

"Bear with me, Sandra. What did he look like."

"He was a big fellow. Looked like he played a lot of sports. Black hair. He was well dressed. Classy, like. His tie had little fishes on it."

"McGonagle."

Surprise, surprise.

Sandra watches me closely now. She senses something is out of whack. She wonders what's going on.

"He was a guard, wasn't he? He showed me identification just like yours."

"Yes. He was a policeman."

"Well, he wouldn't have any reason to remove the files, would he?"

I sigh.

"There's something odd going on, isn't there?" she says.

I shrug.

"Yes, Sandra. There's something very odd going on."

"God."

"I'll be in touch," I say.

I turn to go.

"I suppose they took the tapes as well?" she says.

Huh?

I freeze in my tracks.

"Tapes?" I say.

She nods.

"Tapes," she says.

"What do you mean?"

"Doctor Walton taped all his sessions."

"Where did he keep the tapes?"

"At his home. He has a surgery there, too."

Don't I know it.

Hope springs eternal.

"Did you mention the tapes to the other guards?"

She shakes her head.

"There was no reason to. At least there didn't seem to be."

"I'd better run," I say.

"Good luck," she says.

"Thanks," I say.

And I leg it.

32

I call Davy Mullen on the mobile.

"Did you drive to work today?" I say.

"I did," he says.

"Good. I need to borrow your car."

"When?"

"Now."

"Where are you planning on going in such a fierce hurry?"

I tell him.

"I'll go with you," he says. "I'm finished my classes for the day."

I look at my watch.

"Already? It's barely past noon. You have a great job."

"You should have gone to university," he says. "Where are you now?"

"Dame Street."

"Walk down the front gates of the college. I'll be there in ten minutes."

Ten minutes later, on the dot, Davy pulls up at the front gates of Trinity College. He's still driving the red Mercedes. I get in. We head for the country.

It's *déjà vu* for Milo.

Walton's place looks as deserted as it was four days ago when McGonagle wasted Nuala and the doctor and tried to put an end to my sojourn on earth. We drive past slowly and check the place out for lingering coppers or evil bastards with big guns. There's no sign of either.

Davy drops me round a bend and does a three-point turn. I keep watch as he drives back to the house. He parks on the road and gets out of the car. He's the picture of nonchalance. He opens the gate, rambles up to the front door, as if he's just calling on a whim. He rings the bell. If anyone answers he'll ask for directions to Ballykissangel. Not a creature is stirring.

I trot down and join him at the door. It's locked. We try the surgery door. Locked. We go around the side of the house to the window of the surgery, where McGonagle took a pot shot at me and missed the bull's-eye by a few hairs. The window has a hole in it. Guess what? The hole is the size of a bullet. A spider's web of cracks and splinters emanate from the centre.

I crack the glass with my elbow. I reach in and open the window. Davy goes back to the surgery door. I climb in the window. I land softly on the carpet. Talk about feeling the creeps. My scalp tightens. My skin crawls. My scrotum puckers. Goose bumps emerge all over my body. The room is frigid. Desolation weighs heavily on the atmosphere. The bodies are gone, of course, but there's blood all over the place. And a lingering, powerful sense of evil deeds done.

Jesus.

My heart pounds. I desperately don't want to be here. In this colonial outpost of Hell. Lucifer came here for plunder and he left his spoor, marked this house forever as his territory.

I go through the waiting-room to the hall and the surgery door. I open it. Davy sees the look of me and his eyes widen.

"You're white as a sheet," he says.

"Come on," I say.

"You look like you've seen a ghost."

"We should spend as little time here as we can."

I turn my back on him and go back to the room where the murder took place. He closes the door behind him. He audibly shivers as he moves into the house.

"Mother of God. I see what you mean," he says.

I try to ignore the dried blood as I check the desk and bookcase in the surgery. Davy searches the waiting-room. I look on the floor under the furniture. No tapes. No tape recorders. I go look in the toilet where I puked. Someone cleaned up my vomit. The toilet is clean. And empty.

We move back into the main house. The sitting-room. Armchairs and telly and ornaments and stuff. A *nice* room. Cosy. No tapes. No tape recorder. The window looks out on the garden, where McGonagle tried to finish me off.

There's a door in the wall opposite to the door to the surgery. I open it. It's Walton's study. Very male. Dark wood and leather. Decorated in various deep shades of brown. It's full of books on wall-to-wall shelves. There's a small desk with a computer on it tucked into a corner. One of those reclining chairs with a little dais for your feet that emerges when you lie back.

With some rooms you get a sense of their true purpose. This is where Doc Walton did his thinking.

Beside the reclining chair there's a coffee table with two sets of headphones, one big and one small, lying on it. The small headphones are the kind joggers use and they're plugged into a Sony Walkman, which rests beside them on the table.

The larger set is connected to what looks like a very expensive sound system. Mitsubishi. There's a CD player, a cassette player, a turntable for records and a receiver. They're encased in a rich-looking mahogany unit, above which shelves reach up to the ceiling, where the speakers hang, tilted at a forty-five-degree angle to the wall.

The top two shelves hold albums. On the three below there are CDs. And below the CDs there are shelves full of cassettes, all stacked in containers, so that each shelf holds three layers of tapes. I check them out. The upper two shelves hold the music. It's mostly classical — Beethoven, Chopin, Mozart and the like.

The bottom shelf is full of home-made recordings. Each cassette has someone's name written on it. Each name has a number of cassettes, varying from two to a dozen, depending, I suppose, on how long the person had been coming to see the doctor. The tapes are listed in alphabetical order and, lo and behold if I don't find under C a bunch of cassettes with Nuala Cooley's name on them. There's eight of them. I touch them.

"Success?" says Davy behind me.

"We're in business," I say.

We're both whispering, subdued by the creepy, ominous ambience of this haunted house.

"Let's get the hell out of here," he says.

I can't agree more.

I scoop the cassettes out and put them in the deep pockets of my army jacket. I take the Sony Walkman from the table and put that in with the tapes. I check the tape in the machine – *The Three Tenors*. I leave it. I have one last perfunctory look around the place to make sure we're not overlooking anything. I don't see any ghosts, but I feel the evil spirits rubbing up against me. Slithery serpents sliding through the vulnerable landscape of my soul.

Mocking me.

We get the hell out of there.

33

The closest safe haven is Davy's four-bedroom semi-detached in Donnybrook. We make a beeline for it. The house is quiet and peaceful. The kids are at school and Lynda is visiting her mother. Davy leads me into the lounge and sits me down. He fetches a bottle of Black Bush and a glass. Sets them down on a coffee table beside me.

"I'll make a pot of tea," he says. "You do your business. You won't be disturbed."

I take *The Three Tenors* out of the Walkman and put in the tape marked *Nuala Cooley – 1*. I put on the headphones and press the play button.

For the next two hours I trespass on the private estate of Nuala Cooley's inner world, as she works with the doc and gradually unburdens herself. How little I knew of her and the load that she carried. I cringe as I listen and contemplate the cruel weight of the cross she carried through her short life.

Ah, Nuala.

I thought I knew her. I thought I was plugged into her mindset. For at least a few short months back in the innocence of our glory days, I fancied I was tuned into the *zeitgeist* of her life, that we were on the same wavelength. At least for a while.

I had no idea.

Really.

I was deaf, dumb, blind and stupid.

Nuala resorted to Doc Walton out of desperation. She was suffering from bouts of chronic depression. She felt that she was beginning to crack under the strain. Sometimes she even contemplated suicide.

My Nuala.

Her secret was pressing down on her. Closing in on her. Cutting off the escape routes — the distractions of merriment, humour, frivolity and sexuality that she'd been using most of her adult life to keep the demons of her past at bay.

It didn't take Walton long to get it out of her. He had her sussed the first day he saw her. Recognised the symptoms straight away. He was good at his job. He steered her deftly along the road to acknowledgement, recognition of her blamelessness and, perhaps, in time, recovery.

Nuala was brave. And in a hurry. She took the

bull by the horns right from the start. She faced the horrors eyeball to eyeball. She courageously confronted the perpetual nightmare that constituted her childhood. She relived the fear, the dread of the approaching footfalls. She suffered anew the awful violence of the assaults. The childhood rapes. And she ripped the mask off the face of the monster who perpetrated the abuse. And the scavenger who destroyed a young girl's innocence and love of life and living was – you guessed it – dear old, dear old Dad.

No. Daddy. No. Nodaddy nodaddy nodaddyno.

The perverted swine was molesting her since she was seven tiny years old. It lasted until she was fourteen.

God in Heaven.

The Big Man.

The Great White Hope.

The would-be Saviour of the Nation.

A degenerate. A pus-filled scab on a boil on the arsehole of humanity. A dirtbird. A child-molester. A molester of his own child.

Don't touch me, Daddy. Please.

The pain in her voice. Such suffering. How could he? Her own father. How could he visit such horror on his own daughter. His little girl. The immensity of the crime, the betrayal of trust, is so huge it's virtually incomprehensible.

I'll take the bastard down for this. I swear.

For this I could kill a man.

I fast-forward through most of the sessions. Nuala is talking the monsters out of her mind and I don't want to be intrusive. Nor do I want to hear all the pain and grief and despair.

On the last tape she's psyching herself up to confront him. Walton says it's a good idea. It will help her come to closure, he says. She's come a long way and she's as ready as she'll ever be, he says.

So, she tells Walton, she sent the Gaffer a letter inviting him to accompany her to a session at Walton's. And how do you think the scum of the earth responded? The bastard telephoned her. And he chided her. He actually had the gall to lecture her. Honest. The Cooley family doesn't air its dirty linen in public, he said. And he threatened her. He told her not to back him into a corner. This is bigger than both of us, he said. Don't be foolish, Nuala.

He said.

Saints above us.

The man is a barbarian.

Even Doc Walton was shocked and, given the nature of his business and the sordid secrets constantly divulged to him, I reckon it took a humdinger of a story to shock that man.

He'd tentatively scheduled the confrontation

that wouldn't happen for last Thursday. The day they were killed. There's irony somewhere in that. Buried in the bloody disgrace.

The Walkman crackles in my ear. I realise I'm sitting, staring off into space, listening to static. The tape stopped running ages ago. My eyes are wet. My nose is running. There's a cup of tea gone cold on the coffee table. The Black Bush is untouched. Davy sits in a chair across the room. Watching me. I take the Walkman off my ears. I wipe my nose with my finger.

I hear chatter and the noise of dishes and cutlery being used in the kitchen. I look at my watch. It's after six.

"Lynda and the kids are having their tea," he says.

I nod.

"Are you all right?" he says.

"Archie Cooley is a child-molester."

He nods.

"He was abusing Nuala since she was seven years old."

Davy shakes his head in sorrow.

"I guessed it was something like that," he says.

"Did you?"

"It was written, clear as daylight, on your face, as you listened to the tapes."

"God help us."

"Have a drink."

I pour myself a couple of fingers. Knock it back.

"How could I not know, Davy?"

He shrugs.

"We were so close," I say.

"Don't punish yourself, Milo. She was hiding it all her life. It was second nature to her."

"I had sex with her. A part of her must have loathed it. Must have been thinking of him. Remembering how she felt when he'd do it to her."

"Don't knock yourself out."

"I feel like I failed her."

"Archie Cooley molested her, Milo. Not you. He did the damage. Focus on that. You can give yourself a hard time later, in luxury, when this is all over."

"Do you think he had his own daughter killed?"

"It looks like it, doesn't it?"

"That's evil. Pure, unadulterated evil."

"And we have him by the short and curlies, don't we?" he says, nodding at the tapes.

"It's pretty strong evidence."

"What we have to do now, Milo, is figure out a way of getting the story out. We've got to expose the bastard."

"I suppose we can't just give the tapes to the cops?"

"And risk a cover-up? If those tapes fall into the wrong hands, they'll vanish off the face of the earth, as sure as God made little green apples. Do you know who you can trust?"

I shake my head. It's time for some high jinks.

We put our heads together.

We come up with a plan.

The end game.

34

Our scheme entails the participation of DV MacEntee, who, I hope, remains my newfound friend. I call him on the mobile.

"It's Milo Devine," I say, when he answers.

"Milo," he says, "where are you? What's going on?"

"I'm not very far away from you and I need your help."

He pauses.

"DV, I didn't kill Nuala."

"I know that. I think. Cynthia phoned me a few days ago. She said you'd called. She said she believed in you. She's Nuala's best friend. If it's good enough for her, it's good enough for me. I suppose. But it's hard to know what to think, Milo."

"I know."

"So, what do you want."

"Can I come over? I'll explain everything."

"Okay. I'm still at work. The door is open. And I promise not to call the cops."

Davy goes into the kitchen and has a word with Lynda. I wait at the hall door. She comes out to say hello and goodbye. She has a gander at me and gasps.

"Is that you, Milo?" she says. "I wouldn't have recognised you."

"Sorry I'm stealing your husband."

"Don't be sorry. Be careful."

She gives me a hug.

"God bless," she says.

"Thanks."

Davy kisses her.

And we're off.

DV is as good as his word and there are no coppers or cruisers loitering at or near *Banba* Films when we get there. The door is unlocked and the reception area is deserted. There's light coming from upstairs. And music. Bryan Ferry singing *Rescue Me*. A fitting selection for the occasion, I daresay. We climb up to the loft.

DV sits on the couch, hunched over a pile of papers.

"Hello in the house," I say.

He looks up and attempts a half-hearted smile. He looks tired.

"Is that you, Milo?"

"It is."

"Great make-up job."

"How's the movie business going?"

"Running me ragged. I miss my partner."

"Aye."

I introduce Davy and they shake hands. We sit.

I fill him in on the whole murky story. I play parts of the tapes to convince him. As he listens his eyes go wet, his lower lip trembles and his body shakes.

"Good Lord," he says, when I finally press the stop button.

"After listening to that, it's hard to believe in God," I say.

"It's hard to believe in anything."

He looks from me to Davy and back to me again.

"Do you think he killed her?"

"It looks that way," I say.

"To be precise, it looks like he had her killed," says Davy.

"It's just incredible. Mind-blowing. What are we going to do?" he says.

"We have a plan," I say.

"And?"

"And it involves your co-operation."

He doesn't flinch.

"I'll do what I can," he says.

"Good man," says Davy.

"So, what's the plan?"

"Cooley is holding a press conference at his home tomorrow," I say. "He's expected to announce that he's officially throwing his hat in the ring and running for election."

DV nods.

"I want to go to the press conference and confront him there," I say.

DV exhales with a whistle.

"You like to make a splash, don't you, Milo?"

"It's the only way. We don't know who we can trust in the police. This way, we nip any potential cover-up in the bud. It's a press conference. The place will be crawling with reporters. Even Cooley can't kill us while the world is watching. And we'll get everything out into the open before he has a chance to smother us with injunctions and whatever other legal chicanery his mouthpieces dream up."

"It's a hell of a gamble," he says.

I shrug.

"That's life."

"And this way we give Nuala what she wanted," says DV. "We give her her confrontation."

I nod.

Milo Devine and the Demagogue's Daughter

He thinks for about three seconds.
"Count me in," he says.

DV takes us down to a sound room in the basement. He splices the tapes into sound bites that succinctly tell the sordid story. He makes a hundred copies. We fine-tune the details of tomorrow's adventure.

Davy drives me to the safe house. We check in with Henry on the mobile. We decide to leave the watchers on duty for the night, just in case McGonagle makes a move. I need a press card for tomorrow. No problem, says Henry. First thing in the morning.

Davy doesn't come in.
"I want to go home and hug my kids," he says.
"I know how you feel," I say.
It's been that kind of day.

I make a cup of tea and watch the late news. Today's poll says sixty-seven per cent of the voters plan to give their yes to Cooley if he runs.
Scary.
I hope there is a Hell.
And on that note I go to sleep.

35

I wake around eight. My gut feels like it's being squeezed in a vice. I'm thinking maybe I should have taken Davy's offer and done a runner to the USA.

This is it.

The big day.

The doorbell rings. I jump. My nerves are in tatters. I go to the front door, lift a corner of the curtain and have a decko. It's a motor-cycle courier. I open up and I sign for an envelope containing my press credentials. The lights must never go out in Henry's office. According to my press card, I'm a reporter for *Medialink Eire*, whatever that is.

Sound as a bell.

I brew up some tea. I boil a couple of eggs and grill some bread into toast. But I can't eat for the gansey-load of butterflies fluttering in my belly. I drink a cup of tea and I watch the morning news on the telly. The talking head says the latest talks up north are moving into a new phase. A sense of optimism prevails, she says. She wraps by musing that peace, this time, may truly be at hand.

I'm a bag of nerves and shitting planks at the prospects of the day ahead of me. Nonetheless I take a minute to contemplate the notion of permanent peace in my land. Who'd have believed it?

Peace.

Maybe there is a God, after all.

DV MacEntee arrives around nine. He's driving a van, the side of which looks like a page out of the Book of Kells. *Banba* Films is written across the top in stylized Celtic script. Beneath that there's the logo, which is an Irish wolfhound standing on its hind legs and gazing through the eyepiece of a movie camera the dog holds in his front paws. His Master's Vision, says the motto written underneath.

"Very derivative," I say.

DV nods.

"That's the idea," he says.

"The Irish stuff is all the rage these days," I say.

"Yep," he says. "Celtic is cool. It's the flavour of the times."

Cynthia Pilkington sits in the passenger seat.

"She insisted on coming along," says DV. "I figure she's entitled."

I nod.

Cynthia stares wide-eyed at me.

"Milo? I'd never have recognised you," she says.

"What are you doing here?" I say.

"I'm going to the press conference. I'm the second camera unit."

She taps a little compact camcorder on her lap. She flashes a grin. Looks at her watch.

"The clock is ticking," she says. "Are you coming or not?"

She makes room for me on the seat. I climb in beside her.

"Okay, DV," she says. "Hi-Ho Silver Awaaay!"

She winks at me.

DV grins.

I grunt.

Cynthia may wink, but she's white as a sheet and DV may grin, but his eyes look haunted. My mouth is dry as a bone. My stomach is tied up in knots.

DV puts the van into gear.

He takes his time. It's twenty past nine. The press conference begins at eleven, so there's no great rush. We stop at a deli at Sutton Cross for coffee, which we drink sitting in the van.

"Were you at the funeral?" I say.

They nod.

"It was awful," Cynthia says. "Nuala's sister, Carmel, was in bits. She wrapped herself around the coffin. Wouldn't let them put it into the ground. John, the brother, had to pull her off."

"It was painful," says DV. "We left after the burial. We were invited back to the house for the wake, but we couldn't face it."

"It's not as if we'd have been missed. There were hundreds there. And I'd only have gone for the sake of the mother, but she was like a zombie at the grave. She didn't seem to recognise anyone."

"She was stoned out of her skull," says DV.

"Who could blame her?" says Cynthia.

"Nobody," says DV.

"How was the Gaffer?" I say.

"Oh, inscrutable as ever. Charlie Chan with a Dublin accent," says DV.

"DV told me what he did," says Cynthia. "I still can't believe it."

"It's hard to swallow, all right," I say.

"The fucker should be taken out and shot," she says.

"Hear, hear," says DV.

A fleet of TV trucks slows down at the lights and turns right onto the back road up the Hill of Howth. We all check our watches. It's half past ten. DV hands me a reporter's notebook and about ten biros. Also, a leather-encased tape recorder with a tape already in it, similar to one he has hung over his shoulder.

"Test it," he says.

I press play. Nuala talks. A voice from the grave.

"My father raped me," she says.

Beside me, Cynthia shudders.

"Jesus, Mary and Joseph," she says.

"That will get their attention," I say grimly.

"Good," says DV.

He clips his press card to his coat lapel. I do likewise.

"I'll get by on charm," says Cynthia.

I rewind the tape. DV cranks up the engine. We pull into the wake of the media train.

The gates to the Cooley estate are open. The minders, their Uzis under wraps, step aside and watch the hacks roll in. There's a uniformed cop pointing directions every fifty yards or so along the drive. They point us towards a rectangle of gravel in front of the house.

This time we're going in the front door.

We park the van and follow the herd. I hang my tape recorder over my shoulder. As well as the tape recorder, DV carries a camera and a tripod. Cynthia brings her camera. She stops at the front door. She tilts her head and whispers.

"There's Nuala's mum," she says.

Down at the gable end of the house, the old woman is bent over, tending her garden. Even at this distance, she cuts a forlorn, dejected figure.

"I'm going to pay my respects," says Cynthia.

DV and I go inside.

They're holding the press conference in the drawing-room where Cooley and I had our little chat eight days ago. The furniture has been pulled back to the wall and replaced by a long, black oak table with two matching leather-cushioned chairs behind it. There's a microphone, a pitcher of water and two glasses on coasters on the table. There are rows of folding chairs in front of the table for the press corps to sit on.

Another table is filled with snacks similar to what was fed to me when I was fool enough to eat and sup in the house of the devil. Reporters are milling around the table, filling their faces.

Behind the conference table, backs firmly planted against the wall, stand four Special Branch men, their eyes incessantly scanning the crowd. One of them is Sweaty Finnegan. His eyes move over me and take me in, but they don't linger or come back.

The TV people are busy setting up their lights and cameras and gear. Davy joins them. He stands up the tripod and sits the camera on it. He looks through the eyepiece and does his adjustments.

I sit. In the middle of the second row of seats.

I press my knees together to keep them from visibly shaking.

After a while a PR man hustles the press gang into their seats. I'm surrounded. Boxed in by the reporters. But also protected by their presence. I hope. The Gaffer's men will have to wade through the crowd to get at me. Everything is going according to plan. So far, so good. I say a little prayer to myself.

Now I lay me down to sleep,
I pray the Lord my soul to keep.

In my state of heightened anxiety, it's the only prayer I can think of.

If I should die before I wake,
Lordy, lordy.

A hush descends on the room and the Gaffer arrives. The media go noisily into gear. Lights and cameras flash. Cooley is flanked by his henchmen, McGonagle and Ned O'Brien. They're well used to this mild frenzy. The politicians sit and the hullabaloo dies down.

McGonagle stands to the side of the table, a few paces back. He nods hello at Sweaty Finnegan and the other Branch men. The Gaffer pours himself a glass of water as Ned O'Brien does the introduction. Ned leans into the mike.

"Ladies and gentlemen, thank you for coming," he says, "Before we move on to the substance of this press conference, Mister Cooley would like to make an opening comment with respect to his family's recent loss."

He moves the mike over towards the Gaffer. Cooley leans forward. The hacks turn on their tape recorders. I don't. Nobody notices. I lick the nib of my pen and make like I'm taking notes.

"Ladies and gentlemen of the press," says Cooley, "and readers and viewers at home, welcome to my home. As you all know, my family and I recently suffered a grotesque tragedy. We lost our daughter Nuala. Words cannot describe our feelings of grief and bereavement. The loss of a daughter at such a youthful age is an affliction no parent should have to endure. But endure it we must and the process of endurance has been made easier somewhat by the wreaths, the flowers, the mass cards and the letters of sympathy and condolence which we have received from ordinary people from all four corners and all four provinces of this wonderful nation of ours. Your response to our tribulation has been unprecedented and unbelievable. So I'd like to take this opportunity to say to the Irish people – compatriots, from the bottom of our hearts, the Cooley family thanks you."

The reporters nod and murmur. They give Cooley a quiet round of applause. It's a gesture of solidarity from decent people in his time of grief. He smiles sanguinely and nods his appreciation.

Cooley pushes the mike back to O'Brien, who is looking behind us at the door, his eyebrows arched quizzically. I turn my head and have a gawk. Stan O'Brien has just arrived. Davy called him, anticipating the likelihood that I may well need the services of a lawyer before this day is over. Stan's arrival is obviously a surprise to his old man. He nods at his da and leans against the wall by the door. His head doesn't move, but his eyes roam round the room, presumably searching for me. He doesn't spot me.

The elder O'Brien loudly clears his throat. The reporters go quiet.

"I, like all members of our party and most, if not all, Irish people, wish our great leader Archie Cooley and his family could enjoy a period of peace and reflection in order to come to terms with their loss. Alas, time marches on and the affairs of state will wait for no man. In the morning of the millennium, we stand on the brink of a new era, an era that could well prove to be another Golden Age for the Irish nation. Here in the twenty-six counties, we're enjoying a period of unprecedented prosperity, which can be directly attributed to the policies of previous governments in which Archie Cooley played a prominent role."

Cooley nods in appreciation of the tribute.

"And in the north of Ireland," says O'Brien, "the prospect of a just and lasting peace has never been more real. At such a crucial period in the history of our small country, the nation cries out for strong, inspired, wise leadership."

He winds down.

"It gives me great pleasure to announce today that Archie Cooley has courageously and selflessly decided to stay in the race. The nation needs him and he'll not deny his people."

O'Brien waxes lyrical and sings the Gaffer's praises for another ten minutes or so. Then Cooley does his thing. He gives ream after ream of chapter and verse attesting to why he, and he alone, should be chosen to walk in the grandiose footsteps of the High Kings of Tara.

"On election day, give me your number one and you'll not be sorry," he says.

"Give me your number one and Ireland will prevail. I promise," he says.

"Trust me."

He says.

Milo Devine and the Demagogue's Daughter

When he finishes, he throws the floor open to questions. The media ask the usual questions. The Gaffer answers expertly. Easily. There are jokes and quips and good-natured banter. He has the crowd in the palm of his hand. It's like a meeting of the Cooley appreciation society. The hacks are leery of asking the hard questions for fear of being seen to be dancing on his daughter's grave.

A lull occurs in the proceedings. It's my cue. My heart is in my throat. I stand up. I suck my anxiety into my gut. My throat is dry as sand. I clear it. I cross my fingers and talk. Fortunately, my voice works.

"Isn't it true, Mr Cooley, that your daughter Nuala was seeing the psychiatrist, Jack Walton, on a professional basis and they weren't actually lovers at all?"

Silence. Somebody gasps. Everybody stiffens. Every eyeball in the room zeroes in on me. The pundits disapprove. That question is out of order at a time like this, the expressions on their faces say. Nonetheless, they're journalists and they're curious about what's going on. You could hear a pin drop. A clock high up on the wall above Sweaty Finnegan ticks loudly. I look at it. It's a quarter to twelve. I look at Sweaty Finnegan. He's staring at me curiously.

Out of the corner of my eye I see DV stealthily

leave his camera to distribute copies of the tape to the press hounds, who look quizzically from DV to the tape to me. Their instinct is telling them there's a big story maybe going down here.

Cooley's blue eyes go steely. Ned O'Brien looks as if he's been kicked in the balls. He's indignant. He's thinking I'm a lowlife from a sleazy tabloid.

Think again, Ned. And prepare yourself for a shock.

"Identify yourself, sir," he says. "What publication do you represent?"

I finger the press card on my lapel and shake it at him. As if it makes a difference. I turn back to Cooley. I'm cool now. The shakes are gone. Likewise the stage fright. It's like when I was on the operetta in primary school. Once I got the first few words out, I was unstoppable. I'm into the action now. And relishing it.

"Isn't it true, Mr Cooley," I say, "that your daughter Nuala had to seek psychiatric help from Doctor Walton because you had been sexually abusing her since she was seven years old?"

The pundits are rapt at attention. They're slipping the tapes DV gave them into their pockets to keep them safe. O'Brien looks apoplectic. Cooley cocks his head like a hawk would. He stares right at me. His expression remains inscrutable, but I can feel the heat off those laser eyeballs of his boring right into my soul. I sense the hatred emanating out of him. I eyeball him right back.

Fuck you, Cooley.

How sweet it is.

"This is monstrous," says Ned O'Brien. He's fit to be tied.

"Indeed it is," I say.

I hold up the tape recorder.

"This is the voice of Nuala Cooley," I say. "The man on the tape is Doctor Walton."

The pundits gasp in concert. Cooley glares at McGonagle. "You fuckin' eejit, there were tapes," his look says. He glares at me again. I wink. *Gotcha*. I glance at Sweaty Finnegan. He's eyeballing me relentlessly. His memory is tugging at him. He recognises me but he doesn't know it yet. Can't put a name to the face.

I've been there. Done that. It's frustrating as hell.

I press the play button.

"My own father abused me," says Nuala.

Cooley comes into the play. He raises his voice over the action.

"The contents of those tapes are discussions shared between a doctor and his patient. That's confidential information and I advise you to turn off that tape immediately," he says.

I have to give him credit for coolness under fire. I'm shooting the heavy guns at him and he's still scheming, searching for a means of containment.

Nobody else says a word. Nuala now dominates the room.

"Daddy warned me," says Nuala.

"He threatened you?" says Walton.

"Yes," says Nuala. She breaks down in sobs.

"This is preposterous," says Ned O'Brien.

Cooley turns to McGonagle.

"Confiscate that tape," he says.

McGonagle starts to move towards me. Sweaty Finnegan too.

I raise my arm, forefinger extended, and point it accusingly at Cooley. The cameras lap it up.

"Isn't it true, Mr Cooley," I say, "that your daughter Nuala wanted to confront you with your crime? Isn't it true that you were afraid you'd be exposed for the child-molester you are? And isn't it true that you ordered Inspector McGonagle here to kill her?"

Cooley glares at me. For once he lets his guard down. His eyes narrow and open. I see behind the mirrors. And I behold stark, vicious, unmitigated evil.

He knows who I am now.

Ned O'Brien doesn't.

"This is bizarre," he says. "Identify yourself, sir."

I brace myself.

"My name is Milo Devine and I'm an innocent man."

Pandemonium breaks loose. The press gang bursts into business. It's stampede time. The cameras zoom. The lights pop and flash. The reporters jostle and muscle each other to get their microphones close to my mouth. I'm half blinded, but I spot McGonagle bearing down on me through the throng. He has his gun out.

"Arrest that man," shouts Cooley.

I presume he means me. He never gives up.

McGonagle is almost on top of me. He raises his hand with the gun in it. He's about to clock me. Someone grabs his arm. It's Sweaty Finnegan. McGonagle makes like he's going to have a go at Sweaty, but Sweaty's cohorts come up on either side of him. The jig is up and McGonagle knows it. Sweaty takes the gun from his hand. The cameras flit away from me and zoom in on McGonagle and Sweaty and the gun.

"What in Jasus' name is going on here?" says a talking head.

"STOP."

The voice behind us shuts everyone up. It's the voice of authority. Soft and feminine but firm and undeniable. The voice of motherhood. The fracas stops. The room goes quiet. We turn in unison.

The voice, of course, belongs to Margaret Cooley. She stands in the doorway, bent and tired and old beyond her years. But there's grit still in those old bones. For her daughter's sake, it seems like she'll fight the good fight till it's over. The look in her eye would drill through steel. Cynthia stands beside her.

Just as I did, Margaret Cooley raises her arm and points the finger of indictment at her husband.

"You bastard," she says. "You sick, arrogant, megalomaniac bastard. You killed my Nuala."

Ned O'Brien's head snaps back. He looks stunned. He half stands and pushes his chair with his arse, back, away from Cooley, desperate to get out of the range of the arc of condemnation cast by Margaret Cooley's judicial finger.

All eyes are on the Gaffer, as are the cameras. They snap, crackle and pop. He's apparently oblivious. He sits there, his lip zipped, his face a mask, as if he hadn't a care in the world. Then he shakes his head. It's not denial, though. It's more a subtle acknowledgement of defeat. As if he's finally been confronted with the one obstacle he couldn't overcome. The one messenger he couldn't kill. The mother.

The truth, exposed and undeniable, fills and chills the room with all its grim, sordid reality.

Cooley sits there. All alone.

While his wife pours out her grief.

"You murdered my little girl. First you took her innocence. Her peace of mind. Her joy in living. Then you killed her for her silence so that you could rule the roost, be master of your domain. You're a malevolent, soulless, evil pervert and I hope you spend eternity in hell for what you did to my little girl."

Her shoulders shake. The strain and pain prove too much and she cracks. She breaks down into convulsive spasms and her body crumples. Cynthia catches her and takes her in her arms. Half steers, half carries her out the door.

Stan O'Brien moves in beside me. Sweaty Finnegan puts McGonagle's gun in his pocket.

"You'd better come down to the station," he says to McGonagle. "I have a few questions for you."

He turns to me.

"You too," he says.

I shrug. Stan O'Brien nods. The press hounds circle us in a scrum, shouting a cacophony of questions. The noise is deafening. Stan the Man raises his arms, palms out, in supplication.

"Later, lads and ladies," he says, "we'll answer all your questions. For now we have nothing to say."

The pundits recognise him for the lawyer he is and ruefully acknowledge they'll get nothing out of us. They grumble and growl, but they leave us alone and start to disperse. They talk frantically into their mobiles, type madly into their laptops.

"Stop the presses."

"Here's the scoop."

"You won't believe this."

I spot Cooley's back as he heads into the main house. I grab Sweaty by the shoulder.

"What about Cooley?" I say. "Aren't you arresting him?"

"I'll have to refer that up the chain of command," he says.

I glare at him. He shrugs.

"That's life," he says.

Outside, there's a soft drizzle falling. Down by the flower beds, Cynthia sits on a bench, holding Mrs Cooley's hand. The old woman mutely gazes at her garden. Her diminished, broken figure is the picture of grief personified.

Stan leads me to the car park where DV is putting the gear away. Sweaty Finnegan comes over to me.

"I'll let you make your own way to the station. Do you know where it is?" he says.

"Yeah."

He clears his throat and talks low, close to my ear, so that only I can hear.

"I never figured you for a murderer, Devine," he says.

"Thanks," I say.

"That doesn't mean I'm going to start liking you," he says.

36

Stan the Man drives me down to the police station in his Rover. DV follows in the van. Behind him comes a convoy of press hounds. The rest of the day goes by in a blur. The cop shop is besieged by the media and bedlam reigns.

Given his feelings for Nuala, Stan O'Brien must be demolished by the doings of the day and the revelations about the nature of Nuala's life and death, but he's a soldier. He keeps his chin up and does the legal thing. He keeps the coppers off my back. At turns he's agreeable, effusive, smartarse or indignant, as the situation warrants. He smokes like a trooper.

"This will break my father's heart," he says. "He was devoted to Cooley. He would have walked on hot coals for him. That treacherous bastard. Hanging would be too good for him."

Stan is well known in legal and political circles for his long-standing, passionate opposition to capital punishment. I say nothing. Child-molesters bring out the lust for retribution in the best of us.

Sweaty Finnegan and another cop I don't know give me the third degree for a while, but I can tell Sweaty's heart isn't in it. He may be an arsehole and he may hate my guts, but he's not hopelessly inefficient as a cop and even he can recognise a set-up when it's laid out in front of his eyes. His main focus of interrogation is McGonagle and after I sign my statement he says he's more or less finished with me for the day.

"You can go if you like," he says.

I say I'd like to hang around. To hear what McGonagle has to say for himself. Sweaty says that's cool. If McGonagle starts talking I can help separate the reality from the bullshit.

"I always figured that McGonagle for a psycho, but I never envisaged anything like this," he says.

"Who could?" I say.

Sweaty puts a small cubby-hole of an office at my disposal.

DV stays outside and plays spin doctor for the media. Gives them the true version of the story. Even the hard-bitten, cynical veterans of the press corps are flummoxed by the day's revelations. They walk around shaking their heads in amazement.

After an hour or so, Cynthia arrives. She got the Cooley's maid to call the family doctor, who gave the old woman a pill to put her to sleep.

"How come Nuala's brother and sister weren't there today?" I say.

"They're gone back to the States," she says.

"They didn't stay long."

"They flew out last night."

"The night of the funeral."

"Yeah."

"They were in a hurry."

"So much for family solidarity and helping each other through the grieving process."

"Yeah."

We're quiet for a while.

"Are you thinking what I'm thinking?" I say.

Cynthia nods.

"They knew?" she says.

"They must have. About the abuse, if nothing else. A normal son and daughter would stay at least a few days, if only for the mother's sake."

"God, Milo. It's all so dirty."

"And that leads us to the next question."

"Did the mother know?"

"Yep."

"How could she not know, living in the same house for all those years?"

"Sometimes the mothers don't know. Usually they do. Often they repress the knowledge and live their lives in denial."

Cynthia squirms.

"God," she says.

"Sexual abuse is a dirty business. It's psychological dynamite. It spares nobody in the house."

"I feel manky. I'm going to have a long, hot bath when I get home tonight."

Cynthia holds my hands and keeps me supplied with cups of coffee and kind words. She goes out to a chipper and fetches fish and chips for lunch. I realise I'm starving. The chips are soaked in salt and vinegar. They're luscious.

"I haven't enjoyed a meal so much in ages," I say.

"At least a week, I'd say," she says.

Davy arrives around four and joins me and Cynthia and DV MacEntee in our cubby-hole. He opens his briefcase and extracts a bottle of Black Bush. There's a stack of plastic cups on the desk. He pours the drinks and hands them out. He takes my hand in both of his and shakes it.

"Free at last," he says.

We drink.

"Henry and Tom send their regards," he says. "They'd prefer to keep a low profile. Henry says he'd be obliged if we'd keep the company name out of the press. He doesn't want any hassle with the law. Technically, they were committing a crime in not turning you in."

"Fair enough," I say.

"But they'll come to the party."

At around seven the bottle is empty and Sweaty comes to tell us that McGonagle has spilled the beans. He's confessed to Nuala's murder. He says Cooley put him up to it.

"You're off the hook, Devine," he says.

"What's his story?"

"After he got Nuala's letter asking him to meet with her and Walton, Cooley got worried about Nuala going public. That's when he made his mind up to kill her. He set McGonagle on her. McGonagle followed her to Walton's on the Thursday and tied the two of them up. He fed them drugs to put them to sleep while he and Cooley spent the weekend dreaming up their plot. On the Monday, McGonagle went to see you."

"And I jumped at the chance to be a gilly."

"It was like leading a fish to water, according to McGonagle."

I grunt.

"Who picked me for the fall guy?" I say.

"Cooley came up with the idea of a patsy and McGonagle picked you. With your prior relationship with Nuala and your spoiled career in the Gardaí, he figured you were perfect for the part."

"He was right."

"You're a lucky man, Devine. You're supposed to be dead."

"I came close."

"What does McGonagle get out of all this?" says Stan.

"Money."

"How much?"

"Half a million pounds."

Stan whistles.

"That's well over union rates for a hit-man," he says.

"Cooley's not short of a few bob. And he wanted to keep it in the family, so to speak."

The system takes over. Sweaty's boss is on the blower to the Justice Department to talk about the possible prosecution of the Gaffer. This case will put the shits up the bureaucrats. The Gaffer's status means he'll get the kid-gloves treatment. There will be no such thing as sending a couple of the lads out to *Saoirse* in a cruiser to put the cuffs on the likes of Archie Cooley.

"Will he be charged?" I say.

"He will if I have anything to do with it," Sweaty says. "But we'll see. I hear there's already a battery of high-powered legal eagles holding a council of war out at Cooley's place. He's a powerful man. You can rest assured he'll claim that McGonagle is a psycho and took it on himself to waste the pair of them in a fit of misguided loyalty. Cooley's career in politics is over. The child-abuse thing in itself is too big and too dirty to finesse. But as far as getting a conviction in court goes — well, it will be his word against McGonagle's."

"And his money. And his clout," I say.

Sweaty nods.

"There are the tapes," says Stan.

"All they prove," Sweaty says, "is that Cooley was a pervert."

"The whole thing is incredible," says Stan.

"Grotesque," I say.

"Bizarre," says Sweaty.

I part with Stan the Man in the car park.

"Thanks for your help," I say.

He nods.

"Are you all right?" I say.

"I'll survive. I'm going home to get good and drunk."

"I'll be in touch."

I walk away. Stan pauses by his car, his key half in the door. He stands there, his head down. He cuts a sad, lonely figure.

The Burke brothers and Billy Cartwright are drinking cans of beer in the car park. They shake my hand and slap me on the back. I have a word in Billy's ear.

"I need the lend of a car for tonight and tomorrow," I say.

He slaps the bonnet of the Cortina under his arse.

"Will she do you?"

"She'd be grand."

"Do you want it now?"

"Can you park it outside my flat? It will be the last favour I'll ask of you."

He nods.

"I'll get the Burkes to drive me home," he says. "I'll leave the keys in the exhaust."

"Thanks, Billy."

We say our goodbyes.

Davy drives me home. Cynthia sits in the back. DV MacEntee passes us in his van and honks the horn adios. Davy toots back.

"What do you want a car for?" says Davy.

"Just to keep me going till I can get my own yoke back. I left it in some side street in Dun Laoghaire."

"I could drive you out in the morning."

"We'll see," I say.

Davy stops the car outside my flat.

"Home, sweet home," I say.

"Do you want us to come in?" he says.

I shake my head.

"No thanks."

I shake Davy's hand. He gives me a funny look.

"Are you all right?" he says.

"Never better," I say. "But I'm knackered. I'll call you in the morning."

I kiss Cynthia goodnight.

"Tomorrow," I say.

The vibes in the flat are like when you come from the holidays. The place has that quiet, empty, abandoned feeling about it, as if it's been missing you. It doesn't take long to fix. You just have to reinvest some of yourself, restore your energy to the ambience.

I make a pot of tea and take a cup into the bathroom. I drink it while I shave. I brush my teeth and take a long, hot shower.

I'm towelling myself dry and my gaze falls on a framed print on the bathroom wall. An old girl friend gave it to me the day she blew me out. It's a picture of a hibiscus. Beneath the flower there's a poem, a Japanese *haiku*.

Now that my house is burned down,
I have a much better view of the moon.

It says.

Bollix to that.

37

I get dressed. I put on a pair of black jeans, a black T-shirt, black socks and black Reeboks. A black leather jacket. I'm the Man In Black. Johnny Cash, eat your heart out. I top the outfit off with a navy blue NYPD baseball hat I picked up many moons ago when I was still on the force and paid a fraternal visit to my fellow law-enforcers in the Big Apple.

In my bedroom there's a poster on the wall that an old flame got for me in Spain. It's a picture of a bullfight. I take it down. Where it was, there's a safe embedded in the plaster. It's where I keep my passport, my mortgage agreement and my emergency cash. It's where I also keep my gun, an old Colt, and a box of ammo I bought under the table around the time I quit the cops and feared some hopped-up, pissed-off copper might take it into his head to give me what he regarded as my just and final desserts.

He didn't, but I kept the gun. I've never used it. There's always a first time.

I load it and put it in my jacket pocket.

I leave the flat and find Billy's Cortina two doors down from my place. I fetch the keys out of the exhaust, get into the car, start the engine, check the fuel level, which is okay, put the car into gear and take it out onto the Howth Road.

It's dark and there's a light drizzle still falling. It's that quiet time on the streets between bedtime for the kids and pub closing time. The roads are practically deserted. Nonetheless, I drive carefully, two miles per hour below the speed limit.

In Howth, I drive to the summit of the hill and past the entrance to the riding school and stables that back onto the Gaffer's place. I turn into a residential street, where I park the car.

I walk softly back to the stables. I check out the lie of the land. There's not a soul in sight and I'm over the wall in a flash. I land on wet grass. I stand still, steady my breathing and get my bearings. I'm nine years old again and stealthily tracking a band of cut-throat Commancheros across the prairie, awaiting a chance to rescue my sidekick, Tonto, from their dastardly clutches. Warily, I pick my way across the fields, through a small wooded area and I emerge at the fence that borders Cooley's land.

I climb over it, struggle through a growth of rhododendron bushes and, lo and behold, before me there's the well-manicured lawn with the bushes sculptured into animal shapes. I'm at the back of the Gaffer's house. There's only one light on inside. It glows through the window of the room adjacent to where Cooley earlier held his press conference. The kitchen is on the other side of the lighted room.

I go down on my hunkers beside a rhododendron bush. I watch the house. Out in Dublin Bay a ship toots a lonely foghorn. Half an hour passes. There are no Uzi-toting minders back here. They'll be warm and snug in the gatehouse. They'll figure your average urban guerilla is hardly going to see any advantage in popping Cooley, now that he's a *persona non grata* and may be looking at a long stretch behind bars.

A silhouette shifts behind the curtain on the window with the light in it. The figure moves across the window and out of sight. A door opens with a soft screech. I move my eyes to the kitchen area, where I first made my entrance into this miserable affair. The door is open. A man walks out onto the lawn. There's a scratching sound and the smell of sulphur. A match flares. The man raises it. Fires a cigar. The flame lights up his face. *Him*.

He blows smoke into the rain. Runs his hand through his hair. Sighs. He's wearing dark pants and a white shirt. The shirt collar is open, the sleeves rolled up. He looks like he's been working. Scheming, no doubt, with his legal eagles, how to beat the rap. The cigar smoke drifts in my direction. It smells like a million dollars. He throws the match away. There's a tiny hiss as the drizzle extinguishes the flame.

I stand up, knocking droplets of rain off the petals of the rhododendrons. Splish, splash, they land on my jacket and my jeans and my hat. I stretch the stiffness out of my legs.

Cooley hears the rustle of the rhododendrons. And maybe my tired old bones creaking.

"Who's there?" he says.

I step out of the shelter of the bush. Onto the lawn. He holds a hand over his eyebrows to keep the rain out of his eyes. I step gingerly towards him, my hands in my pockets, scanning the landscape behind him for a bypassing Uzi. The coast is clear. I'm about six feet away from him when he recognises me.

"Is that you, Devine?" he says.

I take out the gun. Point it at him. He grins.

"A gun?" he says. "This country is going to the dogs with the guns. It's getting more like America every day."

"Ha ha," I say.

"I expected to see you again, but not quite so soon as this," he says.

"We're going for a little walk," I say.

"I could use a breath of fresh air," he says. "Can I get you a cigar?"

I shake my head.

"There's nothing like a good Monte Cristo," he says.

He's extremely light and airy for a fellow who's just been confronted by a gunman in the middle of the night on the edge of the high country.

Weirdo.

I point him towards where the sea below laps and bashes up against the cliffs. He rambles across the wet grass as if he's out for a Sunday stroll. There's a skinny concrete path between the edge of the lawn and the gorse that grows over the side of the hill. He steps lightly across the path and onto the gorse. He juts his chin out to sea and sucks in a huge breath.

"Ah," he says. "I love the feel of the sea spray on my face. It's elemental. Timeless. Nature in the raw. One of the greatest thrills in life is steering a good sailboat through a storm at sea. Are you a sailor, Devine?"

I shake my head.

He looks at me curiously.

"Do you plan on killing me, Devine?" he says.

"I didn't come all this way for a chat," I say.

"Have you ever killed a man?"

"There's a first time for everything."

He chuckles.

"You know, I have a soft spot for you. You've got balls. You have the courage of your convictions. That's a rare thing nowadays. You're not afraid to get stuck in, do the job and suffer the consequences. I admire that in a man. I really do. You remind me of myself when I was your age."

"You were never my age."

"Ah, you're outraged. Your sense of moral propriety has been offended. I understand. Honest. I'm not a monster."

I snort. I beg to differ.

He's getting to me, despite the best of my intentions. I'd made my mind up not to get into any chitchat, not to give him the recognition of conversation. The dignity of acknowledgement. But the man angers and confounds me so much I just can't help myself.

"You murdered your own daughter, you sick fucker," I say.

"She was going to ruin me. I couldn't let that happen. It was her or me. It was self-preservation, Milo."

"Don't call me Milo."

He holds his hands up, palms out, placating me. The rain on the wind off the sea is soaking us. His white hair is plastered to his head and his shirt is so wet it's transparent. I zip up my jacket, turn up my collar.

"I was just protecting myself," he says.

"Don't you feel any guilt or remorse?"

"No."

"You're damaged goods, Mister. You're a psychopath."

"Call it what you will. I'm just different. That's all."

He grins.

"I would have made a great Taoiseach," he says.

I shake my head in wonder at his moral paucity.

"I can see why Nuala was fond of you," he says. "You're a good and loyal friend. Another quality that's in short supply nowadays."

He contemplates.

"You know, if things had taken a different turn, you might have been my son-in-law. That would have given me pleasure. And Nuala too, no doubt."

He shakes himself.

"Ah, but it was not to be. That's life."

I lift the gun and point it at his head.

"And now it's over. Now you're going to die."

He shrugs.

"Che sarà sarà," he says. "There's not much left

for me here anyway. I'd never get elected now. And the only thing left for me to do in this life was to be Taoiseach. I've done everything else."

His nonchalance is disarming. He flicks his cigar into the wind and the rain. Sparks fly back at us. The cigar plummets into oblivion.

"Maybe it's time to move on," he says.

"I wouldn't be in any hurry to get to where you're going."

"Sure, it won't be long before I'm running the place."

"You're mad as a hatter."

He salutes me.

He takes three quick steps and walks off the side of the cliff. My eyeballs pop. *Fuck*. He just walks right on out into space. Now I see him. Now I don't. He drops like a stone. Without a sound. Not a scream or a whimper. *Jesus*. One minute he's there before me in all his megalomaniacal perversity. The next he's gone. *Puff*. History. Swimming with the fishes.

I freeze. My mind is in turmoil. On the one hand I'm relieved I didn't have to kill him. On the other I'm offended that he did me out of my grand gesture of vengeance. On the one hand I'm thinking mark one up for the righteous. On the other I'm thinking what a waste of a life. Most of all, though, I'm overwhelmed at the blasé ennui with which he did himself in.

I step to the edge of the cliff. I stick my head out to make sure he wasn't pulling a fast one on me and there isn't a platform harnessed onto the side of the hill like in the set-up for a movie shot. Nope. There's nothing below but the craggy cliffs and the sea. This ain't no movie. I look down through the mist and the drizzle at the waves crashing against the rocks below. I think maybe I see the white of his hair bobbing on an outgoing wave, but it could be just the foam.

Holy smoke.

I put the gun in my pocket, scope out the landscape. There's not another soul stirring. I make my stealthy way back to the car.

I go home.

38

At ten o'clock the next morning, I'm sitting in my dressing gown at the kitchen table, my hair wet from the shower, eating an anchovy omelette for breakfast and washing it down with a glass of milk, when the phone rings.

It's Davy.

"Did you hear the news?" he says.

"What news?"

"Aren't you watching the to-do on the telly?"

"No. I've been enjoying a bit of peace and quiet, for a change."

"They fished Cooley's body out of the Irish Sea this morning."

"Go 'way."

"Apparently he was tangled up in some stray fishing nets on the rocks at the base of the cliff just below his back garden. Dead as a doornail."

"Well, that saves the state a costly trial."
"They're saying he jumped."
"Good riddance."
Davy pauses.
"Did you go out yourself last night?" he says.
"No. I had a hot bath and hit the sack early."
He pauses.
"Is there anything you want to tell me, Milo?"
I think.
"No, Davy. Not really."
What he doesn't know won't hurt him. Maybe when we're both in old age, sitting on a park bench wondering where all the years and our teeth went, he'll ask me again. And I'll tell him. Then.

"All right, so," he says. "Are you going for a pint tonight? We'll celebrate your vindication."
"The Palace?"
"Around eight?"
"It's a date."

39

A week later I'm back on the Hill of Howth. I'm standing at Nuala's grave in St Fintan's Cemetery, overlooking the bay. A hearty breeze blows in off the sea. It smells of imminent rain. What's new?

I don't wear glasses any more and my hair is almost back to its natural colour. It took me two days to adjust to being the old me again.

The hullabaloo has begun to die down. In the eyes of the law, I am once again an innocent man. The champagne flowed at the party. The festivities were tinged with sadness, though. Nuala was never very far away.

McGonagle is still in jail. The judge wouldn't give him bail. Said he was too dangerous to be walking the streets and couldn't be trusted not to do a runner. He'll go down for a long time.

Revisionism has been visited on my status with the

peelers. They offered me my job back, at a rank appropriate to my age and the years gone by. Sweaty Finnegan, believe it or not, was the bearer of these tidings. I thought about it seriously, but I turned the offer down. Something to do with the notion that you can't go home again. Sweaty took my card and promised he'd steer a bit of work in my direction.

"This doesn't mean I like you, though," he said.

I guess we'll never be friends.

I can live with that.

I put a bunch of lilies down atop the mountain of wreaths and flowers that surrounds Nuala's grave. I go to the side of the hill, look down at the fishing boats and yachts bobbing on the lively sea below.

It starts to rain.

I take Nuala's knickers out of my pocket. I kiss them. I hold them out into the wind. I say a little prayer and I let them go. They snap and flap and crack and scud off on the breeze towards Wales.

I blow Nuala a kiss.

Across the bay in Dollymount, *Stella Maris* stands majestically above the sea and watches over her wandering sailors. She looks across the water at me and I fancy she winks.

"It's not such a bad life, if you don't weaken," she says.

I sigh.
"Keep you pecker up," she says.
"I will," I say. "I promise."
I walk away.
"Hey," she calls after me.
I stop and turn. I cock an ear.
"Come up and see me some time."
She says.

The End